Sweet Home

By Joseph Zuko

Story by
Josh McCullough & Joseph Zuko

D1456267

This is a work of fiction. Names and characters are fictitious. Any resemblance to actual persons, living or dead, is entirely coincidental.

Thank you to Josh McCullough, Pam Anderson, Katie Zuko, and Linda Kim for helping me edit my book.

Thank you to my Mom and Dad for always being so supportive.

Thank you to Sam for the idea to start writing.

Thank you to my wife Katie Zuko. She cheers me on like I am her local sports team and thank you for not letting me give up on my dreams.

Cover art by Paul Copeland

paulsartspace@yahoo.com

A note from the Editor: Josh McCullough

My name is Josh. I edited Sweet Home and feel I should issue a warning to the reader. If you suffer from any serious medical conditions or are a big baby, please put the book down immediately. It is quite intense and contains an extreme amount of bloody, gory, goopy violence. When I asked Joe to tone it down a bit, his only response was to cackle maniacally for five minutes straight. It was disturbing to say the least. To those brave enough to continue, I advise you to pull out your favorite fainting couch and strap on a second pair of undies. This book is bloodier than a British swearing convention. Get it? Because they say bloody a lot. I'm sorry. Enjoy the mayhem.

Chapter 1

It reeked of ungodly body odor inside the prison transfer bus. The smell reminded inmate number 7532 of a body he had kept for too many days. The hitchhiker he picked up on Highway fourteen had gone sour so fast.

Inmate 2704, in the seat next to 7532, turned and whispered, "This weather is killing my arthritis."

7532 glanced at the old man's gnarled hands. They were swollen and no longer bent at the knuckles. The old inmate's name was Arthur Wright and he was on this bus for the same reason as 7532. Murder.

7532 nodded at Arthur. Head shakes and nods were the prisoner's main form of communication. He had chewed his tongue down to a nub several years ago. He flicked his head back and attempted to whip his greasy locks out of his face. His stringy hair drove him insane. It was always getting in his face and blocking his view. The first week into his life sentence, he had opened a guard's throat and the warden put him on lockdown for six months and then heavy restriction for the remainder of his stay. Barber visits and other prison luxuries had been off limits from then on.

Arthur grumbled, "I hope this fancy hospital we're off to will give me some fucking pain killers." He kept his voice low so the guard wandering up and down the aisle couldn't hear. "I wanna feel absolutely nothing before I get to hell."

He smirked at Arthur.

"Oh yeah, sorry. I forgot about your... condition," Arthur said as he attempted to flex his fingers. He grunted in pain as he continued. "You don't know how lucky you are, brother."

He raised an eyebrow and shook his head.

Arthur looked beyond him, "Goddamn."

7532 tilted his head and gazed out the barred window. Snowflakes melted on the glass. Beyond the window was an endless forest of evergreens. The trees were solid white. A snowcapped mountain in the distance looked like a postcard. Dark clouds blocked out the sun, but he knew they had left at eight a.m. and had been on the road for close to three hours. The sun should be directly above the bus.

"That's majestic. Stare at a concrete wall for thirty years and you forget how beautiful the world really is." Arthur readjusted himself in his seat, "I hope we get there soon. I gotta take a shit."

7532 shifted his attention from his foul-mouthed neighbor and studied the very tip of the mountain. He pondered what the world looked like from that vantage point. He could probably see for a hundred miles in every direction.

Can I see a town from there? Then he wondered.

How many people in that town could I add to The Reckoning?

"Jacob?" Arthur whispered. 7532 didn't turn his head from the window. Arthur spoke a little louder, "Jacob?"

He snapped out of the daydream. It had been a long time since he was called by his first name.

"How long did the quack give you?"

Jacob held up his index finger.

"A year?"

Jacob closed his eyes and shook his head.

"A month."

Jacob nodded.

Arthur sucked at his teeth. "The good news is in thirty days you'll be set free."

But it wasn't good news. He wasn't ready to die. His masterpiece wasn't finished. Jacob was so many bodies shy of his goal. He had rotted in a cell for sixty-three months and now he was on his way to a hospital. The state planned to leave him shackled to a gurney until his number was up.

"I hope I can sweet talk a nurse, male or female I don't give a shit, into cranking my peter one last time before I go. I've been grinding my dick raw on a mattress for ten years. Damn near whittled it away to nothing." Arthur smiled revealing a mouthful of yellow stained teeth.

Jacob grew weary of Arthur's filth. He wished he could lean over and bite out his tongue to shut him up. He closed his eyes placed his head on the backrest. The thought of not hitting the mark he had set for himself was devastating and weighed heavy on his mind.

All that work. He thought. *Was it for nothing?*

"Jacob," Arthur whispered again. The convict opened one eyelid. His pupil drifted to the corner of his eye as he looked to Arthur.

"Is it twenty-seven?"

Jacob opened both eyes and stretched his neck.

"Regan and I have cigs riding on this. Come on man," Arthur asked sweetly. Doing his best to get the info and gain the upper hand.

Regan Straight, inmate 6897 a.k.a. *"The Clutch"* as the newspapers called him, sat directly in front of them. His bald head reflected the overhead lights like a disco ball. A fresh scar ran from the top of his scalp, plummeting down the right side of his skull and stopping just below his ear. He cranked his neck to eavesdrop.

Reckoning human souls was Jacob's legacy. He surmised it was the reason people became doctors, airline pilots or the President. Holding a human's life in your hand was real power.

Jacob gave an upwards motion with his thumb.

"Higher?" Arthur was taken back. "Damn boy, you were busy."

Regan turned back around in his seat. The game would continue.

Nobody but Jacob knew the real number or the true goal that he had set for himself. For ten years, he collected human lives like someone might collect comics. It took real passion to amass the numbers he had.

"The focus and determination... I wish I had that when I was in the game," Arthur said as he licked his bottom lip. "I was all run and gun, flying by the seat of my pants. Killing at random and leaving a damn mess everywhere I went. This one time I had this old gal tied to a chair. I was about to dump a glass of bleach down her-"

Jacob could do nothing but listen to Arthur ramble on. He wanted so badly to silence the man. He needed a few miles of peace. All of this talk was boiling Jacob's brain. He ached to open an artery, but no matter the thrill, he would never take out Arthur. There was nothing to gain from it. Only healthy vibrant lives could be reckoned. A hunter wouldn't take credit if a sick bear stumbled into camp and died next to the fire. That would be cheating. Effort had to be involved. It must take skill and a level of patience. Otherwise, what was the point?

"-I left fingerprints on the glass. Jizz in a towel and hair in the sink. Two weeks later I was arrested," Arthur said as he rolled his eyes at his own stupidity. He noticed he had lost Jacob's interest. "I heard Zarren took out an entire mining town in northern Idaho. Can you believe it? Killing every man, woman and child." Arthur leaned forward and bowed his head. He stretched his shackled hands up toward his face so he could itch his nose. He glanced at Jacob and saw he had the man's attention again.

Jacob looked over the inmates and found the prisoner Arthur was discussing. Zarren Torros was a full head taller than any other inmate. He sat alone at the very front of the bus. The big man needed two seats. He sported a lion's mane of raven black hair and a matching beard.

"No survivors." Arthur cleared his throat. "It was like forty people. He did it all in one night. The bodies were almost impossible to identify." Arthur mimed swinging a hammer down between his legs. He struck an invisible skull and then his mangled hands become the skull blowing apart. He made an explosion sound with his mouth. Arthur's fingers became chunks of the skull that landed in his lap. He pretended to shake them off in disgust. Arthur nodded at Zarren, "That boy's a crusher."

Jacob scanned the entire bus. It was only a quarter full with a headcount of twelve convicts. Only the two guards and the driver were healthy enough to count toward his masterpiece. The other inmates were just a waste of time. Their diseased and dying bodies were nothing but empty husks to Jacob. They sat around in chains and waited for Death to pluck them from their miserable existences. Jacob wasn't going to do Death's job for him. On top of that, every one of the men here was at one time or another a colleague in the murder game. This fact also gave them a pass. It was common courtesy to not snuff out a peer.

Jacob looked at the back of his hands. Rough and jagged scars crisscrossed his skin. One of his favorite scars was in the shape of a scythe. It curved around his thumb and down his wrist. Looking at it conjured up the image of "Death" as portrayed in the movies and on TV. He enjoyed this concept of a black robed, scythe toting Grim Reaper. The entertainment business made Death out to be a workingman. Close to a plumber or garbage truck driver, as if Death worked in a union. Jacob imagined Old Bones wearing a t-shirt on the weekends that read, Local Chapter of Soul Collectors number 666. His pay was good but Grimmy hated the long hours. The endless job of collecting souls must have been a dirty, disgusting grind that no one ever appreciated him for, but some asshole had to do the nasty work.

Reckoning never felt like a job to Jacob. It was often exhausting and troublesome, but never work. The hours zipped by when he stalked his victims. Running his knife through human flesh was better than any other high in the world.

The bus made fresh tracks in the snow as it wound its way up the highway. The sun crept behind the mountain as it headed west.

A guard moved slowly down the aisle as he checked the convicts. He tugged at their cuffs. The bus sped around a tight corner and climbed the switchback when a family of deer bound across the highway. The animals stopped in their tracks when the headlight of the bus illuminated them.

The driver stomped on the brakes and cranked the wheel. He yelled out, "Shit! Hold on!" There was an enormous crunch as the bus plowed through the deer. Blood and gore splashed across the windshield. Antlers exploded through the glass, impaling the driver. The bus slid out of control, hit the guardrail, rolled over the embankment and down the steep tree-lined ravine.

Jacob could feel the pressure of his restraints against his body, but there was no pain. It looked like his month was about to be cut short. The bus tumbled over and over. Tree branches pierced the windows, killing several of the men in chains and both guards. Heads smashed against reinforced metal.

The bus came to a stop on its side. Fluids and smoke poured out of the engine block. It was total carnage inside the bus. Only a few inmates remained alive. The guard laid across Jacob's lap. A set of keys dangled next to the convict's hand.

Chapter 2

Two men circled each other. A fury of punches were exchanged. Drops of sweat spattered onto the mat. Mumbled words poured out over a mouth guard, "Move faster. I hit you with the jab every time." The man giving the advice fired another quick left. His opponent blocked it this time. "That's it. Keep your feet moving. Your enemy won't tell you when he's about to kick you in the nuts." A padded shin and foot launched from the mat. Its destination? The groin of his sparring partner. The devastating kick was blocked just in time.

Another round of punches were thrown. Each man made contact with his intended target and the fists moved faster. The hits were harder. Some of the blows were thrown in anger. The friendly competition suddenly became strained when the man giving the lesson landed too many painful and accurate strikes in a row. A mouth guard flew across the mat. The sparring ended with a powerful hook. A body fell to the floor. The man's arms and legs went limp for a few ticks, his chest heaving.

"Oh, shit! I'm sorry, Ben. Are you alright?"

Ben breathed heavily, his sweat soaked t-shirt clung to his chiseled body. He pulled at the Velcro that held his boxing gloves tight and tugged at the strap to get his protective headgear off. He laid exhausted on his back and rubbed his sore jaw, "I'm fine. That'll teach me to block next time." Ben's vision snapped into focus as his friend, Dominic, knelt down beside him.

He quickly pulled off his gear and examined Ben's pupils. The two of them were clean-shaven, healthy men in their forties with strong, muscular builds.

Dominic steadied his breath as he spoke, "You want to keep going? Or call it a day?"

"Do I want to keep getting my ass handed to me or go get an ice pack from the fridge? Let me see. Yeah, I think I'm done with today's lesson."

Dominic extended his hand and helped Ben to his feet. He threw an arm around Ben's shoulder and gave him a friendly pat. "You're picking it up fast, man. I promise in a few months you'll be right there with me and I'll be the one getting my ass kicked."

"This is one hell of a deal you talked me into," Ben said as he reached down to pick up his spit covered mouth guard. He continued, "Hey Ben, let me workout in your gym for free and I'll beat the shit out of you a few times a week in exchange. Does that sound good?" He stepped over to a bench and plopped his tired butt down on the black vinyl. "It's like I'm paying a bully to give me wedgies and flick boogers at me."

Dominic took a seat next to him, "That's not how I see it. I'm giving you lifesaving lessons that would cost the average consumer a hundred and fifteen dollars a month in exchange for a gym membership that you only charge thirty dollars a month for."

Ben swallowed a swig from his water bottle, "Oh, really?"

"My math says you should be giving me eighty-five bucks a month on top of the free gym membership. So let's see, eighty-five divided by four lessons a week," he paused as he crunched the numbers, "I should be getting seven dollars a beating and I haven't even got one damn nickel off you."

"Deputy Dominic Spence you are a true friend."

They bump fists.

"How's business been?" Dominic asked as he ran a towel over his forehead.

Ben scanned the nearly empty gym.

One man, in his late sixties, walked slowly on a treadmill in the corner of the room. All of his workout gear was clearly from the 80's. From his bright orange foam covered headphones to his hot pink shorts. The man was positively retro.

"Business is booming."

"It's the end of the year. Next week you'll get all those suckers signing back up as they try to stick to their resolutions. You'll be fine."

Ben mulled it over as he pulled off his shin guards.

"How've you and Lisa been?" Dominic inquired as he peeled off the rest of his gear.

Ben tossed his stuff off to the side and got up from the bench. "Have you tried this new post workout drink I got?" He headed for the front counter.

Company t-shirts hung from the wall. In bold font, they read *Sweat and Tears Gym*. Colorful containers of protein powder, vitamins, creatine, amino acids and fish oils were stacked neatly on shelves that covered every inch of wall space behind the counter.

Dominic followed him. Ben pulled out two yellow packets from a box that sat under the counter. He pinched them between his fingers as he swung the packets back and forth to work the powder into one end.

"If you need to talk I'm always here to listen."

Ben raised his eyebrows and shook his head, "I don't know what you're talking about." He tore the packets open and emptied the contents into his bottle on the counter. "Things are going really, really, really great."

A bell chimed above the front door as it opened. An arctic like blast hit both men. Snow fell onto the doormat as a gentleman in his sixties stepped through and quickly closed the frozen door behind himself.

He carried a yoga mat and wore a gray knitted stocking cap. A black eyepatch covered his left eye and a deep scar ran from under the patch to the middle of his cheek. A cigarette hung from the corner of his mouth. His voice was rough as gravel as he spoke. "Hello, fellas. It's a tidbit nipply out there." He wiped the melting snow off his thick and amazingly well-groomed goatee.

Ben smiled at his gym patron and gave him a nod, "Hello, Duke. I didn't think I'd see you here today. Please put out the cigarette."

Duke's good eye floated down to the burning white stick tucked between his lips. He acted as if he forgot it was there. "Gadzooks, how long has this cancer stick been there?" Duke inhaled deeply. The red tip burned bright. In a matter of seconds he had it down to the filter. He stepped back to the door, cracked it open, exhaled the large cloud of smoke and tossed the butt out into a snowdrift. "There we are. I'm never one to be wasteful."

Dominic rolled his eyes, "Why come to the gym everyday if you can't stop smoking?"

"Deputy, I don't trust a man if he doesn't have a few vices, and at my age quitting is for losers." Duke stepped from the door and over to the coat rack. "I come to the gym to burn calories in Lisa's yoga class. If I don't, I won't feel like I earned my six-pack of brew tonight. I can't spend New Year's Eve sober, can I?" Duke asked as he dusted off the last flakes of snow that had fallen onto his broad shoulders. He pulled off his heavy coat and hung it up. His body was trim and it looked like it belonged to a much younger man.

"I think you'll be the only one in her class today," Ben poured the powder into Dominic's water bottle.

"That makes me teacher's pet, I guess." Duke noticed Dominic staring at his eyepatch. "Can I help you with something, officer?"

Dominic replaced the cap on his bottle and gave it a gentle shake. He stared out the gym's front window unable to look at the man as he asked his question, "Why are you still wearing the eyepatch?"

Ben came to Duke's rescue. "Come on, man."

"Doctor Evans says your eye is totally fine. You only had to wear the patch for the first couple of weeks. It's been a year since your accident." Dominic fought his growing smile.

Duke raised his voice, "It wasn't an accident." He caught himself. Paused and allowed the anger to pass. "It was an attack."

"Evans says you have 20-20 vision, and wearing that patch is just your way of begging for attention. What do you think?"

"Well, I'll have to have a chat with the good Doctor about his patient confidentiality practices then, won't I?" Duke pulled off his cap as he stepped closer to Dominic. Shoulder length salt and pepper hair escaped from its wool prison. The hair, goatee, eyepatch and scar made Duke look like he just stepped out of a Lucky Strike magazine advertisement from the 1970's. He was as rugged and handsome as a man could get.

Dominic narrowed his brow and kicked on his Super-Cop voice, "So, why are you still wearing that patch, Duke?"

"We're just wondering, that's all. It has been a year since you went on that hunting trip," Ben said with a friendly smile, trying his best to de-escalate the situation.

Duke lowered his voice and bass resonated from his chest as he spoke, "Well boys, isn't it obvious?"

Dominic pondered what he could possible mean. He looked to Ben for any clues.

"It clearly goes with my *motif*." Duke nabbed a hairband out of his pocket. "Now if you gentlemen will excuse me. I don't want to be late for Mrs. Williams' class." Duke pulled his long hair out of his face and back into a bun. He secured the band and made sure the bun was tight enough to survive Lisa's fierce yoga instruction. He walked away with all the confidence in the world.

"What. A. Kook." Dominic took a swig from his bottle. The second the post workout drink hit his tongue he did a spit take. "This tastes like shit," he said as he wiped the tainted water from his mouth.

"I know." Ben gritted his teeth and choked down a sip. He coughed out the words, "I'm never gonna sell it all."

Duke entered the locker room and stowed his clothes and boots. The other sixty-year-old man in the retro gear entered the locker room.

"Stanley, you sexy old man. How was your walk today?" Duke held out his hand and the two of them engaged in one of the manliest handshakes of all time.

"Excellent, sir, excellent. I see you're here to work on your chakras and drink some snake oil." Stanley teased as he opened his locker and fished out his gym bag.

"That's it, that's it. You nailed it. Hey, how did that date go, with um, what was her name?" Duke asked, not letting the light ribbing faze him.

"Morgan. Oh, I didn't tell you?" Stanley placed his Walkman

and headphones into his bag. "The date started well. Her face was a five, but her body was a solid ten. She laughed at my jokes. Sexual innuendos. Hand on my thigh. I felt like it's locked up and in the bag."

Duke nodded at Stanley, "Nice."

Stanley continued, "I go to drown a urinal cake and when I got back a biker is taking a whisky shot out of her cleavage."

"Damn." Duke dropped his head.

"Turns out she was his old lady back in the day." Stanley pulled a fresh shirt from his bag.

"So that was that?"

Stanley changed out his top. "I was in my going out clothes, so I figured I'd stick around. He ended up being pretty cool and we all headed back to her place."

"Please tell me that's the end of the story."

"I wish I could, Duke." Stanley took a deep breath before he kept going. "Let me ask you something, really personal."

"Nope."

Stanley was no longer listening, only telling. His mind had left the locker room. He was back at the date night, like a Vet telling a horrifying story about his time in Nam. "You ever choke a man? Sexually?"

Duke's upper lip snarled, "Excuse me?"

"It got dark at the end. Real dark." Stanley looked drained. The memory was too much.

Silence.

Duke's visible eye was opened as wide as it could go as was the one hidden under the patch. He could no longer bear the silence anymore and he said, "A man's gotta find release. I guess."

More silence.

Stanley raised his head. His face was beaming.

"Oh, you, joking son-of-a-bitch. You got me good," Duke said as he laughed out the awkward feeling that had crawled into his body.

Stanley's face went flat, "We did have a three way, but he choked me."

Duke's laugh was cut short. He paused and squinted at the man across from him.

"Oh, you got me again. Damn you're good."

Stanley pointed to the faint bruises on his neck. "I mean it Duke. It was the best damn orgasm I'd ever had in my life." Stanley sported half a smile.

Duke swallowed hard and scratched at the hairs on his chin. He searched and searched for something to say. Finally, he landed on, "Cool."

Duke exited the locker room and headed for a room at the back of the gym. The lights were out, but he could hear the sound of worldly trance music creeping out from under the closed door. He turned the knob and flipped on the lights.

A beautiful woman with dirty blonde hair lay flat on her back with both hands pressed against her stomach. A stylish mat was her only comfort from the hardwood floor. She wore a skin-tight black outfit that showed off her perfect yogi body.

"I'm sorry, Lisa, am I early?" Duke paused and waited for her response before he closed the door behind himself.

Her voice was smooth and calm. She spoke without opening her eyes, "I didn't think I was going to have anyone in class today."

"No blizzard or holiday would keep me from perfecting my downward dog," Duke said as he laid out his mat.

Lisa glided up to a sitting position. She looked like Dracula floating out of a crypt. When she got upright, her lids popped open. The whites of her eyes were streaked with bright red blood vessels. Wet tracks led past her temples and the tears had pooled in her ears.

Duke blurted out, "I usually cry after the hard workout."

Lisa huffed out a smile as she rubbed at her eyes and wiped away the tears. "Thank you."

"For what?" Duke knelt onto his mat.

"For not asking me what's wrong."

"I might not be married at the moment, but that doesn't mean I don't understand women. If you wanted to really talk about what's wrong, there is nothing on God's green Earth that would stop you."

"You're right." She breathed out a long, deep and clearing breath. "Are you ready to sweat?"

"I love it when a beautiful lady asks me that," Duke joked.

Chapter 3

Jacob unlocked the last shackle around his ankle. He climbed to his feet and stood on the interior wall of the bus. The steel beast lay on its side and the seats that held the dead bodies hung from the wall on Jacob's left. Snow drifted through the busted windows. It was dark in the ravine and darker inside the bus. Jacob moved his arms, legs, spine and neck to check for broken bones. Everything moved normally.

"Hurry up boy, let me loose," Arthur hung from his chair. Blood caked his white hair. Jacob knelt down and worked at the man's restraints. "Don't worry. I'm not hurt. It's the guard's blood."

After a few twists of the keys, Arthur was released. Jacob helped the old-timer to his shaky feet.

"Oh, God it's cold," Arthur held his arms close to his chest.

Jacob noticed the wind blowing through his long hair. He understood that his orange jumper was damp with blood and melting snow, but he couldn't feel the chill in the air.

"Help me get his coat," Arthur moved closer to the dead guard. He attempted to move the zipper, but his fingers didn't possess the dexterity. Jacob took over and muscled the heavy coat off the limp body. He helped Arthur into the warm fabric and zipped it up tight. Arthur was the son Jacob never wanted.

"That's better. Thank you."

Jacob checked the guard's belt. He found cuffs, zip ties, pepper spray, a handgun and extra ammo. Then he found what he was looking for, a flashlight. He clicked the button. A cone of light flashed over the gore inside the bus. Blood and broken bodies were everywhere. The fact that the two of them were alive was a miracle.

A grunting sound grabbed their attention, "Get me down."

"Regan?" Arthur stepped close to the grunting. Jacob panned the light over to the noise. It reflected Regan's shiny scalp. The man hung from his seat, three feet off the ground and was at

Jacob's mercy.

"Are you hurt?" Arthur crouched in front of Regan.

"I don't think so," Regan said as he pulled against his chains.

Jacob moved closer and reached out with the keys.

Regan lifted his head, "Was it forty-five?"

Jacob paused. He looked back and forth between the two cons. Their faces grew bright with excitement. Jacob extended his hand and raised his thumb into the air.

"Over forty-five. You were a machine," Regan's smile was contagious. The game would have to continue. Rules said they would have to wait until the next day to ask again.

Jacob removed Regan's cuffs and helped him out of his seat. He was a bigger man than Jacob. His chest was shaped like a barrel and his arms were squeezed into his jumper.

"It's so damn cold. My nuts are climbing into my body. Where's the other guard?" Regan's words puffed out in white clouds.

Jacob moved his light over the interior until they found the second guard. His body was a few feet from the front of the bus and his last moments of pain were frozen on his twisted face. Glass crunched under their boots as they moved to the front of the vehicle.

"Sorry Jacob, I hope you don't freeze to death, but that jacket's for someone that can feel this blistering winter air." Regan removed the coat from the guard's body. He wrapped it around his shoulders and zipped it up quickly.

The bus shook around them.

Regan squatted down. "It's rolling over."

A voice boomed from above them, "Get me down."

Jacob aimed the light straight up in the air above them. Zarren twisted his massive body in his seat. He sat only one foot above their heads. Chunks of meat from the bus driver and deer dropped off his broad chest. The flesh landed at the three convict's feet. The monster flexed and strained against the restraints. Grunting like an animal.

"Calm down. We have the keys. Jacob will climb up and get

you out of there." Arthur elbowed Jacob, encouraging him to climb up and release the man.

As Jacob climbed the seats he became a little worried Zarren might not adhere to the same code of conduct he had laid out for himself.

Jacob stood on the lower set of seats, he reached and quickly unfastened the chains that held Zarren to his chair. He was good at reading other humans, but Zarren was like staring at a marble statue. His eyes gave no clue to his state of mind. The last lock popped and the monster was set free. Jacob jumped down and the three convicts stepped back as Zarren climbed out of his chair. The whole bus shook again when his boots hit the ground. The big man straightened his back and towered over the others. He inhaled a lung full of the cold winter air.

"We should get moving," Arthur pointed to the blown out front window.

"Where should we go?" Regan jammed his hands into his jacket's pockets. Jacob stepped passed Zarren and headed for the front window. The safety glass was pink from the mix of snow and blood. The bus driver's body hung from his seat. The deer's mangled torso was cut almost in half. Its head, neck and shoulders were sticking through the windshield and entwined with the bus driver's corpse. A gallon of blood pooled below and the tail end of the deer hung by threads from the front of the bus.

"It'll be hours before the hospital notices we haven't arrived." Arthur inched in behind Jacob. The bus was laying on its door side. All of the windows had bars. The only way out was the windshield.

"We need to get out of the cold." Regan kicked his foot at one of the bodies, testing to see if it was truly dead.

"A town." Zarren's words were as cold as the winter chill itself. He wanted to get back to work. Before the law caught up with them and before they were forced into the state run hospital to wait to die. He wanted to spill blood.

"Yeah, let's find the closest town and play," Regan said as he nodded his head.

Jacob was excited to hear that they were all on the same page. He pointed at the dead corrections officer on the ground close to Regan. He made a gun with his hand signaling what he wanted. Regan squatted down and liberated the firearm. He passed it over to Jacob.

He aimed at the windshield and emptied the gun into it. The glass gave way and the weight of the deer crushed its way through the clear barrier. As the animal fell, its antlers tore the driver in half. A couple hundred pounds of meat fell before Jacob and a gust of icy wind peppered them with snowflakes. Jacob passed the gun back to Regan. Then he climbed over the two carcasses. His hands squished through their organs as he pushed his way through the window and stepped out into the snow. He could see the red stains on his scarred hands but he couldn't feel the sticky texture or the remaining warmth from their slowly cooling bodies. The snow was knee deep and wet. It was going to be a slow and miserable hike off this mountain.

Outside the bus, Jacob could feel something he had not felt in a long time. Freedom. If they hurried and had a bit of luck on their side they could find a nearby town. If they did, he would be able to add to his Reckoning. There wouldn't be time to stalk his prey. He wouldn't worry about properly disposing of the bodies. If he could find a town, hit it hard for one night he just might reach his goal.

The others joined him out in the snow. The fresh air filled their lungs. They sizzled with excitement as they scanned through the thick trees that surrounded them.

Regan tucked the gun into his jacket pocket. His smile spread ear to ear. "I'm fucking rock hard right now. Jesus Christ, I can't believe we survived that crash. You know what this means." His eyes bugged out of his skull as he continued, "The Universe wants us to go on a spree. I know we all like to do our own thing, but we should stay together. If the four of us hit one town. Oh my God."

"What?" Arthur wiped a snowflake from his lashes.

"We could wipe it out. Every last citizen." Regan pointed to the scar on his scalp. "My cancer is back. I've got less than six months. It's time to go crazy, you know, fuck it all. If we hang together, we've got a better chance to make it. A trooper rolls up on us. He'd have a hell of a time trying to take all four of us down. Safety in numbers or whatever."

Jacob and Zarren nodded at him. Everyone was onboard.

"We got a party to get to then. It's New Year's Eve." Arthur gazed up the ravine to the highway. "Boys, it's too steep for me. If I was twenty years younger I could make it, but there ain't no way in hell I'm getting up there with these," he said as he waved his claws at Zarren. The big man just stared through him and never gave an ounce of emotion.

Jacob pointed down the hill toward the end of the ravine. It was difficult to see through the forest, but the highway switched back and laid about three hundred yards down the steep hill.

He led them through the trees and they inched away from the crash site. The pitch was so extreme that it forced them to slide on their butts and crawl down through the snow. They used the evergreens as stopping points to catch their breath and slow their descent. Their cotton jumpsuits soaked up every drop of moisture they came in contact with. It was miserable, but in comparison to prison, it was heaven.

Halfway down, Jacob noticed his legs were not working as well as before and his fingers felt slow.

They must be going numb. He thought.

The trees parted and the highway lay before them. The bus tracks were already halfway filled in. The ground began to level out and Jacob could stand upright. A mighty gust came crashing down the highway. It whipped Jacob's wet hair into his face and the howl of wind filled his ears. It was so loud on the mountain he didn't hear the work van approaching. Carl's Plumbing was stenciled in white on the side of the blue van. Its chained tires dug into the snow as it skidded to a stop feet from Jacob.

The window rolled down, "Damn, buddy. Are you alright?"

Another flurry knocked a chunk of snow off Jacob's jumpsuit, revealing his prison number.

"Oh, shit!" Carl the plumber cursed. He didn't notice the others coming down out of the tree line. His focus was on the stringy haired escaped convict in front of him.

Carl shifted into reverse.

Regan raced, gun drawn and aiming into the open window, "Hands off the wheel!" he commanded.

Carl raised his hands, "Take the van, but let–"

Regan cut him off, "Get in the back," he said as he reached into the window, popped the lock and swung the door open.

"I got kids!" Carl hyperventilated.

Regan pulled himself up into the passenger's side, "Get in the back!"

Jacob observed Regan's work. The hairless man was quick and precise. He climbed in, popped Carl in the nose with the butt of the gun and pushed him out of the driver's seat. Carl disappeared into the darkness at the back of the van. Regan pulled the side door open and let Arthur and Zarren into their new ride. The van swayed to the left as Zarren entered and slammed the door shut. Regan climbed behind the wheel.

"Come on Jacob, move it," Regan called to him.

Jacob's body shook. It could have been from the ice forming on his jump suit. He was born without the ability to register injuries or pain. Doctors called it congenital insensitivity. Jacob had a lifetime of not knowing if his flesh was burned, cut or broken. His disease made it near impossible to know what his body needed or wanted. Maybe it was the freezing conditions, but Jacob was positive it was from the excitement. He was going to be on his way to a town. To spill blood. To add to his list. To continue his Reckoning.

He moved with purpose to the opened door. He slid into the seat, closed the door and then the window. Jacob pressed the button on the glove box. The normal insurance and registration filled the small compartment. He dug to the bottom and found what he was looking for, a map. He had read every sign and street name on the trip to the hospital and felt he had a good idea where they were in the state of Oregon.

The back of the van had pipes of all sizes and tools for the plumbing trade. An extra chair sat with its back to Regan. Arthur took the seat and buckled himself in. He was out of breath and exhausted. Regan stepped on the gas and got rolling. The tires slid at first and then the chains caught hold and they were off.

Carl cowered in the corner of the van. The bulge on his nose oozed blood. Zarren dropped to his knees so he could fit. Carl reached for the latch to the backdoor. Zarren caught Carl by the wrist and yanked his arm away from the handle. The monster sized convict pulled Carl's hand close to his wide chest. At first it looked like Zarren wanted Carl to feel his heartbeat.

"Please let me go," Carl coughed blood.

Zarren used his free hand to clutch Carl's trapped fist, "I didn't say you could touch that." He twisted Carl's hand. His wrist snapped like kindling. Carl's eyes bulged, his jaw dropped. No sound escaped. The skin around the wrist was stretched on one side and wrinkled on the other. His palm faced in the wrong direction.

Zarren took a moment to look over the stash of tools. He popped open a rusty toolbox. On top of the other tools lay a well-used ballpeen hammer.

Carl's lungs filled and let out an ear-piercing howl. Zarren drew the weapon from the rusty box. The head of the hammer ground along the ceiling as Zarren dropped it on to Carl's ankle. His white athletic sock turned crimson. The impact left a divot. The joint was destroyed. The big guy had time to kill and he wanted to play. The wrist and ankle were just the beginning. Carl's end would not be clean or quick.

Jacob unfolded the map and got his bearings. He wished Zarren would just finish off the screamer in the back of the van. He never found pleasure in making them suffer. There was less chance for them to escape if you finished them off quickly. Jacob's index finger glided across the map. He knew they were on Highway 12. Less than ten miles away was the next town. Sweet Home.

Chapter 4

New age music thumped through the room's in-ceiling speakers. The rubber mat under Duke's face had been flooded with perspiration. He had one leg tucked behind his neck and the other driving into the mat. His palm pressed firmly against the ground holding most of his weight. His free arm extended high into the air above him. Duke's toned body twisted and flexed as he held this very difficult pose. Lisa called it the *Destroyer of the Universe.* Duke found that title very appropriate.

Lisa whispered, "Breathe." She was in the same pose as Duke, and made it look effortless. "Ten more seconds... and release."

Duke quickly untangled his appendages and dropped to his knees as he faced Lisa. He toweled away a gallon of sweat, "Something must be really upsetting you. That was brutal."

"I'll see you at the next class?" Lisa remained emotionless.

"Yes, ma'am," Duke said as he gathered his belongings and left the room.

As Duke headed back to the locker room, Dominic was on his way out. He was showered, cleaned and dressed in his dark blue police uniform. A heavy coat was tucked over his forearm and a duffle bag hung from his shoulder. The initials S.H.S.D were marked in gold on the side of the bag.

"Deputy," Duke nodded.

"Duke, Sherriff wanted me to talk to you about your hood ornament."

Duke paused and exhaled a long breath. "Yes?"

Dominic slid one arm into his coat. A shiny-bronzed badge hung from its breast. "It's got to go. Hang it on a wall in your cabin, donate it to The Oasis, but get it off the front of your truck. It's a public safety hazard."

Duke growled, "Some say that about you."

Dominic zipped his coat and puffed out his chest, "Have it down before the start of the new year."

Duke stared the officer down, "Yes, sir, you son-of-a-bit-"

The radio on Dominic's shoulder squawked and cut Duke off, "Deputy Spence? Please head down to the station."

Dominic turned his head and thumbed the transmitter, "I'm on my way." When he looked back Duke had disappeared into the locker room.

Ben sat in front of a computer screen in the gym's office. Photos of Lisa and Ben were on every wall. Their wedding day, trips to Disneyland and Las Vegas, running marathons, dressed up as zombies at Halloween, and the two of them giving each other cheers with flutes of champagne. Framed family portraits were hung proudly. A set of twins, a boy and girl, joined Ben and Lisa in most of the photos. The most recent picture of their family unit sat on the desk next to the phone. The kids were now fifteen.

Lisa stepped past the open door to the office. She had a towel draped over her shoulders.

Ben didn't look up from his computer screen as he spoke, "We only need a hundred people to sign up next week."

"Hmm," her focus shifted around the room.

"If we don't, I'm not sure how we are going to pay… anything," Ben said as he clicked at his mouse.

"I need to pick up a few groceries for dinner. Can you get the kids?" Lisa turned and stepped from the doorway before he answered.

Ben checked to make sure she was gone before he responded, "Sure, I wasn't *doing* anything."

Duke exited the locker room, showered and dressed in his street clothes, he headed straight for the main door as he pulled on his stocking cap. Waiting for him behind the front counter was Ben. He had all his winter gear on and was ready to leave.

"Heading out?" Duke asked.

"I've got to get the kids. I doubt anyone else will show up today." Ben stepped out from behind the counter and flipped off a bank of light switches on the wall next to the door. "Will we see you at the party tonight?"

"Perhaps, Stanley has been harping on me about getting out more. I take it you and the Mrs. will be there?" Duke picked up his coat from the rack.

"I'll be there trying my best to guilt people into signing back up for the New Year. I don't know what Lisa has planned." Ben pulled out his keys as he waited for Duke.

Hearing this stopped Duke in his tracks, "Here is some advice and please take it. It is of the utmost importance that you make sure your lips are pressed against your beautiful wife's the moment the ball drops on Times Square. I missed a year once and my second wife was gone by February."

"I'll do my best." Ben held the door open for Duke.

They stepped out of the gym and onto Main Street. Mountains surrounded the town on all sides. A fresh blanket of snow covered everything in white. Small businesses lined the street and holiday decorations were hung with cheer. Duke's 1974 Ford pickup was parked at an angle in front of the gym. Attached to the front grill was a massive twelve point deer head and neck. It protruded nearly four-feet from the front bumper. Dominic was right. It was a public safety issue.

Ben locked the front door and shook it three times to make sure it was secure.

Duke stepped off the sidewalk and leaned next to his trophy. He slipped a cigarette between his lips and struck a match off the deer's antlers. "Sheriff wants me to take this down, can you believe that?"

"Yes, I can. It's begging to impale someone," Ben said as he turned to face Duke.

"The only blood it's ever drawn was mine." Duke's uncovered eye zeroed in on one of the pink stained points.

"Alright, well if I don't see you tonight, have a good New Year's." Ben extended his hand and the two shook on it.

"You too, Mr. Williams." Duke blew a lung full of smoke out the corner of his mouth. "And I hope you give my advice a second thought."

Ben smiled, released Duke's hand and headed down the sidewalk in the direction of Bill and Tad's Excellent Video Adventure.

Lisa wrapped her knuckles against an impressive solid oak door. The house attached to this marvelous door was a two-story brick mansion at the end of a cul-de-sac. Brass letters were bolted to the exterior, they read Thomas Evans M.D. An elderly man with thick glasses opened the door.

"Lisa? It's a holiday. I'm not open for business."

"It's an emergency." Lisa didn't wait to be asked in, she gently stepped past Thomas and entered the house.

Lisa nervously waited on the examination table in the Doctor's home office. A little red seeped through the cotton ball taped to her arm. The room was furnished with everything a practicing physician would need to see patients. Degrees and diplomas hung with pride next to the main door. Adjacent to the framed certificates of achievement were photos of the doctor and some patients. The pictures spanned decades. One framed photo always bugged Lisa. It was a photo of her and Evans when she was eight-years-old. The chubby cheeks on her fat little face drove her nuts.

Dr. Evans stood across from her as he looked over the test results. He cleared his throat, "So I know how to best deliver the news, what exactly are we hoping to hear today?"

Lisa broke into tears. Her shaking hands covered her face. Dr. Evans put down the test and stepped closer to Lisa. He grabbed her by the shoulders and pulled her in for a hug. She sobbed.

"It's okay. I promise it's all going to be okay. No matter how bad you think it is, I swear, in the end everything will work out." He pulled her away to look her in the face and deliver her an award-winning smile.

Lisa babbled at a rapid pace, "We're about to lose the gym and the house. Ben and I have talked about getting a divorce. I'm forty-five years old and if I'm pregnant on top of that, I don't know who the father is."

Evans drank in all that info. Processed it and managed a quarter of a smile, "It might be years from now, but it all will work itself out and you'll be okay."

A snot bubble formed in her nose, "Are you saying I am pregnant?"

Ben entered the video store. The place buzzed with excitement. A newly released action movie played over the store's speakers. Customers were in every aisle. Two guys in their thirties stood behind the register ringing up customers as fast as possible.

The bigger of the two men had a nametag on that read "Bill." He wore a set of jazzy black rimmed glasses and a luxurious beard. He waved and said, "Ben! Are you here to snag our interns?" Then he rubbed at his potbelly. "The holidays tore me a new belt size. I'm signing up at your gym tomorrow. You can run me through a monster of a workout, cool?"

"Sounds great. Where are they?" Ben stepped out of the way of a speedy video renter.

The smaller of the two men behind the register had a name tag that read, Tad. He proudly wore a mustache that curled up at the ends and a snap-brimmed-hat. He pointed. "Putting away a stack in horror."

"Thanks," Ben said as he side stepped by a young couple and headed for the back corner. Even though it was a longer route he skipped by the westerns. It was in that aisle, twenty-years ago when the store was called Vic's Videos, that he met Lisa. He bypassed the aisle, but the memory of their first meeting played in his mind anyway.

It was 1996. Ben and Lisa both reached for the same copy of *The Quick and the Dead.* He was a big Sam Raimi, *Evil Dead* fan. Lisa was a big Leonardo DiCaprio, *Growing Pains* fan. They started to argue about who was going to rent it, but when Ben locked eyes with her he stopped mid-sentence. Lisa had the greenest set of peepers he had ever seen. They were like staring at two magic emeralds. She was so beautiful. It was as if she hit him with a freeze-ray. Noticing he was catatonic, Lisa took the opportunity. She swiftly reached out, plucked the movie from his hand and said. "Thanks, buddy." Lisa made it halfway down the aisle before guilt set in. She pivoted as Ben started to defrost and asked. "You want to come over and watch it with me?"

The rerun stopped playing in Ben's mind as he turned into the aisle marked horror. A thin, fifteen-year-old girl, held a stack of Blu-rays. She searched the rack for the next movie's location.

Ben called to the girl, loudly, so he could be heard over the movie playing in the background, "MaKelle?"

This spooked the young woman so badly she dropped the movies and let out a scream. "Dang it, Dad. I'm in the horror section. I'm on edge, Pops."

"I'm sorry." Ben chewed at his lip to keep from smiling.

"You have to announce yourself early. People my age can suffer from heart attacks too, you know," she said as she pressed her fingertips to her chest. After the shock wore off, she reached out for her father and gave him a hug. Ben's daughter looked like a clone of Lisa. MaKelle released her dad and bent down to pick up cases. Her dad helped.

"You finish this stack and I'll grab your coat."

"Dad, it's the rush. I can't leave now. They need me."

"You guys work for free rentals. I think Bill and Tad can make it without you. Where's your brother?"

"In the back."

Ben handed MaKelle the last movie and headed to the back office.

He turned the knob and opened the door as he said, "Hayden?"

Two startled teens stopped kissing and jumped away from each other. Their cheeks were flushed. Clearly, they had been smooching for a while.

"Dad?" Hayden yelped. The two teenage boys didn't know what to do with their nervous hands. They shifted from arms crossed to hands on their hips back to arms crossed as they waited for the adult to talk first.

"Hayden, Andrew I was just coming to take you and MaKelle home."

Andrew's voice cracked. "Hello, Mr. Williams. He was helping me find a movie."

"In his mouth?" Ben questioned. "Grab your sister's jacket and meet me at the front?" Ben stepped out of the office's doorframe.

Andrew wiped excessive saliva from his lips. "Do you think he's mad?"

Hayden grabbed the two coats and headed for the door, "No, sweetheart. You're not the first boy he's found me kissing and you won't be the last."

"I'm not your first?" Andrew's heart broke a little.

"Please, I've had my skin in this game since first grade." Hayden gave him a wink and blew him a kiss.

Ben walked through the falling snow. The kids flanked him on each side. Hayden applied a fresh coat of ChapStick to his tender lips as MaKelle playfully jumped from one-foot print to another. Her game was not to leave any of her own prints in the snow.

"I don't think Bill and Tad would appreciate you turning their office into a petting zoo. So, maybe don't drag other boys in there to play tonsil hockey."

"Dad, you're so funny. Petting zoo. Tonsil hockey. Where do you get this stuff?" Hayden patted his father on his back.

MaKelle moved as nimble as a gazelle. She left no trace of her existence in the snow. "It's a small town, Hayden. At the pace you're going you're going to run out of boys by your junior year." She leaped over a fallen tree limb and landed dead center in someone's size thirteen snow print.

"Jealousy's not your style, Sis." Hayden nudged her,

throwing off MaKelle's balance.

Damn it! She left a mark in the snow.

"Getting any old boy to kiss me is easy. Getting the right one takes skill." MaKelle gave up and walked normally now that she had lost the game.

"And who is the 'right one'?" Hayden inquired.

"Please change the subject." Ben pleaded.

"Why are we walking? Where's Mom? Where's the car?" MaKelle asked.

"She took it to go get groceries."

Hayden's eyebrows dropped, "She got groceries last night."

They walked in silence as Ben pondered where his wife might have really gone.

Chapter 5

A loud snap came from the back of Carl's van. Like a length of lumber being kicked in half. It was followed by a muffled scream. Jacob glanced over his shoulder to see what had made the noise. Zarren's wide back blocked most of the view, but it was clear he had been working his way, slowly, up Carl the plumber's legs. The maniac was destroying each joint on his way to the hips. Thankfully Zarren took one of Carl's dirty socks and jammed it into the man's mouth to stifle the screams.

Jacob wanted to climb back there and end the man's suffering, but figured it would anger the behemoth. It was better to keep the peace than take away the big man's toy. Jacob was confident in his skills, but had no desire to square off against that wrecking ball.

Snow dumped onto the highway. The wiper blades could hardly keep the windshield clear. They crept down the mountain and slid at every switchback. They silently enjoyed their freedom and plotted their first kills.

Snap. Zarren forced Carl's other hip out of socket. Jacob glanced into the back of the van again and Zarren looked like a toddler squishing Play-Doh in his hands.

Jacob tapped Regan on the shoulder and motioned to the back.

Regan grimaced. "I know." He itched at the scar on his scalp and spoke out the corner of his mouth. "Big guy, can you put the poor bastard out of his misery?"

"No." Zarren hit Carl again with the hammer.

Regan shrugged his shoulders at Jacob. "I asked him, man. What do you want me to do? I ain't pulling the van over and giving him a spanking, that's for goddamn sure."

A light flashed on the dash.

"We'll need to gas this bitch soon," Regan said as he turned the heater down a notch. Jacob eyed the map. It claimed a gas station was on the horizon.

Regan's concentration never came off the road as he spoke, "If we find a place to fill up, it's all you. I wanna see the master at work."

The thought of an occupied gas station thrilled Jacob to the bone. It had been so long. Two-thousand days had passed since he had last added to his list.

"Where are we?" Arthur asked as he rubbed his tired eyelids.

Regan spotted a sign that read GAS 1 MILE on the side of the highway, "About to stop and fuel this thing."

"You're gonna waltz in there dressed like this? We'll have the cops raining down on us in no time."

"Jacob's taking care of it. All we gotta do is kick back and watch." Regan laughed until he began coughing from it. "Damn cigarettes."

Arthur turned in his seat. "Can we take another guess, before you add to the pile?"

Jacob ignored the question as he searched through the center console. Among the pens, paper clips and business cards he found a rubber band. It was not perfect, but it would work. Jacob pulled his locks of hair out of his face and put it back into a ponytail.

"Come on, one more guess." Regan begged.

Jacob held up one digit and motioned it at both men.

Arthur spun around as far as he could in his seat. His head bobbed between Regan's and Jacob's. "Sixty?"

Jacob slowly raised his hand and then motioned with his thumb. Higher.

Regan's knuckles blanched as he squeezed the wheel. "More than sixty? That's bullshit. You were convicted for murdering three and you're telling us you hit over sixty?"

"Calm down." Arthur patted his friend on the shoulder.

"I am calm. I just don't like getting lied too. I'm not an idiot. If you had done more than sixty we would have heard about it."

"Why would he lie?"

Regan's pupils zigged back and forth, as he rationalized the number in his head.

Fluorescent lights shone like a beacon a quarter mile down the highway. A neon sign hung above the building. *One Stop Mountain Shop* blazed in bright green.

Jacob raised his hand and signaled for them to stop. Regan tapped at the brake and pulled over to the side of the road. Jacob reached for the door's handle.

Regan grabbed Jacob by the sleeve. "Was it really higher than sixty?"

Jacob turned his head and two cons were locked in a stare down. Jacob's gaze never wavered. His disfigured features burned with intensity. Regan released his hold and Jacob disappeared from the van.

He sprinted like a ghost down the side of the highway. He veered out behind the shop. Jacob quickly vanished into the shadows of the evergreens.

"He didn't bring a weapon." Regan stated as he slowly pulled ahead.

Arthur clicked his safety belt and moved to the front seat next to Regan, "He is the weapon."

As Jacob moved closer to the back of the building, he realized this was all new territory for him. In his old life, he would spend a full week stalking a victim. First, he would verify they were good enough to add to the Reckoning. Then plot how he would take them down without witnesses. Jacob had not had a fulltime job in decades, and in order to keep himself fed he had to strategically steal from each person he added to his list. Then dispose of the body so they could never be found. It was quite a process he had developed, but now there was no time. He had only a few moments to decide if he could add whoever was in the store to his list and then take them down fast. Only the strong and virile could truly be Reckoned.

A man in his early fifties walked passed a rack of knickknacks and magnets that read One Stop Mountain Shop. He held a phone to his ear as he paced. With his broad shoulders, strong jaw, thick hair and choice of clothing, he closely resembled a model in an *L.L. Bean* catalog. A green nametag hung from his shirt. KEVIN was engraved on it with white text.

"Sweetheart, I'll be home in an hour. I promise I won't make you late for the party." He listened to the voice on the other end of the phone as he brushed some dust off a wooden Sasquatch figurine. The little hairy Bigfoot held a yellow sign in the shape of the state of Oregon. The store had row after row full of crap for tourists, snack food, drinks, hunting and fishing equipment plus outdoor clothing.

"I'm almost finished counting stock and then I'll close early..." He pinned the phone between his ear and shoulder as he lifted a big heavy box up off the floor and onto the front counter. "Tell the kids I'll pick up a movie for them at Bill and Tad's... You already got the champagne, or do you want me to bring one from the store? It's not that cheap. It's totally drinkable... Okay, I'll see you soon. Love you." Kevin hung up the phone and placed it back on its charging station. He picked up a tablet and a scanner from the front counter.

He stepped over to the back of the store and entered an aisle filled with tools. Kevin worked left to right and methodically scanned the UPC sticker on each item. He softly whistled to himself as the numbers tallied into the tablet.

He was halfway down the aisle when he heard the door swing open and the electric bell chimed. He turned to give his customer a smile and to say, "Hello." Kevin's deep voice called out across the store, but no one was there.

Maybe it was the wind? He thought to himself. Sometimes when it's stormy out it sounds like the door opens, but it doesn't normally set off the sensor. A loud squeak echoed through the store. It sounded like a wet rubber sole twisting on the linoleum.

"Hello?" Kevin called again.

Nothing.

He trotted over to the front door. Fresh snow and wet

footprints covered the welcome mat. There were no vehicles at the gas pumps.

How could someone have walked here in this storm?

The sound of metal scraping on metal grabbed Kevin's attention. Something heavy was flung up and crashed into a bank of fluorescent lights at the back of the store. The plastic cover and all four glass tubes rained down from the ceiling as that corner of the store went dark.

"Show yourself!" He jogged over to the front counter. Kevin heard someone scurry down an aisle. They were getting closer.

"I've got a gun."

Ding-ding.

A van pulled next to the gas station pump. Its side door slid open and a few men in orange correctional jumpsuits crouched inside. They sat and watched.

Kevin dropped the scanner and tablet on the countertop. In an instant, he had a snub-nosed revolver out from under the register.

"I'm calling the cops!" He shouted as he reached for the phone. A pane of glass shattered. The noise stole his breath. He could tell it was the display case for his hunting knives. Sweat accumulated on his forehead. Kevin sucked in sharp mouthfuls of air. Another object flew through the air and crashed into a bank of lights. It shrouded that part of the store in darkness. With the gun extended shoulder high, Kevin raced to the hunting section. Shards of glass covered the remaining blades. One knife was missing. The tag below the empty spot claimed it was a *Cold Steel Trail Master O-1 Bowie Knife* and retailed for two hundred and fifty dollars. Its nine and a half inch razor sharp blade was made out of high-carbon steel. Perfect for flaying meat from bone.

Fuck!

Kevin dialed nine-one-one on the phone's pad and pressed call. Something hard flew into the back of his skull. Excruciating pain caused him to drop the phone and clutch his scalp. He blind fired two shots. The phone's case cracked on impact and spun on the floor at his feet. The can of green beans bounced off the linoleum and rolled away.

A tiny voice inquired from the phones speaker, "Nine-one-one, what's your emergency?"

A third bank of lights were smashed by another flying can of food. It did not break all of the fluorescents tubes. The remaining bulb flickered intermittently. The green labeled tin can of food rolled to a stop in front of a row of candy.

It was a can of beans? Jesus Christ that hurt.

Kevin spun three-sixty. The place looked empty. Half of the lights in the store were now broken and the remaining bulbs cast jagged shadows. He checked his hand. It came away from his head slick with blood. Kevin's eyes no longer held their focus and his lids blinked quickly as they flicked away drops of sweat.

"Take the money in the till and leave," he begged as he backed himself into a corner. A bright colored blur raced between two aisles. Kevin fired two more shots and took a few large steps toward the gap. The aisle stood empty.

"Shit!"

A standalone cardboard display holding bags of organic trail mix and jerky fell forward on to its face. He fired two rounds in its direction and clicked through two more pulls of the trigger. The box of extra ammo was tucked back behind the counter. He turned and dashed for the front of the store. The van outside caught his attention again. Kevin's mind raced.

What are they waiting for? Didn't they hear the gunshots? What the fuck do they want?

He grabbed the box of ammo and dumped it onto the countertop. Out of nowhere a man appeared. He stood fifteen feet away. His orange overalls were darkened with moisture. The knife in his hand reflected a glint of light. It was the man's face that gave Kevin the biggest fright. He had dark circles around his sunken eyes, long stringy hair pulled back into a ponytail and horrible scars. His skin looked like the surface of the moon and deep, dark railroad tracks crisscrossed every inch of the convict's face. The scarred convict took off in a sprint. He moved with all of the grace and speed of an Olympic athlete. Kevin pushed out the cylinder and the spent shells dropped from the gun. His shaking hand reached for a fresh round, but before he could load it, the convict had hurled himself over the countertop. The look of joy on the lunatic's face was terrifying. The inmate crashed into Kevin, knife first. The blade entered just below the storeowner's nametag.

A powerful, scar covered, hand wrapped around Kevin's open mouth and stifled his scream before it could escape. Kevin felt all nine and a half inches of the blade pass through his skin, into the muscle, break the bone in his chest, stab the speeding heart and split the shoulder blade before pinning him to the wall of sheetrock. Kevin did a full-body spasm. He dropped the gun and the round. There was no life flashing before his eyes. No heavenly light shining down on his soul. There was just the godawful stink of body odor from the convict and the pain from this mortal wound. His body was already shutting down. Kevin's final thoughts were on his younger brother, Don, and how he had told him to spring for the Glock.

It is Christmas. Kevin and Don are standing around the tree. They sip spiked eggnog from festive cups. Don's elbow pressed gently into Kevin's ribs as he jested with his older brother, "Spend a little more money on the gun for the store. It holds seventeen rounds. You might need all of those shots someday."

Kevin choked out his final words, "I should have listened to Don."

Jacob was perplexed by the man's last sentence. Over the years, he had heard a lot of people's final thoughts and dying words, but that was by far one of the weirder phrases he had come across. He studied the dying man's eyes. The confusion. The pain. In those final seconds, this stranger told Jacob all of his secrets and all of his fears.

Jacob's body tingled with excitement. Even though he was going to die in the next month, he felt more alive than ever. He couldn't remember the last time he had been shot at. This shop owner was a perfect start to Jacob's final chapter. He was worthy of being Reckoned.

Number two hundred and fifty-three. Forty-seven more bodies to go and I'll complete my goal. The thought of it filled Jacob with a sense of pride. He wished he still had his tongue so he could thank the man. Jacob noticed the nametag. He would have said, "Thank you, Kevin. I'm one step closer to achieving greatness because of your sacrifice."

The front door chimed. Jacob's head snapped in its direction. His three comrades entered with a flurry of wind and snow.

Arthur's voice cracked as he asked, "Did he call the fuzz?"

Jacob shook his head as he slowly inched the blade from the dead man's torso and laid the body onto the floor behind the counter.

"That was some crazy fucked up shit, brother. You got mad-dog abilities." Regan grabbed a bag of zesty tortilla chips off an endcap and popped it open as he walked slowly over to the counter. "Color me impressed." He dropped a salt covered triangle into his big mouth. As he chewed, he continued to speak. "Get his wallet. We'll need a credit card for the pump." Some of the chip dropped out of his mouth and onto his chest.

This drove Jacob insane. Well, more insane. A slob, talking with his mouth full, and barking orders like Jacob didn't have a damn clue. He was juiced from the kill. The adrenaline pumping through Jacob's veins felt like high-octane jet fuel.

Regan could feel the tension radiating off the deadly man behind the counter with the knife. He decided to offer Jacob a chip from his stolen bag of yum yums, "Good job, killer," he said with a wide-eyed smile.

Jacob declined the snack.

Regan turned back toward the full store, "Let's do some shopping fellas."

Jacob vanquished the urge to slit Regan's throat and settled the storm raging within himself. It took a few minutes to regain total control of his emotions. The others had begun filling shopping baskets with all of the snacks the prison commissary never stocked. Something inside Jacob was off balance. His sickness made it difficult to know what the body needed. It had been five hours since his last meal.

That must be it. I'm hungry. He scanned the store. I'd kill for a SNICKERS. Jacob looked at the dead body next to his feet. I guess I already did.

Chapter 6

The eyepatch wearing Duke Allen wandered an aisle at the local Sweet Home Safeway. He had only a few items in his cart so far. A carton of cigarettes, a twelve pack of premium India Pale Ale from Deschutes Brewing and a pint of Tillamook chocolate chip ice cream. He pushed his cart toward the wall of freshly cut meat. Shiny packages of USDA approved beef sat before him. He picked the thickest steak they had on the shelf and tossed it into the basket with the other "bad for you" items.

Out of the corner of his eye, he spotted his yoga instructor, Lisa Williams.

I should go and say hey. He thought. Then Duke noticed she was shuffling across the store like a zombie. Whatever had been bugging her earlier had apparently gotten worse. She didn't see him so he headed in a different direction to avoid the awkward public interaction.

Duke veered toward the front of the store to purchase his items. When he was halfway there he remembered he needed eggs for breakfast. He doubled back and headed for the other corner of the store.

Duke passed a magazine rack on the way toward the refrigerated food. A sexy revolver on the latest issue of *Guns & Ammo* caught his attention. He came to a stop and picked up the high-gloss magazine. Duke thumbed quickly to the section about the gun on the cover. He was a full paragraph in when a raspy female voice whispered.

"Duke?"

A shiver raced down the man's spine. He raised his head from the page and said, "Did the devil let you out of hell for bad behavior?" He placed the magazine back on the shelf, turned and faced the demon. "Hello, Sharon." A hint of disgust floated in the air.

A woman in her fifties with platinum blonde hair stood in front of him. A plastic basket hung from her forearm filled with healthy organic food. She placed her well-manicured hand on her curvy hip, pulling open her winter coat and revealing a fabulous hourglass figure.

"You're not fat. Anymore," Sharon said with an amazed huff. She reached out and poked Duke in the stomach. "Nice and firm. You actually look handsome. Except for that stupid eyepatch. Are you hitting Lisa's yoga class every day now?"

Duke brushed away her poking finger, "Don't touch the merchandise."

She looked over his cart, "Still a bachelor?"

Duke's eye narrowed and he nodded at her basket, "You finally quit eating babies?"

Sharon smirked. "So clever. Tell me, how is Duke Allen going to spend his New Years? Any big plans for the evening?"

"I'm going to spend it happy and alone." Duke reached for his cart to make his escape. Sharon caught him by the arm and turned him to face her.

"It just so happens that I'm also single this holiday season. Why don't you bring that new body of yours over to my place tonight?" she asked as her hand gently massaged Duke's bicep.

"Playing hard to get, Sharon?" he asked as he brushed away her hand. Again. "Even though I miss the girls..." Duke surveyed the wonderfully deep ravine that was her cleavage before continuing, "...I have no desire to throw my meat into your grinder."

She closed her eyes and shook her head. "Classless until the end." She stepped closer and invaded Duke's personal space. "The girls can't be the only part of me you miss. What about...?" Sharon leaned forward and whispered in Duke's ear for a fraction of a second Duke's knees trembled and were about to give.

"Now who's classless?" Duke said as he took Sharon by the shoulders and moved her out of his bubble. "It's a new year. Go make someone else miserable." He released her, pivoted and made his final escape before she could think of something evil to say back.

A cruiser zipped down Main Street and pulled into a parking spot in front of the tiny timeworn Sheriff's office. He pulled next to a tan Ford Bronco. Sheriff was written in big bold letters on the vehicle's doors. Deputy Dominic Spence adjusted the gun on his hip as he exited the Crown Vic. He scanned the surrounding buildings, and town's people, looking for anything that seemed...out of place. He had developed the habit even before he started at the academy. The sidewalk in front of the police station had been recently shoveled and salt had been spread across the concrete. Flakes the size of quarters poured from the dark clouds above, but the little chunks of salt kept them at bay.

Dominic put his shoulder into the front door to force it open. The old wooden entrance swelled every damn winter. As Dominic entered the front office a plaque hung on the wall stating the building had proudly been there serving the community since 1952.

"It's me," he said as he pushed the door closed. He had to deliver a quick strike with the palm of his hand to force it closed. He turned into the office. The dim and dark space caused his face to scowl. The front desk phone operator's station sat empty.

Rebecca was scheduled until six p.m. Where the hell is that girl? Dominic thought to himself. *I just got a call from her to come in.*

No purse or jacket.

Rebecca must be at lunch. Sheriff's Bronco was outside. MaCready has to be around here somewhere.

"The lights are off," Dominic stated the obvious as he flicked the switch on the wall. Nothing happened. He flipped it on and off a few more times. Nothing.

"Goddamn it, electricity is out at the switch. Again." He banged his hand against the sheetrock. The lights flickered above.

"Sheriff?" Dominic called out. He flipped the switch again and hit the wall one more time and the lights came up. With the overhead lights beaming, he could clearly see Rebecca's desk. A lone photo of her sat next to the computer. Her chubby cheeks sported a large smile full of bright white teeth. Large thick glasses framed her round face. Next to her was an equally fat calico cat pulled tight into her temple. The poor kitty-kitty was not happy about this forced selfie.

Dominic slid out of his heavy coat and hung it on a hook. The hook snapped away from the wall loudly. The jacket dropped to the floor with a thud. He ran his hands through his thick, wavy hair. He breathed out a long calming breath as he picked his coat up from the floor. A few steps later he was standing in front of a pristine desk, even the paperclips were organized by size and color. His name was engraved on the gold colored nameplate. He draped his jacket over his chair, then tapped a few buttons on his desk phone.

The female sounding computer voice informed him he had, "No new messages." Dominic pulled out his chair and took a seat at the desk. He hit the power button on his computer. A few minutes ticked by before he was able to pull up his work emails. Click, click...and one last click on the folder for new emails. Zero new emails. Unless he counted the spam, but he didn't need to refinance his house or get a bigger penis. Delete all.

"MaCready?" he said as he stood back up from the desk. He moved toward the back and headed for a door with a single word written in black stencil on it. "Sheriff"

He paused at the door and called even louder, "Sheriff." He wrapped his knuckles against the glass. He could hear a voice on the other side of the door. It was only a whisper and it sounded like it was crying softly.

Dominic turned the knob and opened the door. A woman in her early sixties, sat reclined in the leather chair, her crossed legs extended up onto the corner of the desk. She lazily tapped out a beat with a set of dirty gray cowgirl boots. Large black headphones covered both ears as a pop hit played loudly over the little speakers. She sang the up-tempo song softly to herself. A tan colored cowgirl hat hung from an angular, engraved crystal award on her desk.

"Sheriff?"

MaCready pulled her headphones off and paused the song mid chorus. "Dominic." The Sheriff did not bother to put her boots down or sit up as she continued, "I didn't hear you. Noise cancelling headphones. I got them for myself this Christmas. Come in. Sit down."

"Where's Rebecca?"

"Sent her home. She hadn't got a call all day."

Dominic forced a smile as he pulled out his chair. "How can you hear the phones if they are noise canceling?"

"The little light blinks red on the console when a call comes in. Have you heard this new song?" She hit play and let the music flow out of the headphones.

Dominic shook his head no, shifted in his seat and folded his arms across his chest.

"It's so good. I've heard it four times today. I can't get enough of the chorus."

"You called me in."

"Did you talk to Duke?"

"I told him that you requested that he remove the trophy from the front of his vehicle."

"How did he take it?"

"I think Duke wanted to shoot me and hang my head from the back of his truck."

MaCready chuckled to herself. Then a memory clicked. "I heard back about your transfer request."

Dominic sat forward and uncrossed his arms. His throat squeaked out a, "Yes."

"Let's see. I put the papers somewhere." MaCready's eyes shifted over the desk then over to the cabinets.

Dominic gritted his teeth, "What did it say?"

She sighed and made two obnoxious clicks with her mouth before she began, "Looks like the big city isn't ready for you, yet. Maybe next year."

The deputy's gaze flicked to the floor and he gnawed at his top lip. His strong hands gripped the armrests at his side. Veins popped. The steel frame of the chair groaned under the pressure.

"This is such a cushy gig. Why the hell are you itching to get out of Sweet Home so badly? You get the same level of pay and you don't have cracked out trailer trash trying to gun you down?"

MaCready's desk phone rang.

"Maybe it's some action," MaCready jested as she lifted up the receiver. "Sheriff MaCready, Sweet Home." She listened carefully. Slowly she dropped her feet to the floor, sat up in her chair and picked up a pen. MaCready scribbled a note down on a pad of paper. "Got it. I'll get a deputy out there," and she hung up the phone.

"Someone called 911 out at the One Stop Mountain Shop. They tried calling the landline back but no one's answering. Get out there and see what 'Handsome Kevin' is up to." MaCready eased back into her chair, her boots raised up off the floor and she placed them gently on the desk. Her headphones slid back over her ears and she pressed play.

Dominic released his vise-grip on the armrests and stood up quickly. As he crested the threshold, MaCready spoke loudly over her headphones, "Don't forget about the New Year's party at the high school gym. We need to show up and represent the department. Plus, I overheard Rebecca say she was looking forward to a dance with you." MaCready waved her eyebrows wildly at her deputy and ended it with a wink.

Dominic strained a smile and a nod at her as he closed the door behind himself. He took a few steps away from the door, paused and then threw a silent fit. His fists flew through the air. He kicked at the imaginary bastard that was keeping him in this dump. Dominic picked up his coat and mouthed a quiet "Fuck!" as he punched his fists into its sleeves.

He headed for the door. As he reached for the switch on the wall the lights flickered off on their own. His extended hand twisted at the wrist and he flipped the light switch a wicked bird. He landed a solid right cross to punch open the sticky front door.

Dominic paused for a moment on the sidewalk as he gave his jacket's zipper a quick yank up. His grimace burned. If he saw someone jaywalking right now he would gun them down in cold blood.

Hayden Williams sat at a desk in his bedroom. Posters of

young, hot, male actors and musicians hung on every wall. The room was tidy, but not crazy clean. First place trophies and awards were crammed onto a shelf. They proclaimed him an outstanding athlete. His nimble fingers flew across the keyboard with precision. He was Beethoven and this instant message was his symphony. "MaKelle! Get in here. I need you more than ever."

MaKelle Williams, burst through the half opened door with a dramatic flair that would impress Kramer on Seinfeld. She clutched an electronic tablet between her hands. "What do you need, brother?"

His fingers didn't break their stride as he spoke, "I'm inviting boys over for the night. Which one do you want Andrew to bring?"

"I don't need a boy here." She crossed her arms and slowly shuffled her way toward him.

"I didn't say you did, but if Andrew was to bring someone to keep you occupied and there was a gun pressed to your head, which one would you pick?" Hayden clicked his mouse a few times and then pulled away from the screen to reveal her two choices. On the left side of the computer was a nice boy who was not too bad looking named Steve-o. She had seen him around at school but they had never talked. On the right side of the screen was a boy, that for the last month, every girl in her grade had been gossiping about. Colby. He was new. Straight from California, and looked like a young *Chris Evans*.

MaKelle's eyebrows climbed up her forehead. "They would be coming here? Tonight?"

"That was the plan."

"And I'd have to hang out with one of them, alone, while you're 'busy' with Andrew?"

"That's the plan."

"Gun to my head, he's bringing one of them, no matter what?" MaKelle scratched at her invisible beard and pretended to make a hard decision.

"Yes, just pick one, please." Hayden's patience for her charade was wearing thin.

"I guess, if there is no getting around it and the gun is firmly placed to my head. Ask him to bring... I don't know... Colby."

"Finally, color me shocked." Hayden fired off a quick message to Andrew.

"If you knew which one I was going to pick then why waste the time asking?"

"Having a choice is precious." He continued to type without looking back at her.

"What?"

"If I didn't ask and Andrew showed up with Colby, say you ended up hating him. Say he ruins your night or the rest of your year at school, who would be at fault?"

"You."

"Exactly."

MaKelle shifted her stance and moved closer to the computer screen. The siblings were now ear-to-ear as she watched every move he made on the computer. "What's he into?"

"Who knows, teens are growing up so fast now a days."

"Do mom and dad know they're coming over?"

Hayden stopped typing and with his index finger he pushed her noggin away from his. "I didn't get permission if that's what you're asking. Our folks are intelligent people. They must know there's a high probability that we would have guests tonight."

MaKelle swatted his hand away, "I should stalk him on Facebook. Find out some info. Get the deets'. I don't want the conversation to drag."

"That sounds *fabulous*."

MaKelle fired up her iPad and headed for the door. "You said you're giving up that word for New Year's."

"New Year's starts tomorrow. I'll drop the F-word all I want until midnight."

Ben Williams stood in front of a full-length mirror. He had a purple button up dress shirt pulled up his left arm and hanging from the shoulder. A black shirt hung the same way on his right. He turned and pivoted back and forth modeling the two different shirts. Purple, black, purple, black.

"MaKelle, Hayden?" he called.

The two teens meandered out of their separate rooms staring at electronic tablets. The light from the screens cast an eerie glow over their faces. They shuffled down the hall toward the open door.

Ben turned to face them, "Which one?"

They lowered the screens and gazed at their father. Ben playfully posed and flexed at them. He improvised a quick dance to show off the shirts in action.

"I think you should wear them like that. Start a new trend." MaKelle teased.

"Come on. Help a brother out here." Ben placed his hands on his hips. His focus shifted to his son.

Hayden raised an eyebrow. "What?"

"Which one looks better?"

"I don't know." Hayden's attention drifted back to his iPad.

"Of course you know. Just tell me."

"I see. Dad, I'm not that kind of *gay*. I don't care about fashion. Toss a coin or ask Mom when she gets back." Hayden turned away and headed for his room.

"Thanks bro," Ben laid down a thick layer of sarcasm.

"You're welcome, bro." Hayden threw the sarcasm back at his father.

MaKelle turned off her tablet and stepped over to the bed. She pushed a pile of unfolded clothes out of her way and took a seat. "Which one makes you feel more confident?"

"What?"

"If you feel confident in how you're dressed then you'll portray confidence in how you walk and talk. That's what you're after, right. You want to suavely talk people into signing up at the gym? If you feel like *the man* then you will act like *the man*." The youthful lady spoke with a wisdom beyond her years. She easily picked up on her father's confusion. "I read it in one of your men's fitness magazines."

His confusion grew.

"What? I read the articles too." A devious smile crept across her young face.

Ben slid the purple shirt off his shoulder. "Thanks for the advice." He buttoned up the black shirt and hung the discarded one back in the closet. "What did you guys have planned for the rest of the night?"

"Have some friends over and watch movies."

Ben picked up his laundry from the bed and tossed it into his side of the closet. "Just staying in then?"

"We plan to use a Ouija board to summon the dark lord and maybe start a cult. Haven't decided." MaKelle laid back onto the bed. She picked up a framed photo from the side table and held it above her face. It was all four of the Williams around a campfire. Wieners and marshmallows speared on whittled sticks over the flaming little pit. A set of dome tents sat in the background. The two kids were preteens. "When are we gonna go back to Fort Stevens?"

"I don't know Sweetie. It's going to be so busy..." Ben said as he tucked his shirt into his slacks. The disappointment on her face was so slight only a highly trained parent could have picked it up. "...but I'll talk with Mom and see if we can squeeze a weekend in before the end of spring."

"Cool." MaKelle placed the photo back onto the table and sat back up.

Hayden yelled from his bedroom, "MaKelle! Get in here. I need you more than ever."

"My expertise is needed elsewhere." She slowly got to her feet and picked up the tablet. "You look good Pops," she said as she made for the door.

"Thanks, kiddo."

MaKelle paused for a moment. Her features scrunched up, "Is Mom going with you tonight?"

"Excellent question."

A blue Subaru Forester idled in park. It was pulled next to a sidewalk on a quiet street that was lined with split-level and ranch style homes. The wipers pushed aside the onslaught of flakes as they fell upon the windshield. In the front yard next to the car, two ten-year-old boys were working hard to build an epic snowman together.

Lisa Williams sat in the driver's seat of the Forester. She stared at herself in the rearview mirror. Red rings surrounded her eyes and nostrils. Wet tracks ran down her upper lip and cheeks. She appeared exhausted and ready to crack at any moment.

She spoke to her reflection like a drill-sergeant, "Come on Lisa. Suck it up. Don't be such a pussy." A sack of groceries sat next to her in the passenger's seat. It was half full with goodies. Sitting on top of everything was a bag of barbecue potato chips. She plucked the bag of treats from the sack and ripped open the top. Lisa dug in with a ravenous appetite.

With her mouth full of crunchy chips she continued, "That's it. Stuff your face. Push the emotions down with two thousand empty calories. That'll make you feel better. You're such a mess. A guy pays a little attention to you once and you do something so, so stupid. Way to ruin your family. You're an idiot." For five minutes straight she downed chip after tasty chip without saying a word. The redness around her eyes had softened. The waterfall of snot pouring out her nose had come to a stop.

"Damn these chips are good." She dropped one last big, salt covered, barbecue dust encased chip into her mouth and quickly closed the bag. She tossed it back in the sack with the other treats. A water bottle sat in the center console. She picked it up and drained it.

Lisa took a deep breath at the end of her long drink. She replaced the bottle, gave her eye sockets a good rub and caught another glimpse of herself in the mirror. "I look like shit." She pulled her purse from the floorboard, dug through the mess inside the black bag, found her concealer and went to work covering her sad sack of a face. Hiding all of her misery under a thin coat of skin toned paint.

Outside the car in the adjacent yard, the boys were lifting a massive snowball up onto the body of their snowman. They were so close to completing their masterpiece.

Lisa applied the last few strokes of color to her own

masterpiece, tossed her makeup back into her purse and readjusted her mirror.

"Okay, I can do this," she said with a slight waver of doubt. Lisa put the car into gear and started rolling down the street. She passed eight houses before she pulled into the driveway of a split-level. Christmas lights were hung with care along the eave of the house. The single maple tree in the front yard was wrapped from the base to the tippy-top with little blinking lights.

Lisa looked up into the living room window as she turned off the ignition. Their Christmas tree was decorated with family heirlooms and tinsel. It looked like Christmas had thrown up all over the evergreen, but that is just how the Williams family liked it.

She picked up her purse and groceries. "Get in there and give them an Academy award winning performance." Lisa trudged out into the snow with a perfect smile plastered across her beautiful face.

Chapter 7

"God damn this is good," Arthur said as he took another long pull off an ice cold sixteen-ounce Budweiser. "I haven't had a drink in decades. You want one?" he offered.

Jacob shook his head. He needed to stay sharp. He could not afford to have his mind clouded with alcohol if he was going to try to hit his goal tonight.

"What about you big fella? You wanna brewski?" Arthur yelled across the store to Zarren.

The giant grunted a, "No," back at Arthur.

"More for me then." Arthur slurped down another gulp. Between sips, he walked around the store, kicking over displays and end caps just for the fun of it. Individually wrapped packages of food spilled across the floor. The racket was driving Jacob crazy.

Arthur front kicked a neatly stacked tower of *Castrol* boxes that were filled with quarts of 20w-50 motor oil. The tower toppled and crashed to the tile floor. He let out a wolf's howl and looked around to see if anyone else was as amused as he was. Jacob flashed Arthur a look of disapproval as he leaned against the front counter. Arthur didn't give a shit and kept up his mischief.

Jacob chomped down the last bite of his second *Snickers* bar. Not having a tongue to assist in the eating process meant he had to suck and slowly chew on his food until it dissolved enough to be swallowed. It took forever to eat anything, but it did help keep him trim. He was slowly coming down off the high he got from adding to his list. The tingle of adrenaline had almost completely dissipated and he finally felt like himself. He felt, at peace.

That was a very good start. Jacob thought as he tossed the empty candy bar wrapper to the floor. The knife he had used to take Kevin's life sat on the counter next to him. The blood had already begun to congeal around the edges of the blade.

I must clean it before the next Reckoning.

Jacob picked up the knife and headed for the bathroom. As he passed the counter, he could see Kevin lying on the floor. The body looked so peaceful. Jacob was envious. He was not ready to die, he still had work to do, but he longed for the peace and quiet that only death could bring.

Another crash as Arthur knocked down a rack of camping cookware. Cast-iron skillets and griddles clattered to the floor.

Jacob slipped into the restroom and stepped up to the sink. He could hear Arthur's reign of terror through the thick steel bathroom door. Jacob kept his head down as he twisted the knob and water poured from the tap. He did not want to even glance up at his own reflection. Every time he did catch a glimpse of himself in a shiny surface he couldn't believe that the monster staring back at him was really Jacob Glass. Disfigured, covered in scars, he looked nothing like the face he grew up with. Only the eyes had remained the same. As he began to clean the crimson from the polished steel, he wondered.

Is this the face I was meant to be born with?

Is that monster in the mirror really me?

He slid the blade back and forth under the spout. The dark red turned pink. The knife's finish became clear. The steamy water fogged the mirror above the sink. The blade was clean and ready for the next body. It was ready to continue its job.

This one's a keeper. He thought. *It's as sharp as the devil himself. I'll need a way to carry it safely.*

He exited the bathroom and made for the display where he had found the perfect killing tool. Under the busted case was a cabinet. He squatted down and pulled the door open. Inside the cabinet was a stack of thin rectangular boxes. Jacob reached in and yanked the stack out. They spilled across the floor. He dug through them, found the one with a photo of the knife on it. He popped open the small container and inside was exactly what he was looking for, the matching sheath.

In the hunting section of the store he found a belt in his size and wrapped it around his waist. He eased the steel blade into its leather home and snapped it into position.

Zarren had been keeping himself busy with a project since they arrived at the store. He had a little pile of supplies going, a thick wool blanket, tool belt and a collection of brand new tools. He laid the blanket on the floor and picked up a box cutter. He slid the blade out and made a horizontal slice dead center of the wool. He picked up the blanket and pulled the fabric over his head, forcing his bushy noggin through the new hole. The blanket became a poncho. He grasped the tool belt and wrapped it around his waist to hold the wool blanket in place.

Regan crashed through the front door. "The rig is gassed and ready to roll." He dragged the twisted body of Carl the Plumber with him into the store. "Sorry big guy, I think this asshole died of a heart attack. He ain't breathing. We should leave him here." Regan dusted the snow from his shoulders and wiped the melting flakes off his scalp.

Zarren moved from his corner of the store. He slipped his massive sausage fingers into a set of heavy duty work gloves. His tool belt was full to the brim with screwdrivers, a couple of hammers and a few handsaws. He looked at the dead heap at Regan's feet. Purple bruises covered Carl's neck.

Regan noticed Zarren's new belt. "This boy is ready to work," he barked out a laugh.

Zarren flexed his fingers into claws. He worked the new leather gloves on as he stepped closer to Regan. "You choked him." Zarren was not asking, he was stating a fact.

Regan pulled his shoulders back, "A little." Zarren stepped closer as Regan continued. "I was sick of his whining so I took the bitch out."

"He was mine," Zarren towered over Regan.

"Let's just hit the road, fellas. There'll be plenty more in town." Arthur tried his best to keep the peace. His basket of booze and snacks swung from his arm as he stepped for the door.

It was too late. The pissing contest had begun.

Zarren's brow dropped and he smooshed his lips together. Short puffs of hot air blasted out his nostrils. Regan bugged out his eyes and he held a crooked smile. They inched closer to each other.

Their noses were a hair's width from touching.

"If you wanna go, then let's go, big guy. I ain't afraid of shit. I'm already dead." Regan jammed his index finger into the side of his skull and pounded at his scar.

Jacob folded his arms and waited to see who would make the first move. He did not give a shit if they killed each other, just as long as they didn't drag him into it.

After a long and tense thirty seconds Zarren said, "Don't touch my things," then he walked away.

Regan blinked wildly as he regained his composure. An idea hit and his face changed in a fraction of a second. He was back to normal. "We should torch the place. Leave no evidence."

Arthur took a swig of beer and a little spilled out onto his beard. He dragged his sleeve across his mouth as he asked, "Why?"

"Why not?"

"Good point." Arthur let a burp slip between his lips.

Why waste our time burning the place down? Jacob thought.

"You guys load up. It will only take a few minutes to rig something." Regan headed for a corner of the store that had household accessories. It didn't matter what Jacob thought, the majority ruled and they wanted to blast the place to smithereens. He followed Arthur out of the store and into the van.

Zarren made his way for the door and picked up one more souvenir from the One Stop Mountain Shop. A sledgehammer. The heavy-duty tool hung by itself from a peg on the wall next to some other gardening tools. Its metal head was painted black and it had a thirty-six inch fiberglass handle that was wrapped with a rubber grip. The ultimate crusher.

Zarren followed behind Jacob and the three cons climbed back into their stolen ride. They watched Regan collect what he needed to do the job. The bald man was right, it only took him a few minutes to gather up a handful of supplies. A moment later he was hitting the front door carrying an orange extension cord, duct tape and a set of pliers. He slowly unraveled the cord and fed it through the front door. Regan jogged for one of the fuel pumps. With the pliers he cut the head of the cord and peeled back the plastic cover to expose the copper wires beneath. Then he pinned the cord to the side of a fifty-five gallon garbage can that was sitting next to the pump. He held the cut wire in position, right at the lip of the trashcan, and secured it with a few wraps of the gray tape.

Regan ran Kevin's debit card through the pump's machine, selected a grade of gas, picked up the nozzle, pulled back the black accordion cover and wrapped the end of it with duct tape. The tape held the sensor back and simulated pressing the nozzle into the inlet of a vehicle. Regan tore off a strip of duct tape and wrapped it around the trigger. As soon as the trigger was engaged fuel started to flow. He aimed the gasoline into the garbage can and it chugged at a steady pace.

"This is gonna be so good." He lowered the flowing nozzle into the garbage can and dropped it with a wet thud. With the trigger taped up it kept pouring fuel. He raced around to the driver's side and climbed in.

Regan put the key into the ignition and started the van. "I plugged the cord into a timer. The kind you'd set your Christmas lights on. In about twenty minutes this place is gonna be smoked. I wish we could watch it go up, baby! It's gonna be one hell of a show." He pulled the shifter on the steering column, put the van into drive and stomped on the gas.

The van sped onto the highway. They fishtailed a little on the snow, but he quickly got it back under control. Regan tapped out a fast tempo on the steering wheel with the palms of his hands. "You boys ready to do some hell raising?"

"Fuck yeah!" Arthur belted out another wolf howl, finished his can of beer and tossed the empty to the back of the van. "I haven't felt this good in years." He dug through his basket and yanked another can off the pack. "Help a brother out, would you?" He held the perspiring beer can up to Zarren. The big guy didn't move. "Come on. Be a pal. These old digits are worthless."

Zarren gave in and popped the top for the old-timer.

"Thank you kind sir." Arthur was already starting to slur. He happily gulped down a mouthful of brew when an idea hit. "Hey…" He pointed at Zarren. "You've done this before. What's the best way to take out a whole town...? In one night."

This question grabbed Jacob and Regan's attention. It might have been the most intelligent thing Arthur had said all day. Jacob turned to face Zarren. The big man was clearly caught off guard. It looked like no one had ever asked him for advice or his counsel and now he was forced up on to center stage.

Regan licked his lips and said, "Yeah buddy, lay down a battle plan. Walk us through the night."

Zarren deliberated for a moment, cleared his throat and began with an emotionless, monotone voice. "First, we cut off communication and power. Second, we take out the entire police department. Third, we start a fire and draw away the town's emergency teams. Finally, we move house by house and block by block. We leave no survivors."

The van became silent. They contemplated the plan Zarren had laid before them.

Regan blurted out, *"Conan, what is best in life?"* and in his best *Arnold Schwarzenegger* impression he continued, *"To crush your enemies, see them driven before you, and to hear the lamentation of their women."* Regan smiled enthusiastically at Jacob, but it was clear he had never seen the movie. "Come on, you guys haven't seen *Conan the Barbarian*?"

No response.

"It's a fucking great flick."

Still no response.

"Fuck you guys."

Arthur raised his can in a toast. "Beauty plan, brother."

Jacob nodded at Zarren and turned back around in his seat. He pondered Zarren's concept for the evening.

Cut communication and power.

Take out the police.

Set a fire.

Then add to his Reckoning. He liked it. It was simple and easy to remember. It was unlike anything he had ever done before and that was what excited him the most.

The van thundered down the snow-covered mountain road.

60

Regan had begun to drive even faster. A collective buzz had filled the van's cabin. The wall of trees that lined each side of the road and the thick clouds in the sky made it dark out. It felt later in the day than it actually was.

Jacob's hand stroked the sheath on his hip. *It's going to be a fun night.* He thought.

A green sign on the side of the road said they were ten miles out from Sweet Home. The van slogged through the snow. They made switchback after switchback and the pitch of the mountain increased in its intensity. The van slowed to a crawl as they crested the pass.

Regan came to a full stop on the side of the road. The ridge on their right dropped a couple hundred yards into a rocky basin.

The disease Jacob suffered from made it impossible to feel sensations in his body. No heat. No cold. No pain. As a result he had spent decades accidently biting chunks of his tongue off, until it no longer functioned, but even if he had a tongue in his mouth he would have been speechless. He had reached the top of the mountain. He could see the town and he knew exactly how many people he needed to add to the list. The little fantasy he had back on the prison transfer bus had come true.

Regan eased out a whistle. "What a view."

In the little valley below lay the town of Sweet Home. The snow, Christmas decorations and lights made the town look more like an artist's rendering of a snowy village than a living breathing community.

"Oh shit! Look out!" Arthur ducked into the back of the van.

A black and white Crown Vic, traveling in the opposite direction, pulled up next to them. Jacob slid into his seat and kept his head down. His long black hair covered his guilty face.

The driver's side window rolled down as the cruiser came to a full stop. Deputy Dominic Spence popped his concerned face out and asked, "You stuck?"

Regan gritted his teeth and whispered "Fuck," to himself. He rolled his window down halfway. "No officer, we're fine. Just admiring the scenery."

"All right. Drive safe. Have a Happy New Year." Dominic powered up his window and took off down the highway.

The four wanted men held their breath. Regan watched the cruiser round a corner in his side mirror.

Regan let out a heavy exhale, "He's gone."

Jacob sat up in his seat. Arthur rejoined them from the back of the van.

"Welcome to Sweet Home, boys," Regan giggled as he put the van back into gear and headed down the mountain.

Chapter 8

Lisa's keys rattled at the front door, "It's me," she said as she rushed in from the cold and locked the door behind herself. The smell of pine punched her right in the face. The kids demanded a real tree this year and they got it. It was a lot more work to keep watered and to vacuum up the fallen needles, but the smell of an authentic, old timey, Christmas made the endeavor worth the hassle. The tree held the only active lights in the living room. The overly decorated symbol of holiday cheer gave the whole room a warm glow. She paused for a moment and stared into the living room. Lisa came close to breaking into tears, but she stopped herself and kept the gloom at bay.

"Kids? Ben?" Lisa called to them as she headed for the kitchen.

Kids must be in their rooms, zombied out in front of their tablets.

"I picked up snacks." She set the grocery bag on the counter and slipped out of her winter coat. Footsteps could be heard coming down the hall toward the kitchen. The promise of food always got her teen's attention.

Hayden rounded the corner first. He spoke with a playful, childlike British accent, "What wonderful treats did you bring home, Mother?"

Lisa chimed in with proper King's English. "Only the finest the market had to offer my dear." She lifted the open bag of chips. "Here is a bag of thinly sliced salted potatoes for you, my child."

"How delightful," Hayden playfully clapped his hands together.

MaKelle joined them in the kitchen just as Lisa pulled a pound of Reese's Peanut Butter Cups from the sack. "Some imported chocolates from the far Reese's of the Earth."

MaKelle reached for the candies and donned her British

accent. "Well played pun, Mother. I'm glad to see your Oxford education hasn't gone to waste."

The three of them made goofball faces at each other and Lisa stretched out her arms for the upcoming hug. "Get in here." She commanded.

The teens closed in around their mother. She gave the two of them a firm embrace. "God, I love you kids so much." She planted a smooch on both of them. "I can't believe it's already a new year." She dropped another fresh set of kisses on the two of them.

"Okay Mom. That's enough." Hayden broke free from his mother's prison of love and resumed talking normally. He picked up the bag of chips, noticed it was open and half gone. "What happened here?"

"I was hungry."

Hayden chewed at his bottom lip, "That's weird."

"What?" Lisa turned away from him and continued to empty the groceries.

"Is something wrong?" MaKelle moved in next to her mother.

"Why would you think something's wrong?" It came out a smidge too angry.

"Because you never eat half of a bag of chips, like ever." Hayden stepped closer to her other side.

"I'd skipped lunch and I was starving on the drive home." Lisa carried two cans of chili to the pantry. Her two kids stared her down. "It's New Year's, give me a break."

The twins looked at each other. They didn't say a word, but Lisa was absolutely positive they could communicate through their twin telepathy and they were now talking about her behind her back.

"Everything is fine." They looked back at her. "I was just hungry. It's a holiday. I did a hard workout today and skipped lunch...stop talking about me with your minds."

"Paranoia." Hayden started.

MaKelle was next. "Without a doubt."

64

"It's a classic case." Hayden continued.

"How many times have we seen it?" MaKelle didn't skip a beat.

"Why don't you tell us about your relationship with your mother?" Hayden crossed his arms. They loved to torture her with their pseudo doctor gibberish.

"I'm so glad you two are taking psychology at school."

"She's deflecting." MaKelle copied her brother and crossed her arms.

"Where's your Father?" Lisa left the kitchen in a flustered huff.

Hayden picked up the open bag and held it for his sister to snag the first chip. "Something is definitely up."

Before dropping the savory slice of potato into her mouth she concurred, "Definitely."

Lisa stomped down the hallway as she thought to herself.

They're right, I'm not acting like myself. I don't eat a bag of chips for dinner and I never run to their Father to tattle on them. I have to stop this and get back to normal. My hormones are all out of whack.

Stop acting weird.

Stop acting weird.

It was too late. She had lost control of her emotions and her body was not playing fair. Lisa rounded the corner into her bedroom.

"Ben, the kids are playing Sigmund Freud on me again." Her voice cracked. Lisa was on the verge of letting her secret slip.

Ben sat on the edge of their king size bed. He had just slipped his feet into a set of shiny black dress shoes. He stood up from the bed and said, "Come on Lis', you went to college, you should be able to outsmart them. You're a big girl." He turned and looked at her.

Lisa's face went slack. The fitted black dress shirt hung sexily from Ben's strong broad shoulders. The shirt was tucked in, showing off how trim he was around the waist and the slacks put his powerful glutes and thighs on display. Lisa had not seen her husband in anything other than sweatpants, gym shorts and old dingy T-shirts in months.

Damn he looks hot. Oh God, I'm tingling down there.

She had completely forgotten why she had marched down the hall.

Ben could feel her eyes traveling up and down his body. "What? Is something wrong?" he asked.

"Nothing's wrong. You look... nice." Lisa stepped farther into their bedroom.

He ran his hands down his sides and breathed a sigh of relief. "Oh, good. You looked at me like I was an alien." Ben moved over to the dresser and picked up two cufflinks from his top drawer.

Lisa's voice and demeanor had completely changed as she sat on the corner of the bed. "Where are you going?"

"The New Year's dance, remember?" He turned back to face her and slipped the first link into place.

The dance, oh God he's going to ask me to go with him!

All Lisa wanted to do was curl up into a ball, climb under her covers and hide away from this stupid world. The absolute last thing she wanted to do was get all gussied up, mingle with the town, and try to talk them into joining the gym. Moreover, she would have to come up with a legit reason why she wasn't having a drink tonight.

Fuck!

Ben noticed the rapid changes in her expressions, but he could not figure out why she was acting so unusual today. He needed her on his arm at the dance. She was his good luck charm. His rock. Plus having a beautiful woman at his side would increase his chances tenfold. In a pinch they could gang up on someone if they had to. He was no fan of high-pressure sales, but he was desperate. He quickly came up with a plan. Instead of doing his normal thing and ambushing Lisa into a confession or interrogating her until she finally gave up her deep secret, he was going to kill her with kindness.

"Hey, can you help me with this. You know I'm no good with

my left." He stepped over to the bed and sat down next to her. Ben placed the cufflink in her soft hand and held up his wrist. She slowly worked the link through the cuff's little hole.

"I had a funny conversation with Duke today," Ben said as he studied her.

"Yeah?"

"He said, 'It is of the utmost importance that I make sure my lips are pressed against my beautiful wife's the moment the ball drops in Times Square.' And I agree with him."

Lisa fished the link through the last hole and locked it into place. She took the moment to configure the perfect combination of words to maximize her answer.

"Yeah?" Was unfortunately the best she could muster.

"Yeah." Ben took her by the hand and dropped to one knee. He cleared his throat and attempted to sound exactly like a teenage boy asking a date to prom. "Will you please go with me to the Sweet Home New Year's party, please?"

Lisa struggled to find a response. Ben brushed a strand of hair out of her face and tucked it behind her ear.

"*Help me Lisa Williams. You're my only hope.*" He grinned at her with a twinkle in his eyes.

"*Star Wars*?" Lisa pushed Ben away. He stood up and fell playfully onto the bed. "You're going to use *Star Wars* on me?" She climbed up, straddled him and launched a few light punches into his torso. He acted as if they were killing him. "You think quoting one of my favs is going to help you get me to the dance?"

With an overly dramatic, Christopher Walken style, he said, "I'm desperate. You left me no choice." He bucked up his hips, throwing off her balance and then he trapped her arms. At the same time Ben rolled onto her and in a flash he was now on top. He pinned her arms to the mattress. His face was inches from hers. "What do you say? Will you help me talk these suckers into a membership and save... the gym?"

She attempted to free herself from his grip. Lisa hated to lose the wrestling match, but Ben was too damn strong. His hips were pressed against hers as he lay between her thighs. They breathed heavily into each other's face. He released her wrists but kept her trapped under his torso. It had been an eternity since the last time they had kissed passionately or made love. Too many stupid arguments and too many nights they had gone to bed angry. It felt like they had forgotten how to touch each other with love and care.

He feels so good between my legs. I need to kiss him right now. Lisa closed her eyes, lifted her head toward his and just as their lips were about to touch, someone was standing at their bedroom doorway. The presence of this unwanted, unwelcome person watching them grabbed their attention and both of their heads whipped in that direction.

Hayden coughed out an, "Ew, you guys. Close the door next time." He reached into their bedroom and pulled the door shut. The teen just killed the mood. Ben pulled away and Lisa felt too out of practice to lure him back.

"I need to get something to eat before I go," he said as he got to his feet. "Are you coming?" he begged sweetly.

Duke rumbled down Main Street in his Ford pickup. A cigarette smoldered between his fingers and a sneer was perched on his face as he replayed in his head the encounter with his ex, Sharon.

"...*go make someone else miserable.*" He repeated to himself. Just then, perfect cosmic timing was about to occur. As Duke mulled over his relationship with the she-devil he rolled past one of her many business signs she had strategically placed around town.

It was on the back of a bus stop bench. Sharon, smiled perfectly, her platinum blonde hair was professionally styled, someone had worked magic with Photoshop because she had no trace of crows feet or wrinkles. The block letters under her read:

Linn County's number one Realtor. Three years running. Sharon Cox.

Someone had taken a Sharpie to her sign and added a throbbing, veiny, monster sized dick shooting her in the face. The image hit Duke like a fleet of diesel Mack trucks.

"Son-of-a-bitch, I could've gotten laid. What the hell was I thinking?" He tucked the cigarette into the corner of his mouth and struck his palm against the side of his head.

Duke's cell chimed just as he pulled up to a stop sign. He looked at the phone's screen. It was a text he was dreading would come. Stanley, his friend at the gym, sent him a one word message.

"Oasis?"

Duke took a long drag from the burning stick in his mouth. He had been planning to head straight home all day long. He felt a knot in the center of his back and he wanted to go and relax, but something about his run in with Sharon had turned the idea of being alone sour.

He thumbed at his phone's screen, "B right there." Duke made a U-turn at the intersection and zipped back down the street.

"I hope he doesn't want me to choke him tonight." Duke talked to himself with the cigarette hanging from the corner of his mouth. "It would ruin our friendship... I think."

Deputy Spence pulled up to the One Stop Mountain Shop. He noticed how dark it was inside the building. The busted fluorescent lights were still blinking with an irregular pulse. Kevin's red Pathfinder was parked next to the building. A butterfly fluttered around in Dominic's breadbasket as he parked the cruiser at the edge of the lot. He killed the lights and ignition.

As he stepped from his vehicle he was pelted with snow. The only sound out here was the falling flakes and the wind whipping across the highway. He stepped with hast over to the SUV.

With a gloved hand he brushed away the white powder from the driver's side window. It was empty inside the Nissan. He looked over at the store. A breath was stolen from his lungs and his hand instantly went to the Glock on his hip. Two tiny holes surrounded by spider-webbed glass were in the storefront's window.

He reached for the radio on his shoulder and tried to calmly speak into the receiver. "Sheriff." He waited for a moment. "Sheriff, do you read me?" He wiped the flakes off his eyelashes. "Damn headphones."

He inched himself closer to the building and peered inside. No movement, but there were clear signs of a struggle everywhere.

"Shit!" Dominic jumped out of his skin. A distorted body lay on the floor at the front of the store. He pulled his gun and stepped with caution.

When was the last time I pulled my piece? Five years ago? Six?

He eased the front door open and tried not to make a sound as he stepped into the building. The body on the floor was clearly dead. The man's open eyes bulged out of his skull. There was a dark purple bruise around his neck. His limbs were bent and twisted in the wrong direction, but it was not Kevin. The name on his blue work shirt read, Carl. Dominic's memory flashed to the van outside of town and to the weirdo with the scar on his head. He was driving a van with, Carl's Plumbing on it.

It's a crime scene! Don't touch anything! Breathe and remember your training.

He scanned the room. The place had been tossed.

"This is the Police! Show yourselves!" The words fell out of his mouth without thinking. His heart tried to beat its way out of his ribcage. Even though it was freezing outside the Deputy had begun to sweat. He stepped past the dead body and pulled out his flashlight.

"Kevin?" he called as a bright cone of light fell upon the floor before him. He held both the gun and light out in front of his chest, just as he was trained to do. Dominic carefully moved through the store, making sure he didn't touch anything and desperately trying to remember what came next in a situation like this.

"This is the pol-!" He spotted Kevin sprawled out behind the counter. Dominic stepped to the body. A look of terror was frozen on the dead man's handsome face. A lake of blood had collected under his broad shoulders. The crimson stain spread from the incision below his nametag down the front of his torso.

Double homicide!

I have to radio for back up.

We need the State Police or Homicide Detectives. Maybe even the fucking FBI.

Dominic's world began to have a strobe effect. The lids of his eyes were blinking twice as fast as normal and he was hyperventilating.

Take thirty seconds, check every room, make sure that's all of the bodies and no one else is here. Then get the hell out of the building.

Dominic marched back toward the bathroom. He kicked open the door, leveled his gun and growled, "Police!" The one stall was wide open. No bodies, alive or dead. Back out into the main floor. He raced down the short aisles, hopping over knocked down displays, but found no one. Dominic huffed his way for the front door, and crashed through it. The freezing wind felt amazing on his perspiring skin. He jogged back for his Crown Vic to call the Sheriff on his cell. He made a checklist in his mind of what he needed to do next.

Call Sheriff MaCready.

Explain the situation calmly and tell her exactly what I found.

Inform her of the van I saw heading toward town.

She'll tell me what to do, wait here for someone to take over or head back to Sweet Home and hunt down the man driving the van with the scar on his scalp.

Inside the store Regan's timer sat at the one minute mark.

Dominic extracted his cell and took a few deep breaths as he dialed the direct line for MaCready. It rang two times.

Click. One hundred and twenty volts went shooting down the orange extension cord. It took only a millisecond for the juice to zip out the front door, across the parking lot and up the side of the fifty-five gallon trashcan by the pump that was over flowing with gasoline. A spark jumped from the exposed copper wires. The gas fumes caught and the place erupted into a colossal ball of fire. The flames engulfed the pump and the front of the store.

Dominic could not hear himself scream, "FU...!" over the explosion that shook the ground under his feet. The heat hit him first and singed off his eyebrows. Next, the concussive blast rocked the Deputy off his feet. The man flew ten yards before touching back down to Earth. The back of his skull hit the snow-covered asphalt first. He slid another five yards and came to a stop against a curb. The skin on Dominic's face was bright red. White blisters had formed on his nose and cheeks. Sweet Home's only deputy lay unconscious in the snow as the One Stop Mountain Shop burned to the ground.

Chapter 9

A chainsaw's two-stroke motor pulsed from idle to full power as its operator buzzed off the limbs of a fallen tree. The evergreen's branches tumbled to the snow-covered forest floor as the lumberjack worked methodically along the thick timber. Behind him lay a frozen logging road that sliced a jagged line through the clear-cut. The rolling acres looked so peaceful with the blanket of white covering the hundreds of stumps and logs waiting for transport. At the far end of the dirt and gravel road sat a cell tower. The steel structure blended nearly seamlessly with the gray clouds in the background.

"Reggie! Reggie!"

The lumberjack cut off his saw when he realized someone was yelling his name.

"Yeah?" Reggie called out as he shifted his stance and angled toward the person calling his name. It was his buddy Hank, a fellow lumberjack, and he stood dead center on the dirt road with his saw flung up onto his shoulder.

"I'm calling it. Are you heading out soon?" Hank asked as he stepped off the road. A fully loaded semi barreled past them and headed for the highway.

"Nah, I got two hours of overtime approved. Someone's gotta pay for fucking Christmas."

"Stay safe. I'll see you on Monday," Hank said as he waved bye to his friend, turned and began his hike back up the hill to clock out at the company trailer.

"See ya, Hank," Reggie said as he readjusted his safety glasses. He knew it was a little dangerous to be out here by himself, but it wasn't the first time he had done this work alone, nor would it be the last.

"It's time to give this tree a haircut." Reggie yelled to hear himself over his earplugs. The saw in his hand hissed with steam as snow dropped on its blistering hot motor. A quick yank of the cord and Reggie was back at it. Wood chips blasted the top of his steel-toed boots as he sliced and diced the branches. His sinuses were assaulted with the smell of fresh cut pine and exhaust. His body worked on autopilot. Twenty years of lumberjacking made limbing a tree second nature and it allowed his mind to drift.

Reggie sung an improvised melody as he gave the tree a buzz cut, "Ten more trees to limb, before I can head home and crash. It's cold, wet, miserable work, but this asshole has to bring home the cash." He continued to hum the tune as he played back last week's Christmas morning in his mind.

The daydream begins. It's six o'clock in the morning on December 25th. Reggie can hear screams of excitement from the living room. Both of his heads are throbbing with pain. He'd had one, or maybe it was four, too many rum and eggnogs last night. That explained the searing agony in his skull. It was the type of pounding headache that would stay with him all fucking day. No matter what he ate or drank, it was going to jackhammer his brain for the next sixteen hours. The little head in his boxer-briefs felt like a busted up hotdog that had been cooked in a microwave for ten minutes too long. He and the wife, Debbie, had been having messy drunk sex until one thirty in the morning. Something about Christmas made Debbie insanely horny. Every year they'd had the same routine of drinking heavily and finishing the night with the old lust and thrust. What started as some Mr. and Mrs. Santa Claus role-play, turned into an hour-long session of crashing their uglies together until finally, after some raunchy sex talk, they achieved orgasm. In the haze of his rum hangover, Reggie couldn't recall the exact phrase that pushed them over the edge, but he believed it was something about shoving a wad of candy canes up each other's butts.

Debbie burped out, "The kids are up." She whipped back the covers and sat up too quickly. "Oh, shit. I'm going to puke."

"I get to puke first." Reggie joined her and sat up on his side of the bed. His stomach felt like it turned one-eighty and he battled to keep the rancid eggnog down.

"My pussy is tore up, bro," Debbie said as she rubbed her thighs.

"Mine too. I mean, you know what I mean." They giggled through the pain at what a mess the two of them were.

"Merry Christmas," Debbie said with a hint of sarcasm. She lifted herself off the bed and headed for the living room.

"Merry Christmas." Reggie grunted as he did the impossible and got to his feet. A Santa hat and fake white beard sat on his nightstand. They were the two props that got the whole bang session started. He put them on and followed her down the hall. The sweet smell of Debbie was still on the beard. Reggie made a mental note not to kiss any of their children while he wore the beard.

Four young children sat crisscross around the tree. Handmade socks laid in each of their laps and were full to the brim with toys and candy. Their little faces sported grins spread ear to ear as they waited patiently for their shuffling parents to enter the room.

The children sang a chorus of, "Merry Christmas, Mom and Dad."

Reggie belted out a, "Ho, ho, ho. Merry Christmas."

The tree was surrounded by gifts. Debbie had burned through the Christmas fund and then spent a full grand more on the kids. The next hour was a blur of ripping open wrapping paper and the kids screaming with excitement. Reggie tried with all of his mental powers to hold on to this moment and remember it forever. His children's joy and happiness made all of the miserable hours cutting down trees worth it. The daydream ended, but he would play it a few more times before his shift was over.

Reggie got to the end of the tree, stepped over the log and walked to the next tree to be limbed. His thoughts turned to the credit card bill coming this month.

He continued his song, "It's the reason Ol' Reggie's workin' so hard. To pay the bills Ol' Debbie had charged." He was the sole provider for his family and it was a challenge to keep the creditors happy and paid in full.

Debbie was a great wife and mother but she was too hot blooded to be someone's employee. If she was criticized about an email being sent incorrectly the woman was sure to toss boiling hot coffee in her bosses face. It was safer for upper management if Debbie stayed home to take care of the kids. Reggie had come to terms with Debbie's spicy personality. It was a double-edged sword that he loved and hated. Paying for everything with a single income was a tremendous grind, but the constant makeup sex was heavenly. After every bedroom encounter he could have written this letter.

Dear Penthouse,
I couldn't believe it happened to me...

He hummed his melody and inched alongside the timber. He was starting to conceive a romantic plan for the night. New Year's wasn't as big a turn on for Ol' Debbie, but he was ninety percent sure if he got a bottle of champagne or maybe two plus a wad of clearance candy canes he was positive he could wrangle up another night of ground and pound. It was the simple pleasures in life that kept him going.

Reggie was suddenly overcome with the sensation he was being watched. As he turned, a flurry of wind whipped up a dusting of snow. He was surrounded in a whiteout for a brief moment. Then as the gust settled to the ground it revealed a monster of a man standing ten feet from him. The size of this person was startling. He wore a blanket like a poncho and a tool belt wrapped around his waist. His head was covered in a wild mane of curly dark hair and a matching beard. He held a sledgehammer in his hands. The head of the tool looked like it was painted red.

Reggie's mind raced. *Wait, that's not paint. It's blood.*

Action up by the company trailer caught his attention and he looked beyond the large figure. A thin man in an orange jump suit, with long black hair had Hank pinned against the exterior of the trailer. The stranger's forearm was jammed into Hank's neck. The hand wielding the knife slashed and stabbed in and out of Hank's torso at a fevered pace.

Dread wiggled its way through Reggie as he scanned the

work site. His manager was standing in front of the bay window of the trailer. A bald man was draped over his boss's back, with his thick arms wrapped around the supervisor's neck, choking the life out of him.

The fully loaded semi had come to a stop next to a blue van with the name Carl's Plumbing written on the side. An old man with white hair stood next to the semi. He held a pistol at the rig and barked orders to the driver, but Reggie could not hear the exchange.

His face went pale. Adrenaline and panic spiked with a jolt of terror at the horror taking place only a hundred yards away. Everything was happening too fast. The giant with the hammer began to charge. He stomped toward Reggie like a Silverback gorilla. The lumberjack turned to make an escape. The chainsaw still idled in his hands, but the thought of using it as a weapon did not occur to him at that moment.

Reggie plotted.

I'll head for the woods and lose him in the forest. Then head to town and get the Sh-

A powerful impact hit him between his shoulder blades. It knocked the wind out of him instantly. Reggie could hear the crunch of his vertebra. The blow sent him tumbling to his knees. This was the worst pain he had felt in his entire life. As he fell, his trigger hand flexed and the chain spun around the blade of the saw. It bounced back and forth between his legs making a mess out of his thighs.

He landed in a pile at the foot of a stump. He couldn't catch his breath. He couldn't scream. He knew right away the saw had sliced the femoral arteries in his legs. The sledgehammer that hit him in the back lay on the ground next to him. Seconds later the big man was hovering over him, surveying the damage. He knelt down, flipped a switch on the saw, cutting it off, then he picked up both the saw and hammer.

Reggie's body had entered the first stages of shock. His lungs snagged short and painful bites of air. He was unable to take a full breath to ease his suffering. Reggie stared into the big man's eyes. They were ice cold and black to the core. The emotionless face gave no comfort as it watched the life slip out of him.

Reggie could feel the ground rumble under his limp body. It was a familiar sensation he had felt a thousand times before, just never while lying on his back. The semi, loaded with timber, was heading back down the logging road. It raced by him and out of the corner of his eye he could just make out the bald man that had killed his boss behind the wheel.

The big man didn't move a muscle as he continued to watch Reggie meet his end. The lumberjack's heart slowed to a crawl. The falling snow covered his safety glasses and he could barely see out of them. As he crept painfully toward death, he wondered why this had happened to him.

Were these guys a new form of eco-terrorist, hell bent on stopping the logging industry?

As he drew his final breath his mind focused on his family.

How would they make it without me?

His sight was now completely blocked by the fallen flakes. Everything was white. His body was cold. The sound of a collision at the tree line grabbed his attention. At this distance and with his earplugs in it was difficult to tell exactly what had happened. The ground shook under his body. His eyelids fluttered and weighed a hundred pounds each. He drifted off to the next world hearing the noise of galvanized steel groaning under an immense pressure, followed by the crash of the cell tower.

Chapter 10

A battered old pickup with an animal's head mounted to its grill made its way into a sparsely populated lot and skidded to a stop. The exterior of the building was covered with slats of bamboo and a neon green palm tree hung from the front of the bar. In the center of the palm tree's leaves, Oasis was written in neon pink cursive.

A cigarette hung from the corner of Duke's mouth. The amber tip was close to the filter. "The hot spot of downtown, Sweet Home," he said as he sucked down the last of the cigarette and plucked it from his lips. Duke mashed the butt into the sole of his boot and swung his truck door closed.

The lot was starting to get icy so he moved carefully for the front door.

"This will be fun after a pitcher of beer," he said as he grabbed onto the front door and drug himself through the threshold.

It was dark inside and it took a few seconds for his sight to adjust. The Oasis was a wonderfully tacky tiki lounge. Fake palm trees, tiki statues, cypress umbrellas over the tables, a tropical island mural stretched along the back of the bar. Hula music wafted from tiny speakers. It was a stark contrast from the blizzard Duke had stepped out of.

Right away Duke noticed a couple of women in the back corner of the lounge. They were sitting more on each other than next to each other and passion had gotten the better of them. Kisses were exchanged. Secrets whispered back and forth. Love was in the air.

"Hey partner!" Stanley called to his friend.

Duke stopped watching the blossoming romance and moved farther into the building. Stanley was decked out in some fancy duds. The fitted jeans and button up shirt made him look like a new man. He sat at a table with a pitcher full of beer and three glasses at the ready.

Duke slid out of his coat and hung it on a hook attached to a tiki statue. He nodded to the young and pretty barkeep, "Hello, Christy."

"Mr. Allen, nice to see you this evening," she said as she polished a mug with a bright white towel. "It's been too long."

"I've been avoiding empty calories." Duke ran his hand down the front of his smooth stomach.

"Good for you," she said as she gave him a wink.

Duke tugged at his chair and as he sat down he noticed the third glass on the table. "Are we expecting company?"

"Uhm, well." Stanley sipped his brew as Duke poured himself the first round.

The door to the ladies room swung open and a woman in her mid-fifties breezed back into the lounge. She had jet black rock-star hair, wore a skin tight *Led Zeppelin* T-shirt and black leather pants with boots to match. She strutted her stuff straight toward the empty chair at Stanley and Duke's table.

Stanley stood up quickly and slid out her chair like a gentlemen. "Duke, let me introduce you to... you know I never got your first name."

She plopped into the chair. Her hand shot out across the table toward Duke, "Just call me by my last name." Duke shook her hand.

"This is Morgan. She's the lady I told you about." Stanley took his seat and poured her a fresh drink.

Duke couldn't stop the look of surprise on his face as he said, "Nice to meet you, Morgan."

"Likewise." She took her glass from Stanley and raised it up. "To the New Year."

The guys joined her and clinked their glasses together. "To the New Year," they said in unison.

Morgan continued, "I hope this year starts off with a *bang*." She playfully elbowed Stanley as she chugged down a gulp.

Duke choked mid sip.

Stanley's gaze lowered as he drank his beverage.

"So Duke, what do you do?" asked Morgan.

"I'm retired now, but I was an electrician for thirty years."

"*Shocking.*" Morgan laughed loudly at her silly joke. "Now what do you do for fun?"

Duke grinned, "Good one. I enjoy hunting."

"Duke's got a great story about hunting." Stanley chimed in.

Morgan leaned forward. "Do tell."

Duke ran his hand over his goatee as he looked to his friend. Stanley had a nervous energy to him, and Duke couldn't figure out why. "I'll need a few more beers in me before I hit you with that tale. What about you? How do you earn a living?"

She set her glass down, held up her hand and extended a digit every time she listed a job, "I've done construction, I was a roadie for a heavy metal band, worked the docks, did some transcontinental truck driving and in my younger years, I did a little softcore porn."

Duke was taken back. "Really...?"

She smirked and said, "I know it's hard to believe, but I was a damn good roadie." She belted out a monster laugh that had her rocking her chair onto its back legs.

Duke stammered, "I meant... I mean..."

She calmed herself. "I know. The softcore stuff throws everyone for a loop. I'm dating myself, but it was like twenty-five years ago. Back then it was easy money. They had coke and weed on the set. You'd get a little high and they'd film us taking showers or giving a lady a sexy massage. We'd do a little making out, suck some titty." She finished off the last of her beer.

Duke searched for something to say and landed on, "That's... interesting."

Stanley poured her a new one.

"Thanks babe." Morgan leaned forward and gave him a big kiss on the cheek. As she pulled away she noticed a shiny wet spot that she had left on him. Morgan brushed it dry and said, "I left a little extra sugar on you there."

"Would you like to order something to eat?" Stanley asked

as he handed Morgan back her glass.

"Naw," she said as she shimmied a little dance in her chair. "I wanna stay light on my feet. So we can dance to the beat." She waved her eyebrows at Duke. "If I fill up on food I won't wanna be jostled."

"Are you two heading over to the dance later?"

Morgan downed half her glass and let out a giggle. The drink was taking hold and she was a few steps beyond tipsy. "The only dancing I'm talking about will be done, *horizontally*." She let out a snort. "Duke, I hear you got a nice big cabin up in the woods outside of town. Stanley says there's a steamy hot tub on the deck and it's big enough to comfortably hold, *three*." She held up that number of fingers and sang a little melody. "*Three's the magic number...*"

Duke stared Stanley down, but his friend would not look back at him. "Yeah, it's pretty nice."

Morgan dropped her index finger onto the table as she laid out the plan, "I propose we order up one more pitcher, finish that bitch off and head out to take a dip in that hot tub. What do you say Duke, are you in?"

Duke slowly sipped his drink until he finished it. "This beer ran right through me. I need to visit the men's room, excuse me." Duke rose from his chair and patted Stanley on the shoulder. "Can I talk with you?"

"That's sweet. Are you guys going to hold hands as you piss side by side?" Morgan burped out a loud laugh.

Stanley joined her with a laugh of his own. "You're so damn funny."

Duke stopped halfway to the restroom and hissed, "Stanley?"

He set his glass on the table and got to his feet. "I'll be right back. Why don't you order us up another round?"

Morgan swatted him on the ass as he stepped away from the table. She waved to the barkeep. "Sweetheart, can you wrangle up another pitcher?" Again, she sang, "*Three's the magic number...*"

Stanley entered the restroom and found Duke standing with his arms crossed.

Duke angrily whispered, "What in the hell? What's going on out there?"

Stanley raised his hands innocently into the air. "I don't know what you're talking about. Damn, I didn't have to piss when I was out there, but now that I'm in here, I've got to go." He moved for the first urinal on the wall and undid his jeans. "You think it's like a *Pavlov's dogs* kind of thing. You step into the bathroom and your brain plays a trick on you, making your bladder suddenly have to go?"

"I think you're trying to trick me into a threesome with your *softcore* girlfriend out there." Duke paced back and forth.

"You're being ridiculous."

"Am I?"

"It's New Year's and I thought you'd like to spend it out with a friend." Stanley finished, zipped his fly and stepped for the sink.

Duke stopped pacing and glared at Stanley in the mirror. "Look me in the eye and tell me you aren't planning to get me drunk so I'll choke you while you bang Morgan the ex-roadie."

Stanley kept his head down as he reached for a paper towel.

"Tell me that's not what you're angling for."

Stanley dried his hands, tossed the paper into the trash and faced Duke.

"Tell me."

"What do you want me to say, buddy?"

"Oh god! I knew it." Duke resumed pacing.

"Sorry man. I'm chasing the dragon here. I tried to get her old man to spend the weekend in Sweet Home but he's back with his goddamn wife. Morgan doesn't have strong enough hands and-"

Duke cut him off, "Please, shut up."

Stanley grabbed Duke by the arm and stopped his pacing. "I'm sorry."

"What in the hell were you thinking?"

"How long have we been friends?"

Duke did the math, "Two decades."

"Right. You're my best and oldest friend."

"Why risk ruining that friendship with a weird sex act then?"

Stanley took a deep breath. "I'm not getting any younger. I want to expand my horizons, experience life, be more passionate, live every moment to its fullest and share those memories with the people I care about most."

Duke's scowl softened.

"Honestly, I thought if I had to have my oxygen supply cut off while I'm busting the sweetest climax humanly possible, who better to help me with that than my very best friend?" Stanley held out his arms for them to hug it out. "I love you, man."

Duke exited the restroom and b-lined straight for his hanging coat. Stanley was hot on his heels with his arms still open for the hug that was never going to happen.

Morgan flashed a saucy smile at them. "I was about to join you guys in there. I thought maybe you started without me."

Duke grabbed his jacket.

Morgan looked to Stanley, "Are we leaving? I just ordered the beer."

"It was nice to meet you, Morgan and I'm sorry I have to take off so suddenly, but something unexpected just *popped* up." Duke quickly pulled his coat on.

Stanley pleaded. "You don't have to go now. Stay and have a few more beers."

Morgan sounded like a child getting a new toy taken away. "What about the hot tub and the-"

Duke jumped in before she could finish, "Sorry, no hot tub tonight. We'll talk later...buddy." He headed for the door and as he passed Christy, he gave her a wave and said, "Goodnight, Christy."

She was on her way to their table with the new pitcher. "Take it easy Mr. Allen." Christy exchanged the full container for the empty one as Duke hurried through the front door.

Morgan smacked Stanley's thigh with the back of her hand as she said, "You told me he was down."

Stanley slumped into his chair. "I thought he was, baby. I thought he was."

Christy ignored the botched threeway and headed to the back of the lounge where the two women were wrapped up in a human pretzel.

Neither of them slowed down the heavy petting as the barkeep approached the table, "Do I need to get the hose to cool you two down?" Christy asked with a laugh.

"Let go of me, Heidi," said one of the ladies. She squeaked out a giggle as they unraveled their little game of Twister.

"Can I get you two *lovebirds* anything else?" Christy asked as she picked up their empties.

Heidi cleared her throat and straightened out her shirt. "What do you say, Gwen? Should we have a few more before we hit the road?" They picked up their drink menus.

"What do you recommend?" Gwen dug through her purse, found her glasses and put them on her squinting face.

"The Lava Lava is good if you like vodka and Kahlua."

"Let's have two of those, but kick them up a notch." Heidi elbowed Gwen.

"Yes, two Lava Lava's with double shots, please." Gwen elbowed Heidi back.

"Wait, which one are you doubling. The vodka or the Kahlua?" Heidi set down her menu and turned to her friend.

"I don't know. Both?" Gwen dropped her menu and the two of them faced Christy.

"Can we double-double it?"

"They call that a quad, silly."

"No way, it's the double-double, stupid."

"Shut up, you're stupid."

"You're stupid."

"I'll be right back with your drinks." Christy left the table and headed for the bar. She couldn't take any more of the lovers quarrel. "New Year's brings out the fuckin' weirdos." She whispered to herself.

Chapter 11

Zarren cut a wedge into the base of a large evergreen with Reggie's chainsaw. Seconds later a loud crack rocketed from inside the core of the tree. Snow dropped from the limbs as the evergreen slowly tipped out of the sky. It creaked and moaned as it fell to Earth. Its branches broke and snapped on impact. The thick timber lay across the main highway into Sweet Home and successfully blocked the route.

The big man downed the tree a hundred yards away from the blue van parked on the side of the road. He stepped from the fresh stump and moved for the next target.

Jacob was happy Zarren stepped up to the plate and knew his way around a chainsaw. In Jacob's early years he tried to take someone down with a motorized saw and he almost lost his leg. He had seen it done in a movie once and the man with the Leatherface made it look so easy. Chop, chop and the body hits the floor. It was not the case for Jacob. He found the chainsaw to be messy, loud, heavy and unreliable. In the movies they don't show you all the cleanup required after you end someone with a power saw. He remembered swinging it at the escaping person. The chain tore into his spine, but it didn't kill him and the weight of the saw plus its momentum brought the hungry teeth into Jacob's left thigh. The damn thing cut a four-inch gash but didn't hit the bone. He had to stitch himself up, finish the screaming human off. Then spend hours cleaning up the mess.

Jacob looked at his prison jumpsuit. It was filthy, wet and splattered with blood. He needed a fresh set of clothes before he got going on with the night. His knife lay in his lap and was due for a cleaning.

Regan tapped a beat on the steering wheel. "He's really good with that saw. I'd end up dropping the tree on my goddamn head."

"What's next on the list?" Arthur grunted through a yawn.

"Cut the power."

Noise came from the back of the van. A duct tape bound young couple shivered in the dark corner. The woman had on a black cocktail dress and the man sported a matching suit. Strips of silver covered each of their mouths. They were tethered back to back. An empty beer can flew at them and bounced off the man's forehead.

"Nailed it." Arthur laughed.

The man let out a pathetic whimper.

Arthur nudged Regan's shoulder, "What are we doing?"

"Zarren's blocking the streets." Regan answered sharply. He rolled his eyes at Jacob, who was sitting in the passenger's seat. He was now cleaning the blood from his knife with a rag.

"I know that. I mean what are we doing with them?" Arthur pointed at their captives.

"I'll show you." Regan popped open the driver's door, hopped out and closed it.

"What's he doing?"

Jacob shrugged his shoulders and went back to cleaning the blade. The chainsaw blared outside as Zarren started in on another tree trunk.

The van's back doors swung open. Regan flashed a box-cutter. The couple strained against their restraints and screamed through their gags.

"Shut up! I'm not gonna cut you." He reached into the van, slid the knife through a few bands of duct tape that held the two victims together. He yanked the woman out into the snow. Regan thumbed the razor back into the cutter and lightly tossed it at Arthur. "Hang on to this."

Regan dragged the woman to her knees and faced her back into the van. He made sure she was face to face with her man.

He pointed to the man as he leaned on the woman's shoulder. "Are you watching this? Okay, this is choking 101." Regan chuckled and dropped his thick arm around her neck. The man writhed in the back of the van. He inched his way toward the open doors.

"This move earned me a nickname. *The Clutch*."

The woman's body went limp with fear. Regan caught her by the shoulders and lifted the woman back to her knees. "Hold on, I haven't even done it yet. Arthur, watch. You want to line your bicep and forearm up with the arteries running down the sides of their neck. Then add pressure." Regan flexed and the woman's eyes bulged. He let go after a few seconds. The man wiggled to the edge of the van until he was about to fall out.

"Hold on Mister." Arthur caught him by his collar. "He's givin' a lesson. Wait your damn turn. Sorry Regan, do it again. I missed it."

"Bicep and forearm on the arteries. Your hand gets tucked into the pit of your elbow and the other hand puts pressure on the back of their skull. Then you squeeze. Ready?" The woman shook her head, but Regan didn't care and he put full pressure on her neck. His arms contracted like a boa constrictor. The man kicked his legs at Regan and howled through his gag. Tears streamed down his cheeks and his eyes burned bright red. Her pretty mascara covered lashes fluttered and then closed forever. Regan released her neck and she fell face first to the snow. Regan gave her body a nudge with the toe of his boot and she slid down into the neighboring ditch.

In the distance a loud crunch signaled another tree was about to come down and block another exit out of town.

Regan caught his breath and gave his arms a stretch. "Damn, I'm out of practice. I ain't been *The Clutch* in a while." He moved in closer and held his face inches from the man. The captive human's features burned with pure white hot rage. Regan licked his lips and rubbed the scar running down his scalp. "How you doing? Whatcha feeling right now? Alive? Dead? You hate me? You wanna kill me?"

"You're an excellent teacher." Arthur shook the man's collar. "Ain't he?"

Regan rubbed his freezing hands together and asked, "You want revenge?"

The man nodded.

The tree fell from the sky and landed on an intersection.

Regan straightened his back and took a few steps toward the highway. "Cut him free."

"You sure?" Arthur questioned.

"Yes, sir. The man deserves a chance at revenge. Now cut him loose."

Jacob placed his knife back into his sheath and thought.

Just get it over with and quit making the poor bastard suffer.

He plucked a *Butterfinger* out of Arthur's basket, tore it open and chomped on its chocolatey goodness. Outside Zarren moved to another evergreen.

Arthur cut the man's restraints. The man ripped out across the snow. He belted a battle cry through the silver rectangle adhered to his mouth.

Regan looked at peace. He waited, with his arms pinned to his side, as the furious man charged at him. The convict cocked his head back and stood at an angle to his attacker.

The man threw a set of wild haymakers. Regan easily blocked them both and countered with a blow to his sternum. Regan stomped forward and hit him with a clothesline, but instead of knocking him to the ground like a professional wrestler, he wrapped both arms around the man's neck and skull.

Regan made it look effortless as he squeezed the life out of the flailing human. He whispered into the man's ear so the others could not hear. It sounded like a quiet prayer or a priest giving this dying man his last rites. "I'm so sorry. I'm sorry for what I have done to your woman. Please, relax. Let go. It's your time. I'm sending you to a better place and she'll be there waiting for you."

Then the man was gone.

Regan slowly lowered him to the snow and let his body slip into the ditch.

Zarren cut the last notch out of the final tree. It snapped, creaked and joined the other two.

He killed the saw and as he walked back to the van he yelled, "All quick escapes out are now cut off."

"It's time to cut the power, right?" Regan closed the back doors of the van and headed for the driver's seat.

"Yes." Zarren climbed into the side door and slammed it shut.

Regan cranked on the engine and headed into town.

The four of them shared a collective thrill. Every part of the plan had gone off without a hitch and they were inching closer and closer to the outskirts of Sweet Home.

They traveled less than a mile when Regan shouted, "Look at that beat up truck. It's got a fucking deer's head mounted to the goddamn grill."

The truck turned onto a private tree lined road.

"I'm gonna follow him."

Regan killed the lights and kept his distance. Through a meadow in the woods the convicts spotted a beautiful luxury cabin on the hill. The sun was now dipping below the horizon and eerie shadows spread across the ground. Nightfall was rapidly approaching Sweet Home.

Chapter 12

Ben stood at the front door of his home and tossed his winter jacket up on to his shoulder. He checked himself in the mirror that hung next to the kitchen entry. Hair, teeth and clothes all checked out.

"How're ya doing?" Ben asked as he used a fingernail to scratch some plaque off his incisor.

Lisa grunted from around the corner, "I'm figuring out my shoe...situation."

An off tempo march echoed from the hall then she appeared, beautiful as ever, in the mirror's reflection. Ben turned to face her. His attention went straight to her feet. Lisa had a totally impractical high heeled leather boot built for fashion on one foot. On the other was an ugly old snow boot. Anguish stretched across the woman's face as she hobbled into the living room.

"Look good, feel good? Classic dilemma." Ben teased. "You know where I stand."

"MaKelle?" Lisa awkwardly pivoted back into the hallway and headed for her daughter's room. She pushed the half open door. MaKelle lay backwards on her bed so that her sock covered feet rested on the pillow at the head of the mattress. A set of headphones blasted classic rock into the young girl's ears.

"MaKelle!"

She rolled to her side and removed one of the speakers from her head.

"Yep?"

Her mother pointed to her feet. MaKelle's faced scrunched and one eyebrow raised.

"It's gonna snow six inches. You don't want to slip, fall and put a crack in your butt." She smiled, reset the headphone and rolled to her back.

Lisa sighed, and hobbled for her bedroom. A moment later

she emerged with both snow boots on.

"I look ridiculous," Lisa said as she clipped an earring to her lobe. A set of black open toed high heels rested on her forearm. "I'm bringing these with me."

"Good compromise. Kids, we're taking off."

Lisa pulled her coat up her arm and called out, "Come say bye."

Their children stepped from their rooms.

"You ready to boogie with the other old folks?" Hayden mocked and did an old man dance. His arms and legs stayed stiff as he gyrated around.

"You have to bite more bottom lip and keep your arms tight to your chest." MaKelle did her own old person dance as she followed her brother into the living room.

"Hehehe and a hahaha. We're old. Time will work its horrible magic on you someday, so don't make fun." Lisa buttoned her coat and reached for the closest child to give a squeeze.

Ben checked his phone. "Call us if you need anything. Wait. That's weird. I'm not getting a signal. Check your phones."

Lisa dug out her cell. No bars. Hayden and MaKelle's phones said the same.

Lisa hit the speed dial to call Ben's phone. The recorded message played.

Sorry, your call could not be completed as dialed...

Concern crept onto Lisa's face as she put her phone back into her purse. "Maybe we shouldn't go."

"They can handle one night without us," Ben said as he grabbed both children at the same time and double hugged them. "Right?"

"Right." They answered in unison.

He released them and opened the front door. "Let's hit it," he said as he charged out onto the porch.

"Love you kids," Lisa followed on his heels.

"Love you too," They said it in unison, again.

Lisa didn't say a word, but every time the twins spoke the same sentences together it gave her the heebie-jeebies. They sounded like the creepy little ghost girls in The Shining.

Lisa locked the door behind her and headed down the stairs. Ben already had the Subaru on with the heater maxed. Her footprints from earlier were gone, covered by the fresh layer of powder. She moved quickly to get out of the freezing cold and climbed into the passenger's seat. Ben put the car in reverse and pulled out of the driveway. A few blocks down the street he made a left.

As soon as their car was out of sight a set of doors opened on a brand new SUV, with California plates, parked half a block away from the Williams' home.

Andrew, the boy caught kissing Hayden at the video store, stepped off the curb and led the way across the street. "I thought they'd never leave." His cheeks and nose were red from sitting in a frigid car for too long.

The driver of the SUV was Colby, the new boy in school MaKelle had picked from Hayden's computer.

"Are you sure they're cool with me tagging along?" Colby asked as he caught up to Andrew.

"Of course. Hayden commanded I bring you."

"We should have stopped and got a pizza. It's not polite to show up at someone's house without a gift or something." Colby's voice cracked.

Andrew paused in the middle of the street. "What?"

"My Mom and Dad always bring something when they go to a party. It's the polite thing to do."

Andrew concentrated on his young friend's expression. "Dude, are you nervous about meeting his sister?"

"No," he lied, horribly. He instantly read that Andrew was not buying his bullshit. "Look, I went to an all-boys Catholic school. I never had to talk with girls until I moved here. It's hard to think of stuff to say. I have no idea what they're into."

Andrew placed his gloved hand on Colby's shoulder. "Don't be nervous. MaKelle is cool and down to earth. Plus, you're the new hot boy from California and in this town, that right there goes a long way."

Colby breathed out a long nervous sigh.

"You alright?" Andrew rubbed Colby's shoulder and gave it a motivating punch before letting go.

"Yeah, I'm good."

They resumed their march through the snow.

"You really think I'm hot?" Colby asked innocently.

"As the sun my friend."

They climbed the steps to the front door and stomped the snow from their boots as Andrew rang the doorbell.

Duke opened the door to his cabin's mudroom. The truck's engine ticked as it cooled in the garage behind him.

"Honey? I'm home," he said to no one. It eased the loneliness if he acted as if someone was there waiting for him to come home. Duke continued, "You'll never believe the day I had. First I did a killer workout at the gym." He swung his gym bag off his shoulder and placed it on the floor. He kept walking and left the mudroom to enter the kitchen. "Deputy Spence told me I had to take my trophy off the front of my truck. He called it a 'public safety hazard'. I called him a son-of-a-bitch." Duke's home was decked out like a rustic hunting lodge. The kitchen, dining room and living room made up one huge great room. Its focal point was a massive stone fireplace. "Then I told Sharon off at Safeway." He set the grocery bag on the counter and extracted the ice cold beer that had been sitting in his truck since he left the store. "And finally my best friend tried to talk me into some goddamn choking sex three-way thing." Duke found a bottle opener in a junk drawer and popped the top off the bottle of beer in his hand. "How was your day?" He took a swig. In the quiet stillness of Duke's home the only noise being generated was the buzz of the refrigerator and the sound of him chugging beer.

The silence was interrupted by the sound of a chainsaw. Duke could tell it was on the property and close to his private driveway, but was unable to pinpoint exactly where the sound was coming from. Duke moved out of the kitchen and slid open the glass door that led to the deck. A hot tub sat next to the door just under the eave of the cabin. He walked past it and toward the snow-covered rail at the deck's edge. From this vantage, Duke had a view of his whole property. A loud snap echoed through the woods and the chainsaw engine cut off. Duke heard the familiar sound of a tree falling.

Duke shouted at the top of his lungs, "Asshole, stop cutting down my trees and get off m-!" Duke's cabin went dark. He spun and looked back into his home. From his driveway he heard footsteps. There were more than one of them and they were getting closer. The snow reflected the last shreds of light given by the sun, but inside the cabin it was pitch black.

Duke whispered, "Shit." The revolver in his nightstand flashed into his mind.

As he raced back into his cabin he was shrouded in darkness. Three steps in, his shin met the corner of a table and sent him crashing face first to the hardwood floor. The bottle in his hand shattered on impact. The sweet aroma from the hops slapped him in the face and his shirt mopped up the spilled brew. As he righted himself on the floor a triangle shaped chunk of glass buried itself deep into his palm.

There was a loud thud as something big ran into the front door. A window shattered on the opposite side of the house. Duke could hear the intruder's heavy breathing as they climbed through the busted glass. Duke rolled onto his back and held his injured shin. He fought through the pain and forced his wobbly leg to hold his weight.

The intruder kicked on a flashlight and a yellow cone searched the great room.

Duke ducked it and disappeared into a hallway. Another loud crash at the front of the cabin rocked the solid oak door from its frame.

Duke limped down the hall with his hands outstretched in front of him until he found the wood paneled wall. It meant his bedroom was on his right. He reached for the knob, opened the door and slipped inside the room just as the light from the intruder was about to touch him.

Duke leapt across his bed, his fingers frantically searched for the little handle on his nightstand. Jackpot! He yanked it open.

Duke had once joked he kept his guns like he liked his woman on a Saturday night.

Loaded and ready for action.

Duke raised the .44 magnum, thumbed back the hammer and aimed it at the open bedroom door. Footsteps seemed to be everywhere in the cabin. It was impossible to tell if the intruders were coming down the hall over the sound of Duke's heart crashing into his ribcage. The pain in the palm of his hand spiked every time he took a breath.

Duke brought his palm to his mouth. Using his teeth as tweezers, he pulled at the glass shard. It tasted like a disgusting combo of beer and blood. Once it was clear of his flesh, Duke spit it out onto his bed.

Now what? He thought to himself.

Do I go out guns blazing or hang back and let them come to me?

How many of them are there and what the hell do they want?

The flashlights in the great room clicked off. The hallway and open bedroom door went black. The footsteps stopped.

Silence.

Duke felt something deep in the pit of his stomach. It was a sensation he had not felt in a year.

Fear.

Not since he was attacked by the deer had he felt this level of pure fear.

The nasty four-letter word was crippling him.

This fear was different. A year ago he was in the woods. He was in the home of the animal. Duke was trying to take the animal's life, but the tables turned. Duke recalled that moment with vivid details.

It's the end of hunting season. The sun has been up for only thirty minutes when he spots the magnificent creature. It grazes a hundred yards away in a field. Duke pulls the butt of the rifle tight to his shoulder and sights in the dear. BANG! The bullet fired. A direct hit. The animal bounds out of the meadow, but it won't get far. Not with that good of a shot. Duke makes his way through the forest with his rifle slung over his shoulder, filled with a sense of pride. The bright morning sun warms his face. This was a good day.

He finds the spot where the deer was eating. A trail of blood leads him north. He walks to the edge of the meadow and without warning, a flash of antlers and hooves explodes out of the tree line. There's no time to ready his rifle. The creature is too fast. A hoof catches Duke in the chest and sends him to the forest floor. The wind has been knocked out of his lungs and he can't breathe. The antlers come at him like a dozen knives. What happens next takes less than three beats of his heart.

Duke grips the rack and pushes them away with everything he's got, but the deer is too strong. One of the points finds home and hits Duke's skull. The tip of the antler was like a razor blade cutting through his scalp. Duke screams. No one is there to save him. He went hunting alone. Stanley couldn't make the trip so it's just Duke and the buck.

The antler crosses Duke's eye and he goes blind. Blood fills the socket. It was the worst pain he had ever felt in his life.

This is it. He thinks to himself.

I'm about to die.

Will anyone ever even find my body to give it a proper burial?

In the panic and fear Duke's brain clicks into a primal autopilot. Next thing he knew his hunting knife was in his hand and the blade was slicing its way toward the deer's skull. He felt the tip of the knife pop through bone and he pushed it to the hilt. The eight inches of steel scramble the deer's gray matter. The buck reared back, stumbled and fell to its side.

Duke's hands went to his face. He howls in agony. His body thrashes along the ground. It takes a long time to get ahold of the pain, come to terms with it and accept what has happened to him. He keeps a tight hold on his wounded eye. Duke was convinced if he let go his eyeball would fall out of its socket. He got to his feet, his knees like Jello. Steam rose from the deer's carcass.

What now? He thought.

The animal was too big to carry with one hand. The meat would spoil before he could get patched up enough to come back out here and collect his prize, but he was damn sure he wasn't going home empty handed. Not after what he just went through.

Duke made up his mind and shuffled over to the dead body. He retrieved his knife from the deer's skull and cut into its neck. It took an hour to hack, one handed, through all of the skin, muscle and bone.

He pulled his trophy six miles through the thick forest to get back to his truck. Then he drove himself to the hospital. On the drive to the emergency room Duke came up with an epic idea. He was going to mount the creature that almost snuffed him out to the front of his truck. Come hell or high water Duke Allen was going to show the world what happens to you if you try to end his life.

He had lost a lot of blood and was not in the best frame of mind, but it sounded like a kick ass plan. Duke did not do it out of anger or spite. He did not blame the deer for fighting back. After all, he was in the deer's house and he tried to kill it first. It was more for flair and he loved the idea of standing out in this small town. The deer's head was an exaggerated version of bullhorns on the front of a Cadillac.

Now, a year later, Duke was the deer and a hunting party had entered his house.

Are they going to mount my head onto the front of their vehicle?

A flashlight kicked on at Duke's bedroom doorway. It blinded him as he fired the magnum. The light went out. The sides of his head stung as he went temporarily deaf. Without earplugs in, it was incredibly painful to fire the gun indoors.

The room was pitch black again and he could not tell if he had hit his target. His nostrils filled with the smell of gunpowder. Then the smell turned sour and morphed into body odor.

Duke spoke with a whisper. "What's that horrible stink?"

Suddenly someone was standing right next to Duke. The intruder cleared his throat and signaled Duke to where the body odor was coming from.

Duke swung his gun arm in the intruder's direction. The mystery man caught it by the wrist. Duke fired again. The muzzle flash illuminated the attacker. The sight stole Duke's breath.

The scarred face standing next to him was more horrifying than anything he could ever have imagined. It was straight out of a nightmare and now it had his gun.

Duke tried to escape the man's grasp. He yanked his arm back. Duke couldn't see the knife slashing through the air toward his face, but he felt its impact as the blade sliced down his forehead, over his good eye, blinding him for real this time and finishing its work at the top of his cheekbone.

Before Duke passed out from the blow to his skull, he heard a raspy old voice beg, "Let me kill this one."

Chapter 13

Lisa flipped down the sun visor and checked herself in the tiny mirror. She dug through her purse, found the makeup she was searching for and went to work adding some finishing touches to her already beautiful face.

Ben cleared his throat and said, "Thank you."

She hit him with an *I'm not sure what you're talking about* look.

Ben did not realize how nervous he was until that moment. It had been so long since they had gone out alone, he stammered, "For coming with me. Thank you...for coming to the dance I mean...with me." It ended with a twinge of embarrassment.

Lisa couldn't help but giggle at her husband.

He changed the subject quickly to shake off the anxious feeling swimming around in his gut. "I think we need to offer everyone half off the signup fee or maybe even waive it completely. I don't want us to sound like a slimy sales team or that we're super desperate, but we need to offer them something...right?"

"We are super desperate," she said as she lifted the sun visor.

"They don't know that."

"Maybe the town should know it. What if we pleaded to them? Tell everyone just how much we need their help right now."

Ben mulled over the idea. He weighed the pros and cons of coming clean and telling the people of Sweet Home his family needed their help. It was not like they were a shady fly-by-night insurance company that did not deserve the help. If someone signed up and came to the gym they could only change their lives for the better, get healthy and live longer. Who wouldn't want that?

"Hot damn." He popped the vertebrae in his neck. "That just might work, but how do we do it? How do we tell them?"

"I don't know. We'll figure it out when we get there." Lisa

beamed with pride. She loved it anytime she had an idea that got Ben excited. Her pride was short lived. Lisa's hands moved from holding her purse to pressing against her belly.

Babies.

Sweet, lovable, precious bundles of goddamn joy. She thought to herself.

Lisa had friends her age that were on their second marriages or just wanted one more child and they were trying everything modern science had to offer to get that baby into their body. For Lisa it took only one stupid mistake and one faulty rubber to make the miracle of life happen. As they approached the school her thoughts drifted to this concept.

No matter what happens tonight, my life is going to change dramatically this year.

MaKelle filled two glasses with Coca-Cola. Her gaze moved excitedly from the task to the new boy standing in her kitchen. She watched as he snagged his third Reese's Peanut Butter Cup in as many minutes.

MaKelle smiled brightly as she slid his drink across the island, put the cap on the bottle and put the two-liter back in the fridge.

Colby gobbled down the chocolate and took a swig of his Coke. He reached for his fourth candy. His hand froze in the bag as MaKelle started to talk.

"Those are my favorite too. I once ate a whole pound of them in a day. I didn't puke, but I was damn close toward the end."

His hand slowly retreated from the bag. He worked the wrapper off the candy and MaKelle could tell he was really struggling to find something to say.

She decided to keep it simple and ask him some easy questions about himself. "Where in California are you from?"

"Burbank."

"You ever see any famous people?"

"Weird Al Yankovic? Well my dad pointed him out. He just looked like an old guy with big curly hair to me."

Her jaw hit the floor. "You've never heard of Amish Paradise?"

She might as well have been speaking Latin. MaKelle continued despite his confusion. "It's a great song and video. The guy is freakin' hilarious." She snorted out a laugh.

The boy just smiled back at her. He was not much of a talker, but damn he was hot. His attractiveness was throwing MaKelle off and made it super difficult to keep the conversation going.

She stumbled onto the idea that a change of scenery might help. "Let me give you the tour." She picked up her glass, a few extra candies for the road and headed out of the kitchen.

He followed her like a puppy. The living room was her first stop. She headed for the Christmas tree.

Once he was standing next to her, she pointed out an ornament sitting at eye level. It was a star with a photo of the twins in Santa's lap. "That's us at four-years-old."

Colby leaned forward to study the picture. They were wearing matching holiday outfits. Hayden's face was bright red with tears streaming down his chubby little cheeks. MaKelle couldn't have looked happier. Her little face was smiling ear to ear as she gave the camera a set of double thumbs up.

"You look so happy," he said as he straightened his spine.

"I was. It was like meeting a movie star. At four-years-old Santa was as big of a deal as they got."

"My older sister told me he wasn't real when I was four. She got grounded, but it ruined Christmas for me that year." Colby sipped at his drink.

"What a bitch."

Her reaction caught Colby off-guard and he did a spit-take all over the tree. "Oh God, I'm sorry." His cheeks went flush.

She laughed hard and slapped him on the back. "Shit man, I've never seen that good of a spit-take. Don't worry about it. Come on." She kept laughing as she led him down the hall for her bedroom. Hayden's bedroom door was closed.

She banged on it and yelled, "Hayden, don't get Andrew pregnant."

Her brother shouted back through the door, "It gets funnier every time you say it."

"This is my room." She headed for the bed and took a seat.

Colby inched his way through the threshold and for the first time in his life he stepped into the wonderful world of a teenage girl's bedroom.

The walls were plastered with movie posters from the early 90's and rock bands from the 70's. A shelf was bolted to the wall. It was a more impressive display of awards than her brothers.

Colby pointed at each trophy as he said the sport, "Wow, track, gymnastics, archery and soccer...even martial arts. That's a lot of first prize awards."

"My folks own the gym in town. We were raised doing all kinds of sports. I love to compete and hate to lose."

Colby zeroed in on the four different martial arts trophies.

"You wanna see some moves?" she asked as she jokingly raised her hands into a fighting stance.

"Sure." Colby set his drink on her dresser. "What do you want me to do?"

MaKelle dropped her arms to her sides and extended her throat. "Put your hands around my neck."

"Okay, nothing weird about this. I'm choking a girl I just met. No way this ends badly," Colby said as his fingers wrapped around her slender neck.

They both felt the charge of electricity between them.

"Ready?" She asked.

"R-" Before he finished the word she had broken his hold and thrown an elbow, knee and hammer fist at his groin, sternum and jaw. Her moves were fast and accurate. She never made contact with her target, but she came damn close. "-eady." Colby gasped the last half of the word. His eyes were the size of dinner plates. MaKelle had a tight grip on his wrist and she was putting a lot of pressure on the joint. "Ouch." He attempted to pull his arm back, but she had too painful of a lock on it.

"Sorry." She released his wrist.

He rubbed at his forearm and hand. "That was pretty cool."

The physical contact between them, even though it was violent in nature, was very exciting.

"Show me some more." He tried his best to hide how eager he was for her to throw punches at his face and groin.

MaKelle hit him with her patented devilish smile.

Stanley poured out the last of the beer into Morgan's glass. He kept his voice down. "Maybe we should hit the dance at the school."

Morgan slurred. "Isn't it for kids?"

"No, no. The mayor saves up all year and throws a big New Year's bash. There's a live band, free booze and most of the town shows up. We might be able to snag a drunk, single and willing party person there."

"Hell yeah. That sounds like a plan. Let's bounce." Morgan started putting on her black leather jacket. She got panicked and blurted out. "Where's my purse?" The bag sat right in front of her on the table. "Oh shit, here it is." She giggled. "I'm buzzed."

Stanley tossed two twenties onto the table. He nodded to the bartender, "Will we see you there, Christy?"

She loaded out a rack of glasses from the dishwasher, "Yep, I'll be closing in about fifteen. No one's going to come in tonight. Why pay for drinks if they can get them for free, right?"

"We'll see you there," Stanley hooked his arm under Morgan's to steady her as she rose from her seat.

Christy came out from behind the bar with an empty tray. She cleared the table.

Morgan reached and took Christy by the hand and said, "You are pretty...too good for this place. Get out...get out before it's too late and you're trapped." She pulled the young bartender closer, narrowed her eyes and whispered a secret. "Don't call the cops...if you see Stanley's van rocking...in the parking lot. We're gonna knock one out real quick before the main event." Morgan raised her index finger to her lips and said, "Sshhh." Then she gave Christy a wink.

Stanley mouthed, "Sorry." To Christy, behind Morgan's back

and then dragged her semi-limp body toward the front door.

Our lovebirds, Gwen and Heidi, were back at it as Christy came to their table. She coughed to get their attention and began to clear the glasses and napkins. "Last call."

Gwen unlatched her suction hold on Heidi's face. "I think we are good for the night."

"Are you heading to the dance?" Christy made small talk.

Heidi refreshed her lipstick. "We should swing by to check it out."

"Is it fun? We're new to town," Gwen asked as she whipped out her credit card and handed it to Christy.

"People in town cut loose on New Year's. There's always something to talk about the next day." Christy left the table to close out their tab.

"Let's do it."

"And if it's lame we head home?"

"Deal." They sealed it with a kiss.

Sheriff MaCready sat reclined at her desk with her boots up on the corner of the table. She looked at her watch. It had been awhile since she had sent her Deputy to see 'Handsome Kevin' at the One Stop Mountain Shop.

"Dominic should have checked in with a status report." The Sheriff talked to herself as she slid her noise canceling headphones down around her neck and picked up the cell on her desk. She clicked Dominic's name on her phone.

Sorry, your call cannot be connected as dialed.

"Damn AT&T." MaCready set her phone on the table and picked up the landline. She held the receiver to her ear.

It was dead. No dial tone. She reset it a few times, but couldn't get a tone. The Sheriff set the receiver back on its cradle. She thumbed at the radio receiver on her shoulder. She knew if he was still at the gas station he would be out of range and couldn't respond, but it was worth a try.

"Deputy? This is Sheriff MaCready, copy?"

There was only static on the other end.

"Goddamn it." She removed her headphones and pulled her feet down off the corner of her table. "Snowstorm knocked out communications." MaCready stood up from behind her desk, picked up her cowgirl hat, cell and keys. She patted her belt and made sure she had all of her gear. She did.

MaCready shut her office door and muttered to herself the rest of the way out of the station. "I get to drive all the way out there... In this mess... To check on his ass."

Deputy Dominic Spence opened his eyes. Everything was dark gray. He panicked and thought the blast of the gas station had blinded him. His body felt ice cold, but his face stung like he had a sunburn. His brain took a few seconds to reboot, register what had happened to him and where he was in the universe. He squeezed his fist and felt the snow around him. The deputy sat up quickly. He was covered by four inches of powder. He looked like he was at the beach and someone had buried him in the sand. His body shook and his legs felt numb.

As the clumps of snow fell from his face, it uncovered his eyes. The gray that was blocking his view went away and he could see again. The gas station was still on fire, but most of the structure was a burnt out black shell. Ash floated in the air and mixed with the snow. He raised his hands from the mounds of snow at his sides.

"Holy shit!" He vomited when he noticed that his cell had melted to the palm of his hand.

The edges of his jacket had also been singed and the receiver on his shoulder looked like a lumpy mutant version of its former self. The deputy rolled to his side and inched his way toward his patrol car. The driver's door was still open and a pile of snow had accumulated in the seat. He crawled fifteen yards to his cruiser. His pants were soaking wet with melted snow. His legs ached as blood flowed back through his veins, it felt like a thousand needles stabbing him at once.

Dominic forced a knee under his body and an elbow onto

the driver's seat. He scooped out the snow, grabbed the steering wheel and dragged himself into the vehicle. He found his keys, started the cruiser and cranked on the heat. He shivered uncontrollably as he waited for the warmth to creep back into his body.

Dominic caught a glimpse of himself in the mirror. The skin on his face was bright red and little white blisters were speckled across his forehead, cheeks and nose. "Oh, good God," Dominic growled as he examined the damage. Both eyebrows were gone and he was going to be in a lot of pain for the next week or two, but none of the injuries would be permanent. Heat began to pour from the vents. It was a mixed blessing. Dominic's legs were freezing, but his face was on fire. He turned a knob on his console that aimed the heat from the lower vents.

He took a long deep breath.

Dominic thought to himself.

Lungs still work and blood is still pumping. It could have been worse.

As he defrosted, his memories flooded with what he had seen in the shop before it blew to smithereens.

I've got to get ahold of the Sheriff, get back to town and find that blue van.

He raised his hands to grab hold of the wheel. His cell still clung to the flesh. He hissed as a spike of pain surged up his forearm. It seemed impossible but he had forgotten the damn phone.

"This shit is going to hurt." Dominic pulled at the phone. It sounded like Velcro strips ripping apart. He yelled and grunted through the anguish. At the end of the tear, Dominic came close to passing out. He tossed the phone across the car. Every nerve ending in his palm pulsed. It felt like he was holding a red hot coal.

I need to get a bandage on this. Then I can hit the road.

Dominic popped the trunk of the cruiser, climbed out and went for the first-aid kit he had stowed in the back. His feet felt like cinderblocks as he hobbled toward the back of the car. He grabbed the white case with a red cross on it. The burns on his face were making him nauseous. It was worse than any sunburn he had ever suffered, but there was nothing left in his stomach to vomit.

He rested on the bumper with the kit held tight to his chest. It was quiet out here on the highway. He was surrounded by only the sound of snowflakes falling to the Earth. For sixty seconds he fantasized about hitting the road for the nearest hospital and leaving Sweet Home in the dust. Pain meds and the safety of a warm hospital were so compelling.

Could I live with the feeling of being a coward?

Being the chicken-shit that abandoned his town in their hour of need?

The rational parts of his brain were not playing fair. It told him that the Sheriff and he were no match for these guys. Dominic needed to get the State Police.

Damn it. That would take too long, by the time I'd get back with reinforcements more people might be dead.

The idea gnawed at his guts. He signed up for this life.

To protect and serve.

He had to get back. Dominic psyched himself up.

I have to make sure she-.

He reset himself.

I have to make sure that the town is safe.

He raised up off the bumper and got right with the idea he was about to inflict more pain as he bandaged himself. After that he was heading back to town.

Chapter 14

Jacob carried a battery operated lantern that he found in the cabin's garage. The lamp casted a yellow glow over their captive's bedroom. A red stain the size of a dinner plate sat on the carpet. Quarter sized crimson drips could be traced across the floor and out the bedroom door. His three accomplices were keeping themselves busy out in the great room of the cabin.

Jacob was on a mission and wished Zarren wasn't so cut and dry about killing the power to every house. It would make his snooping around a little easier. He stepped toward the closet, opened the door and was amazed by the room's size.

This guy's walk-in-closet is bigger than the cell I've been rotting in for the last five years. Jacob thought to himself.

He combed through the racks of shirts and jeans until he found something suitable. He settled on a black long sleeve shirt and a pair of black jeans. He carried them out of the closet and headed for the master bath. Jacob laid them next to the basin and set his lantern close to the mirror. The light reflected off the polished surface and sufficiently lit the room. Under the right circumstances, the ambiance of the room would have felt romantic.

He kept his eyes low. Not wanting to look up at his reflection.

Not yet. He told himself.

Jacob tugged open a set of drawers on either side of the sink and found a pair of scissors. He placed the shears on the countertop. Jacob worked at the zipper on his disgusting prison jumpsuit and peeled it off his shoulders. Lastly, he pulled the rubber band from his hair and let his greasy locks fall to his face.

He raised his head and stared at the abject horror that was his body. Gnarled, jagged scars crisscrossed his entire body. Each one had a story. Every healed laceration had a tale. Most were given as a lesson while he worked on The Reckoning. Some of the dark purple marks were from when he was a child and too young to understand knives were sharp and ovens were hot.

At fifteen years old, Jacob's parents left and took his two younger siblings with them. They abandoned him when they could no longer take the financial burden of a child that was constantly in the emergency room. Years later Jacob found his folks. They were the easiest two people he ever added to The Reckoning.

Forced to steal every ounce of food and sleep under bridges or inside condemned buildings, Jacob's life was a constant fight for survival. At nineteen he heard chatter from the other homeless that college students were setting up matches and paying money to video tape them fighting. Desperate for cash, he tagged along one night.

What he found that evening was as revolting as it was thrilling. The fights took place in a filthy, dark, dank basement. Fifty frat boys and a handful of coeds would encircle the two fighters. They yelled insults, flung empty beer cans and cheered at knockouts. Jacob fought his first bout that night. He had no idea how to throw a basic jab let alone knock someone out, but what set him apart from the other contestants was his ability to take a vicious beating and keep fighting. He exhausted his opponent until he was able to land a knockout.

It didn't take long for him to become a local legend. Stories circulated that he was unbeatable. More people showed up at the fights and the prize pots grew. The stories brought better fighters to the matches and more and more guys came down to the basement to test their mettle against this homeless superstar.

Jacob spent years down in that basement, earning cash and developing his own style of street fighting. He gave the audience one hell of a show as he honed his killer reflexes.

His reign as an underground fighting champion ended after he won a match, went to collect his prize and was denied the money. Jacob recalled every second of that night. The entitled college punk's name was Blake and he ran the whole fight circuit. He wore his hat backwards and cocked to the side like an asshole. He reeked from too much cologne and his skintight Affliction shirt looked ridiculous on his chubby body. Only half of Jacob's tongue was missing at that point so he talked with a horrible speech impediment.

The punk told Jacob, *'Get the hell out. We're tired of watching you win every week.'*

Jacob protested and demanded that he be paid first.

Blake laughed at the way Jacob talked and said, *'You sound retarded.'* He threatened Jacob and told him if he didn't leave that minute, Blake's crew would beat him to death. Jacob was outnumbered five to one so he took off.

A hate filled Jacob's heart. A hate he had not felt since his family abandoned him. The hate turned to blind rage. He earned that money with his sweat and blood.

Jacob saw red.

He followed Blake home. He watched and waited for a week. An opportunity arose one morning when Blake was alone. Jacob knocked him out, forced the asshole into the trunk of his own car, and drove him to the basement. When Blake woke, the match began. This was the start of The Reckoning.

Jacob made sure it was a fair fight. No weapons. In one corner there was Blake with a chance to win and walk away with his life and in the other corner was Jacob Glass.

He beat Blake viciously. The fight wasn't even close. After he knocked the punk out Jacob kept delivering strikes. He didn't quit until he noticed the young man's lungs were no longer filling with air. He left the body there on the cold cement floor for the others to find. He searched Blake's pockets and found two thousand dollars. The high he felt as he walked away from Blake's cooling body set him on a path. He left the basement for the last time. He checked Blake's car and discovered more money in the trunk. It was enough to get Jacob started. He hit the road and became an untraceable ghost.

The cash eventually ran out and Jacob had an itch he needed to scratch. He set out to find his second victim. They needed to have a little money. Be healthy and strong. Just like the fight with Blake it had to be fair. If they had a weapon, Jacob could use a weapon. If they were unarmed then he had to use his bare hands.

During a recon mission for a person to possibly add to The Reckoning, Jacob wasted a little time and read a newspaper he found in the candidate's recycling bin. Inside the paper was an article about a recent serial killer that had been caught and sentenced to life in prison. The psychopath had been convicted of thirty-five murders and claimed he was only half way to his goal. Up until that point it never occurred to him to have a goal. A number of bodies to reach before he could say he was done.

Having a target number would help him stay motivated and focused. If he nabbed the person he was stalking, Jacob would have a total of twenty-two. He dwelled on what would be a challenging goal. What number could push him to achieve something incredible? He crunched the numbers. If he did one every two weeks for ten years he would be close to three hundred.

That settled it. Three hundred became the high water mark for Jacob. After that he knuckled down and got to it. His purpose. His reason for being. The Reckoning.

Jacob stared into the cabin's bathroom mirror. His fingertips traced a scar that ran like a zipper down the side of his chest. The old wound had taken his left nipple. Not that the nipple did him any good. He couldn't have felt it if someone gave him a titty twister anyway. Three years of fighting in the basement, nearly ten years of hunting humans for sport and five years of prison had left him with this wreck of a body. He picked up the scissors he had set on the counter and began to cut his hair.

After a short while, a pile of hair was left in the sink. He washed himself and cleaned the filth from his body. Then he slid the shirt and jeans on. In one of the drawers he found some pomade and used it to slick back what was left of his black hair. Last but not least he worked the belt through the loops on his jeans and attached his new knife to his hip. Lucky for him the clothes fit quite well and now he could blend into the shadows with this all black outfit.

I'm not handsome, but I look and smell better. Jacob was not sure why it hurt his feelings so much when the cabin's owner said 'What's that horrible stink?', but it did. He also hoped that with the new clothes he could sneak up on people without them shrieking, "Help! There's an escaped prisoner!" Jacob picked up his lantern and the soiled prison jumpsuit from the floor. Satisfied with his new look he returned to the great room with the others.

Regan was finishing a knot as he helped Arthur tie the knocked out prisoner to a dining room chair.

Arthur had removed the man's eyepatch and had it on as a joke. "His other eye looks totally fine. Crazy man was wearing the patch for no reason." He choked out a rough laugh.

Zarren placed a fresh log on the fire he had just built. He readjusted the logs with the poker. The fireplace filled the whole room with light.

As Jacob emerged from the hallway, he noticed the look of shock on the others' faces.

Arthur raised up a pilfered bottle of the prisoner's beer and toasted Jacob. "Dang boy, you clean up good. I hardly recognize you. Except for... you know... the scars."

Regan pulled with all of his might on the ends of a rope as he secured the knot around the prisoner's wrists. "That... should... do it. Alright this old dog ain't going anywhere."

Jacob joined Zarren by the fire. Flames filled the alcove. Jacob noticed the slight shift in Zarren's features. The big man was proud of the fire he had built. The burning logs popped and sizzled as pockets of sap caught ablaze.

Jacob wished he could register the feeling of heat. He was jealous of the way people really seemed to enjoy the feeling of warmth they got from a roaring fire. Jacob lifted the dirty jumpsuit and nodded toward the flames. Zarren understood and gave an approving grunt. Jacob tossed the jumpsuit. The fabric burned rapidly as the fire erased its existence.

Arthur grabbed a dining room chair, slid it in front of their victim and took a seat. "Fellas, it's been an exciting day and I thank you for dragging my wrinkled ass along, but you should go without me. I'm gonna stay here. Drink more of this rich prick's beer and work him over for a while. If I have any energy left I'll take his truck, head into town and see what kind of *trouble* you've gotten into."

The last of Jacob's old outfit turned to ash before him, he stepped away from the fireplace and headed across the room toward Arthur. Jacob offered his hand and Arthur took it.

As they shook Arthur asked, "Was it over a hundred?"

Jacob looked back and forth between Regan and Arthur. The two of them were anxious to hear his answer. Jacob let go of Arthur's arthritic hand and raised his thumb into the air.

Regan blurted out, "More than a hundred? Fuck me!"

Arthur let out a big laugh and pointed at Regan. "I told you he was elite. Pay up boy."

Regan dropped his head and conceded to the loss, "I'll pick you up a pack of smokes when I'm in town. Goddamn it." He muttered to himself and kicked at the coffee table. On the table sat a stack of magazines and a glass ashtray. As the furniture toppled, it sent the glass bowl sailing to the hardwood floor. The sudden loud noise caused the hostage to stir.

"Wakey, wakey," Arthur giggled and placed his thumb over the beer bottle's mouth. He gave it a shake. The brew foamed and fizzed out as it shot onto the man's face. The cold alcohol stung on his open wound and he howled in pain. He jerked awake and fought against his restraints.

Regan followed Zarren and Jacob as they headed for the busted front door. He hollered, "You play nice with the man," just to help wake up the prisoner.

The man blinked beer out of his eyes. His focus darted around the room as he tried to make sense of everything. The look of confusion on the man's face was priceless to Arthur.

"Oh, I will," Arthur said as he gently slapped the wounded cheek of the victim to snatch his attention and get it back on him. "Hey, what's your name?"

The prisoner hissed, pulled his head back and coughed out the name, "Duke."

Duke's brain was slow to connect the dots and it didn't

realize how much danger he was in. His head throbbed and he had the worst migraine of his life and-

Oh God! My eye! He cut out my right eye!

His hands pulled toward his face only to find they were tied behind his back. Everything began to swirl. It felt like his whole body was spinning out of control.

Duke could only process little chunks of info at a time.

The smell of fire and beer.

The constant nagging sting from the slice on his face.

A crew of three nasties heading for the front door.

The crusty fucker in the orange Corrections jumpsuit.

Duke's eyepatch wrapped around the weathered face two feet away.

The magnum on the kitchen table.

And the knife next it.

The old guy with yellow teeth tapped Duke on the cheek again. The pain yanked at Duke's attention and he became laser focused. The fear he felt back in his bedroom just multiplied tenfold.

Yellow teeth spoke. "Eyepatch covering a healthy eye? That's a new one." His breath was so bad it smelled like a skunk had died in a porta-potty.

The three men stepped through the front door and now they were alone. Yellow teeth chugged the last of his beer then he smashed the bottle on the ground at Duke's feet. Shattered glass spread across the maple floor and it made Duke jump.

Yellow teeth reached out and grabbed him by the shoulders. "I'm not gonna lie. I'm a little nervous. I ain't done one of these in thirty years. Let's see what we got in the kitchen." He stood up and headed for the sink. "I'm Arthur by the way. Arthur Wright. Ever heard of me?"

Duke shook his head.

"I was in all the papers and on T.V. too, but that was thirty years ago." Arthur squatted down in front of the sink and disappeared behind the kitchen's island. He opened the cabinets and rummaged through Duke's cleaning supplies. He yelled at the top of his lungs, "We've got a winner!" Arthur reappeared with a bottle of bleach. With a hop and a skip, Arthur was back in front of Duke. It took him a minute to work at the lid, "Damn kid's safety!" He finally got the lid off. He waved his gnarled hands in Duke's face and giggled, "It's hell getting old."

Duke forced out a little courage and he asked, "What do you want?"

Arthur belted a powerful, smelly laugh in Duke's face. "What do I want? What do I want? Boy, you think I want money or the password to your AOL account. No. No!" Arthur picked up the knife from the table. "What I want is to pour this bleach down your throat. What I want is to poison your body with chemicals. I want to watch you die a long, painful and excruciating death. Does knowing that make you feel any better? Does knowing that help you, boy?"

Duke shook his head. He fought to hide just how afraid he was.

"I didn't think so." Arthur inched closer.

Duke shot him a look of disgust.

"What? You think you're better than me? You think because you got this big house and all these nice things that you're a better man than me? You're not!" Arthur angled the knife toward Duke's face and forced it between his teeth. "I've killed richer people than you my friend." Arthur raised the bottle above Duke's face.

"You think I don't know how bad this is going to be? When I was a little boy, my Mama made me drink a glass of bleach every time she caught me swearing and I fucking cursed a lot my friend. I know exactly how bad this is going to be. Now drink up!" Arthur slowly poured the bleach into Duke's mouth. The horrible cleaning product began to flow through the tiny slit the knife made between his teeth. The taste of it turned Duke's guts. He fought to keep it out of his stomach, but between breaths, a little would slip in. Some got in his lungs causing Duke to cough and hack, but the bastard kept pouring it. Duke felt like he was going to drown. At that moment, Duke wished the deer had killed him a year ago.

Chapter 15

Ben and Lisa turned into the school's full parking lot. A banner hung above the main entrance welcoming everyone to the New Year's party. The snow was pounding the earth and the flakes had doubled in size. Four-foot high drifts ran around the full perimeter encasing the school's parking lot in a wall of snow.

Ben surveyed the area and said, "Full house. That's good."

"Something about it being at a school disturbs me." Lisa shook her head.

"I feel like I'm going to get in trouble for drinking on school property." Ben brought the Subaru into one of the last parking spots. He killed the engine, pulled the parking brake, took a long deep breath and started to open the door.

Lisa grabbed him by the arm and stopped him. She wanted to tell him everything. Every horrible truth about what she had done and how she had ruined the family.

"What's up?" Ben asked as they locked eyes.

Do it you scaredy-cat. Tell him. You owe him the truth. Lisa fought as hard as she could to convince herself to say something.

"You all right?" Ben leaned back toward the armrest and hit her with his best smile. It was the same smile he had given her on their wedding day. Same damn smile he did when the twins were born. His happy face knocked all of the wind out of her and the truth suddenly felt like the wrong move.

Why hurt him? She thought. *Don't do it tonight. I need to wait until the pregnancy test is irrefutable. I have to help him win tonight. Save the gym and try my best to right all of my wrongs.*

She squeezed him on the arm and said, "This is going to work."

"Race you inside?" Ben raised an eyebrow.

Lisa's gaze narrowed. Her hand slowly raised to the lever on the door. It was a showdown. As if they were gunfighters squaring off at high noon, waiting for the other to draw first. In one fast move she had the door open, got some traction under her boots, slammed the door shut behind her and was off like a shot.

Lisa wasn't going to lose this race. She hated to lose at any sport. She dug deep and flew across the snowy parking lot. She didn't care about the flakes blasting her in the face. She dropped her head and drove her legs even harder. He was right behind her. She turned on the jets. Her lungs burned as they filled with icy air. He was on her left. The front door was ten yards away. She was about to win. She pushed with every fiber of her body and leaned forward.

She did it. She got to the door first.

"Booyah, mother-*chucker*!" Lisa announced her win to the world.

Ben sucked in wind and placed his hands on his hips, "You got me, but-"

"Don't make excuses," she cut him off as she opened the door.

He puffed out white breaths into the night, "These dress shoes. I can't run as fast in these. No traction."

"Sounds like loser talk to me." Lisa held the door open. Music blasted them right away. She pushed her man into the entrance. "Ladies first."

A wall of gold tassels hung floor to ceiling and shimmered as the wind hit them. Their view was blocked at first until they slid passed the hanging plastic ribbons. The gym was dark and most of the light came from the stage at the far end of the building. A five-piece band was cutting it Foot Loose as the four hundred plus adults were dancing to the classic Kenny Loggins hit.

A crowd of people surrounded the bar that was set up under a basketball hoop.

Someone shouted over the music, "Check your coat?"

A booth had been set up next to the front door. One of the young teachers at the school was manning the coat check.

Lisa recognized her. *Didn't she teach science or was it drama?*

Lisa tugged Ben's arm over to the booth. They pulled off their coats and lay them down on the counter. Luckily she had a nametag on: Brenda Stevens. But it didn't help Lisa recall what she did at the school.

"How's the new play coming?" Ben asked.

Damn it. He always remembers the kid's teachers. Lisa fumed at herself for not being more involved with the kids' school.

Mrs. Stevens nodded at Ben, "It's going great. My two leads are excellent."

"This place is packed." Lisa hollered to Brenda as she took her ticket.

"Mayor Tyler loves her New Year's party." Brenda yelled back.

"It looks like half of the town's here." Ben took his ticket.

"Most people said they had cabin fever from all the snow and decided to come out. Tyler says it's the best turnout in ten years."

Lisa slipped out of her boots, "Can I check these too?"

Brenda stepped aside and showed Lisa the hundred boots behind her. "You won't be the first."

Lisa passed her the boots and then slipped on her dress shoes.

"Have fun!" Brenda gave them a wave as she began to hang their coats.

Lisa and Ben turned toward the raucous crowd. They hesitated, unsure how to proceed.

Ben leaned in to Lisa's ear, "It's so loud. How are we going to tell everyone?"

Lisa calculated their next move. There appeared to be only one option, "We get you a drink to loosen you up, but don't get you drunk. We talk to the Mayor and plead our case. If that goes well, you take the stage and address the crowd."

Ben choked. "Public speaking?"

"I'll be right there beside you. You'll do fine. I promise." Lisa took her husband by the hand. "Let's get you a drink."

Ben beamed with confidence.

Lisa pulled him across the floor and they weaved through the townspeople toward the bar.

Christy, the Oasis' bartender, had the place to herself. She pulled the last rack of glasses from the dishwasher and began to put them away. She loved being alone at the Oasis. No drunks hitting on her, no one there to serve or clean up after. As far as work went, it was heaven.

Her thoughts drifted to what the rocker lady with Stanley had said before they left.

'You are pretty...too good for this place. Get out...get out before it's too late and you're trapped.'

Christy was already trapped. She felt stuck in this town, behind this bar and in this unlived life. Bartending was relatively easy money and there were not a ton of other job opportunities in this neck of the woods. Five years ago she was lured here by her boyfriend.

He said, *'It's mountain living baby, as God intended.'*

At the time it sounded great. As if getting out of the city was going to be an amazing adventure. Perspective and age shined new light on his statement and Christy realized he was just an idiot. She was an even bigger idiot for buying into his bullshit. A year after they settled in Sweet Home the asshole bugged out of town with a new floozy on his arm.

Men can be such pigs, but I don't like women enough to go lesbian. Her brain loved that joke.

She was a year away from thirty, single with no prospects in sight, and the daily grind of life was breaking her spirit. She put the last pint glass away and replaced the rack in the dishwasher. She was just about done. There was only one more thing to do. She did it every night she closed.

Have a damn drink.

Christy reached for the top shelf and took down the *Absolut* vodka. She poured a double shot.

She mocked, "To the New Year," then slammed the booze down her throat. "That burns so good." This was her nightly routine. Close up and snag a free drink. The owner never seemed to notice and that jerk was always out of town.

She placed the bottle back on its shelf and headed for the office. She had planned ahead and brought a change of clothes for the evening so she wouldn't have to drive home first.

She entered the office and flicked on the light. The main desk was covered in paperwork. A beat up leather chair sat in the corner and a full-length mirror hung on one wall. Christy locked the door behind her and began to take off her work clothes. She tossed her t-shirt and jeans to the floor. Christy paused and examined her body in the mirror. The lighting in the office was nice and soft. No harsh fluorescents to make her feel horrible about how she looked in the nude.

Christy unclasped her bra and tossed it onto her jeans. Her breasts were still perky, firm and pointed in the right direction. She always loved her tits. Christy ran her hands along the sides of her hips. Her stomach was trim and the butt was well proportioned. She let down her hair and a cascade of blonde fell to her shoulders.

Hot damn! I look good today. Christy thought as she made pouty lips at her reflection.

Her fingers tiptoed back up her sides and gently crossed her nipples. She wasn't conceited about her body. She was just confident in her sexuality. Christy looked at the leather chair in the corner.

I kind of want to take a few minutes and masturbate. The naughty thought was tempting.

Shit! If I do, my sex drive will go into hibernation for the night.

Her goal all week had been to find someone new in town or a friend of a townie. Maybe they were here for the holiday and leaving soon. Someone good looking and fun that could get in there and knock the rust off her gutters, so to speak.

It had been six months since the last time she had been touched sexually and it was a townie that was truly unavailable. The guy was married with children. It was only a one night stand, just a crime of opportunity. She would occasionally see him around, but they had promised to keep their affair a secret. He wasn't a drinker so there was little to no chance of him stumbling into the Oasis wanting to go another round in bed. She had no future with the man so she let him go. For the last month she felt like she was about to explode from inactivity.

The internal battle continued, masturbate or don't masturbate. Christy talked herself out of churning the butter.

Save it for tonight. It will be better if I wait.

She opened her backpack and pulled out her brand new super tight designer jeans that made her ass look ridiculously hot. Christy left her bra off as she slipped her arms into a skintight shirt.

Her breasts came to a set of perfect points under the shear fabric. *That should turn some heads.*

Christy found her bag of makeup in the pack and went to work on her face. When she was a teenager she dreamed of running off to Hollywood and becoming a big movie star. Two years ago the dream morphed from super stardom to super happy mother. She figured it was just her biological clock kicking into overdrive. It was definitely not something she learned from her own family. Christy grew up with a mother that was a horrible bitch and seemed to hate being a mother. Her grandmother on her mother's side was even worse and detested the grandchildren. She knew she would be different than her parents. Christy convinced herself that if she found a good man and got him to put a baby in her she could break the cycle of being a nasty baby hating witch. It had proven difficult for her to find this nice guy and even harder to talk one into making a kid. Most of the men she dated were still children themselves. She applied the finishing touches to her face and started packing her bag.

Outside the office she turned out all the lights in the bar and headed for the front door. Christy locked the door behind herself and stepped out into the parking lot. There were three parked cars sitting there in the snow, her trusty Jeep Wrangler, Stanley's old van and a new Toyota Camry. Two of the three cars were rocking back and forth. The windows were completely steamed up and clumps of snow fell as the vehicles shook.

Moans of pleasure escaped from the two rides. Whatever Stanley was doing to Morgan seemed to really be working. The two lady lovebirds, Gwen and Heidi, were really putting the shocks on that Toyota through a hard workout and that confused Christy.

They don't have dicks, why are they humping so hard? Then the answer hit her. *You can buy a dick off the internet, duh. I have one in my nightstand.*

That was the straw that broke the horny camel's back. Christy stepped for the front door of the Oasis, unlocked it and headed toward the office to masturbate until her wrist hurt.

Sheriff MaCready turned onto the state route that headed out of town toward the One Stop Mountain Shop. A quarter mile down the road she jammed the brakes and slid to a stop. An evergreen blocked her from continuing.

"Son of a bitch!" MaCready put her Bronco into park, stepped out onto the highway with a flashlight in hand and headed for the tree's stump. She climbed down into the ditch and marched along the fallen tree. She eventually reached the end of the evergreen.

The yellow cone of her flashlight shined on her raised hand as she touched the rings of the freshly cut tree, "What the hell is going on?" She scanned the area and found two more downed trees blocking the main roads out of Sweet Home. She grabbed the receiver on her shoulder, "Deputy Spence? Do you read me?"

Silence.

Only the sound of the wind could be heard from the edge of the highway. "I'm still out of range." She headed back out of the ditch for her Bronco. MaCready froze when her flashlight found the blue colored hand sticking out of the white drift, just off the highway. She moved with caution toward the appendage.

Maybe it's a mannequin? She prayed.

The closer she got to the hand the clearer the painted fingernails became.

It must have been a traffic accident. Hit and Run. She was struck by a car. That's got to be it.

It was rare, but not impossible to have a hit and run in Sweet Home. Four years ago Bobby Jensen was hit by a drunk. He was jogging home from the store when the driver lost control and collided with Bobby on the south side of town. When the Sheriff got to the accident, Bobby was somehow stuck under the back tire of the car. He was still alive and screaming as loud as he could with two collapsed lungs, for them to get the car off of him. At the very end the fifty-year-old man was crying for his mama to save him. He died before the tow truck could arrive and lift the vehicle off him. That night had haunted MaCready for years. She would wake up, covered in sweat, with the sound of Bobby's cries ringing in her ears.

Sheriff MaCready hovered over the hand. She clenched her teeth as she fished out a set of rubber gloves from her belt. She squatted down and brushed away the powder.

MaCready cringed, "Oh, Connie."

Connie Hawkins' eyes were half open and blood shot. The duct tape on her mouth and dark purple bruises around her neck told the Sheriff everything.

This was no hit and run. It was a...homicide.

She started to panic. It had been two decades since she had to deal with a murder in her jurisdiction. MaCready stood up and ran her light over the surrounding grounds, looking for any more clues, then she spotted the black dress shoe a little farther down the ditch. She jogged toward it and again brushed away the snow.

She squeaked out, "Zack!"

Zack Hawkins had the same strip of duct tape over his mouth and bruises on his neck. Zack and Connie lived two more miles down the road out of town.

They must have been on the way to the dance, judging by the way they were dressed. Someone picked them up as they were heading into town and dumped the bodies here.

Maybe it was the freezing weather, but her thoughts were moving in slow motion. Her police training began putting the whole string of events in order. First there was the 911 call from Kevin out at the gas station. The Mountain Shop sat ten miles away. No cell

124

signal in town. The cell tower was six miles away. Zach and Connie lived three miles out of town and they were dropped off here by the downed evergreens blocking the main routes.

Something evil was inching toward her town. A crippling thought flashed across her mind like a neon sign.

I'm not equipped to handle this.

MaCready raced across the highway back for her Bronco. She climbed in and slammed the door behind herself and locked it.

Think. Think. Think.

Ideas raced in and out of her head about what to do next.

Warn the town. Get the state police.

Set up roadblocks.

Find who did this and stop them.

She couldn't do it all by herself. She needed backup. Hell, she needed back up for the backup. MaCready had to find her deputy, but more than anything she had to contact the state police.

The satellite phone. She remembered there was a satellite phone back at the station. The Sheriff had convinced the town treasurer to buy one after a ten-year-old boy went missing in the woods two summers ago. It was the only way she could get service on the mountain. After two days of searching, she found the boy and brought him home to his parents. Then she stored the phone in her desk. She would need to charge it, but that damn phone was her only chance of salvation. She put the Bronco into reverse, did a three-point turn and headed back to town.

She sped as fast as the Bronco's studded tires could carry her. She blasted through intersections as she raced for the station. MaCready rounded the last corner and was facing Main Street. In a blink of an eye the town's power cut off. Every streetlight and traffic signal went dark. The businesses that lined the street became black blurs and only the Bronco's headlights illuminated the road before her.

Chapter 16

MaKelle grunted, "You want some more...? Had enough?" The mattress squeaked as Colby groaned underneath her. He struggled to catch his breath. Her grip was locked on tight. The boy wasn't going anywhere. "Okay, here comes the boom." She swiftly changed positions as Colby tried to roll out from under her. She caught his wrist, tossed her legs over his chest and neck and put him in a well-executed arm bar.

He howled in pain and tapped out, "You got me."

She released him and they both sat up on the edge of her bed. Colby stretched out his shoulder. Their cheeks were flush and a little perspiration had formed on each of their foreheads.

She innocently asked, "You want to go another round?"

"I'm good. Getting beat four times in a row is enough." He forced a smile and massaged his sore neck.

"You almost got me once," MaKelle encouraged him as she wiped the sweat from her brow.

"No I didn't. It wasn't even close." His gaze drifted out onto the center of the room. "Hey, can you do me a favor."

"You don't want me to tell everyone at school that I mopped the floor with you."

"Yes please. That would be nice. I'm new and I..."

"Don't want everyone to know that a girl beat you at wrestling. I got it. You're not the first to ask me that." MaKelle smiled at the boy as she waved cool air into her T-shirt.

All of the nervousness Colby had earlier had completely disappeared and his confidence had grown. He looked her dead in the eyes. "It's not that I'm ashamed I got beat by a girl. You're really good at wrestling. Like, really really scary good at it. I just don't want everyone to know that... We were alone... And all we did was wrestle...like a bunch of kids."

Their hands were next to each other on the edge of the bed.

Colby's pinky reached out and touched hers. A moment later their sweaty palms were pressed tightly together as they interlaced fingers. They entered into that super rare moment, which only happens a handful of times in your teens, they were about to kiss. Time slowed and both were scared to death to make a move.

The question, *will they or won't they accept my kiss,* filled their hearts with dread, but the excitement of the act itself was enough to push them forward. They burned with an innocent longing to touch lips. Colby leaned in a little and MaKelle didn't pull away.

The feelings of fear, excitement, dread, anticipation and extreme joy swirled around the room as they inched closer and closer to each other.

They were a second away from contact and the power cut off. The room went pitch black. They could no longer see the face an inch away.

"Bitch, please!" Erupted loudly out of MaKelle, she fumbled for her cell on the nightstand next to her bed, found it and kicked on its flashlight.

"Storm must have knocked out the power." Colby stated the obvious. The powerful glow of her phone cast them in a romantic light. Again their fingers were interlaced and they continued to lean toward each other.

Their lips were about to touch.

Hayden's bedroom door flung open and he bathed his sister in his phone's light, "Power's out."

"I know," MaKelle said it with a little extra venom.

Andrew joined Hayden at the bedroom doorway.

"Don't get snotty with me." Her brother stepped out of his room and into hers. "I was almost finished writing an epic Facebook rant when the power killed it."

Andrew pulled at Hayden's sleeve, "Should we check the fuse box. Maybe a circuit popped?"

They headed down the hall, back toward the kitchen, phones in hand, lighting their way. Once they hit the living room, Colby pointed out the front window and said, "Power's out down the whole street." They stepped for the window to take a look.

Every house on the block was dark. All the blinking Christmas lights that made the street so festive had gone silent.

"Transformer must have popped." MaKelle concluded as her hand searched out Colby's. She found it and squeezed tightly.

"Probably a drunk driver crashed into a powerline." Colby squeezed her hand back.

"We should build a fire. It would make it kind of romantic in here." Andrew bumped Hayden's shoulder.

"That sounds good. Colby, you're on fire duty. Andrew and I are grabbing candles and food from the kitchen. MaKelle, you find us a board game, not Monopoly, it takes too long." Hayden looked over the other teens. "Ready, team?" They nodded back at him. "And break." He finished it with a clap of his hands, like he was the quarterback on a football team.

Ben sipped on his second whisky and soda for the evening. He rarely drank alcohol and the booze was dancing a jig through his brain. The band was Celebrating Good Times and the audience was singing along. A hand reached for Ben's arm and spun him around, some of his drink spilled out onto the gym floor.

A high-pitched voice asked, "Ben, have you seen Dominic?"

Ben was met with a bright smile and equally large set of glasses. "Hi Rebecca, no I haven't seen him since this morning at the gym."

"What do you think of my new dress?" She waved her arms into the air and did a rotation. Her dress was a little ill fitted, but you could tell she was trying her best. Some cat hair clung to the fabric on her back. "You think Dominic will like it?" She snorted and readjusted her cleavage.

"He'll love it."

"My New Year's resolution is to have a little more Dominic in my life. If you know what I mean?" Rebecca put an elbow into Ben's ribs. "You're like his best friend. Any advice on how to trap him. Ha! I mean catch him. Ha! Wait, I mean catch his interest? I'm nervous. Office romances, they are so...blah." Her face made an awkward twitch.

"Men are easy. You pay him some attention. Ask him if he wants to come over or go out and if he is interested he'll say yes." Ben sipped at his drink.

Rebecca placed both hands to the side of her head and mimed her mind exploding everywhere. "Wow. I'm overthinking it. Okay if you see him here send him my way. I'll be on the dance floor killing these moves." Rebecca clumsily moonwalked out of the conversation.

That poor clueless woman doesn't know Dominic is horribly allergic to cats.

Lisa found Mayor Tyler on the dance floor and signaled for Ben to join her.

In these moments of stress, Ben would often talk to himself with a deep Barry White voice. It helped him to be calm and remember to have fun in life.

Be smooth and relaxed. Because you're never, never gonna give up, babe. That did it.

He strutted across the dance floor and weaved through the crowd as he took a few more sips of his cocktail.

"...I can't believe that!" Lisa laughed loudly at something Mayor Tyler had just said.

"Ben, it's good to see you here tonight. Thank you for coming." Mayor Tyler extended her hand.

Ben looked down at the most powerful woman in town, because she stood four foot ten, even in her heels. She wore her hair long and puffed up onto the top of her head to give herself a few extra inches of height. She held a flute of Champagne and swayed only slightly when she talked.

Ben gently placed his hand on The Mayor's shoulder and moved closer so he wouldn't have to shout in her face. "It's quite the turnout. Thank you for putting on such an amazing party."

"You are welcome my good sir. I love that the community can come together on this magical night to celebrate the next chapter in our lives." Tyler's speech sounded a little rehearsed, but she tossed a friendly arm around Ben's shoulders, which forced him to bend at the waist to accommodate the act of friendship.

Lisa lovingly grabbed him by the arm and played up what an amazing couple they were. "Sweetheart, I was just telling the Mayor about our little issue. Maybe you would be better at elaborating on it."

He took a deep breath, "Well our gym's in trouble, Mayor. We were hoping that you could help."

Lisa tugged at his arm and nervously giggled, "I already covered that part, dear. Ask her about..." she nodded to the stage.

"Right, I was wondering if we could-"

Tyler cut Ben off, "I got it. I'm all about the small businesses. We have to join together and help each other out, right?"

The couple agreed.

"Follow me." Mayor Tyler turned and waved for them to stay on her heels. She navigated her way around the crowd and headed for the stairs that led up to the stage.

She paused at the last step. "You two wait here until I announce you."

The band played the last few bars of their song as the Mayor shimmied and shook her body across the stage toward the microphone. As the last of her imported sparkling wine spilled to the floor, she pulled the mic down to her level. She gave a faint smile, then she boasted. "Let's hear it for the band!"

The crowd gave a ruckus cheer.

"They're dynamite aren't they? Folks I need to borrow your attention for just a moment, then we will get back to the boogeying. One of our family businesses is in need of our help. So let's give a warm welcome to the stage, longtime members of the community, Ben and Lisa Williams." Mayor Tyler motioned for the couple to come out of the wings.

A knot formed in Ben's stomach. Was there anything worse than public speaking? He stepped out from behind the curtain with Lisa by his side.

They were met with crickets.

The four hundred sets of eyes on him seemed to magically multiply. All of a sudden it felt as if there were a hundred thousand people watching him approach the mic stand. A sea of humans stretched out before him. An occasional cough was the only sound in the whole building. Terror seized his heart as Ben stood before the microphone.

He let out an uncomfortable laugh and waved at the crowd. "Hi everyone, uhm, okay, we need your hel-" The power cut, the room went pitch black. The mic kicked off as the crowd gasped with a sudden jolt of fear.

Chapter 17

Deputy Spence clenched his jaw and ground his molars as he made the final switchback to crest the hill that overlooked his town.

Dominic groaned. "No." The valley below was completely blacked out. He continued down the hill and begged for a miracle.

The storm knocked out the power that's all. The assholes in the van were long gone and nobody else is hurt.

He repeated it over and over to himself. He cradled his bandaged hand in his lap. It pulsed with pain. Dominic mumbled to himself. "I could use some Vicodin. Or a stiff drink." He ran through his list. "I need to get to the Sheriff's station and have her call in the state police. Then we need to find the blue van. No wait, we need to alert the town so they can help us find the van." His thoughts drifted back to the pain he felt on his face and hand. It was near impossible to keep his mind on track and focus on what needed to happen tonight.

He zipped along the highway and rounded a bend in the road. The Deputy was close, only a few more miles until he was at the station. Something about that made him feel safe. After almost getting blown to hell and back he craved the sensation of complete safety.

"Oh shit!" Dominic didn't see the evergreen straddling the road until it was too late. He slammed on his brakes, which caused his cruiser to slide, he cranked the wheel to compensate, but it was too late. He lost control and was on a collision course straight for the felled tree.

The front of the cruiser collided with the tree, airbags blew, seatbelt strained under Dominic's weight, his burnt face crashed into the rough surface of the airbag and a bright white spike of searing agony flashed before him.

He awoke to the blare of his cruiser's horn. Once he sat up, the horn fell silent. The skin on his face stung even worse than before, but he couldn't touch it or soothe his suffering. His shoulder ached where the seatbelt had kept him from flying out the windshield. Dominic popped open his door. His brain commanded his legs to work, but they were currently on strike and he fell to the snow-covered road. The icy flakes felt good on his burns, but he had to keep moving. He got his legs under him, popped the lever to open the trunk of the cruiser and shuffled his way around to the back of the vehicle. He grabbed his Mag-lite, the shotgun and a handful of shells. He held the gun in the crook of his arm and fed it shells until it was full. He stuffed as many as he could into his pocket.

Dominic balanced the shotgun on his injured hand's forearm and carried the flashlight in his working hand. It took him a minute to get his bearings. He was a mile from Duke's cabin. He didn't like the idea of asking the man for help after the exchange they had earlier that day, but he didn't have a lot of choices. Dominic began to jog through the snow. That's when he noticed the two other recently cut down evergreens blocking the roads. Dominic picked up the pace.

The Toyota Camry, in the parking lot at The Oasis, bounced once more. Muffled groans escaped through the steamed glass. Inside the car Gwen shivered quietly as a massive orgasm coursed through her body.

Heidi's lips were smeared with bright red lipstick. She whispered. "That was a big one." She extracted a large pink device from between Gwen's legs, put it back in a plastic bag labeled 'Deep-V Diver'. The bag had a *Sharpie* drawing of cartoon diving gear, goggles and an air-tank that lined up perfectly with the pink device so it looked like it was prepared to hit the open sea.

Gwen tugged her bra back into position. "Sorry it took so long to get there that double-double got me super buzzed." She sat forward and reached for the zipper to Heidi's jeans. "Your turn."

Heidi pulled away and climbed off Gwen. She slid into the driver's seat and placed the plastic bag into her purse. "I'll wait until we get home. I like the comfort of my mattress. The passion just hit me and I needed to tap your ass."

"I feel tapped. I'm so sleepy." Gwen rolled to her side and pretended to sleep. "Drive me home, Jeeves."

"Alright Sleeping Beauty, let's hit the showers. I was at work all day I'm tangy down there."

"I like tangy."

"Not this tangy. Hey, all of the lights are out." Heidi turned the key in the ignition, and kicked on her car's exterior lights.

The town around them was pitch black.

"That is weird. It must be the snow." Gwen slid the jeans on the floorboard up her milky white thighs.

"I've never seen snow knock out the streetlights."

"Let's skip that party at the high school and head home."

"Done." Heidi put the car into drive and exited the lot.

Duke coughed up a mouthful of bleach and vomit. His head pounded, his stomach burned and waves of nausea sloshed around his insides.

"The night's still young, boy." Arthur chucked the empty bottle of bleach at Duke's head. "Quit your moaning. That shit won't kill you. Burns like hell, but you ain't gonna die from it."

Duke's face was slick with sweat and blood. The fire at his back was hotter than hell. The stress, heat and spilled bleach had soaked all of Duke's clothes. He strained against the ropes and for the first time he was able to get his arms to move. All of the moisture had lubricated his wrists and Duke began to slowly inch out of his restraints. He moved so slightly that Arthur did not notice.

"I can't believe you ain't begging for your life." Arthur chuckled. "Don't get me wrong. I'm glad you're staying quiet. Most people would be screaming. 'I'll give you all my cash if you let me go!' and it'd drive me nuts." Arthur picked up a towel from the table and brushed away the puke on Duke's chin. "Damn, I wish you were a beautiful woman. That'd be fun." Arthur chewed on his lip as he continued to clean Duke's face. "Oh well. Let's kick it up a notch and see what else you got in there. Drano, maybe?" Arthur tossed the towel up onto Duke's face. "If you drop that towel I'll castrate you right here and now. You got me? I want what comes next to be a surprise. Do you understand? Answer me!"

Duke's throat was raw, but he growled a, "Yes," from under the towel.

"Good." As Arthur raised out of his chair he smacked Duke's gonads and barked, "Cup check." He laughed maniacally. Duke lurched forward, but did not let the towel fall from his face.

Arthur's voice trailed off as he headed for the kitchen. "That was a test, boy, and you passed." Arthur rummaged around under the sink. "Damn, there ain't anything good in here." He pulled out all of the cabinet's contents and kicked them across the floor. "I'm gonna check the garage. If that towel ain't on your face when I get back, you're balls are mine."

Duke heard the footsteps head for the garage and the sound of the door opening and closing behind him. He was terrified that this might be a trick and Arthur was standing in the corner watching him and waiting to see if he would try to escape. Duke decided to risk it. He knew what was in the garage and if this Arthur found it he would be dead either way.

Duke wiggled his arms and twisted his wrists. Thank God for Lisa's yoga class. Duke had enough shoulder strength to slip his arm up and out of the rope. The restraints gave and he was free. Duke paused and listened. The fire roared behind him and his own heavy breathing was kicking off the towel and back into his ears. There it was, faint at first, but he could hear Arthur rummaging through the garage cabinets. There were two containers out there Duke was afraid Arthur might find. Lighter fluid and paint thinner.

Both of Duke's ankles were still tied to the legs of the chair. He was stuck in that seat. So he leaned forward and caught the towel as it fell from his face. He glanced at the door to the garage. Arthur yelled with excitement. Clearly he found something of interest. Duke had to move fast. On the dining table were the revolver and the kitchen knife. Duke stretched as far as he could but the pistol was out of reach. There was noise on the other side of the door.

Arthur slammed his way out of the garage. "I hope you let

that towel fall." He passed through the kitchen. "Dang, you kept it up. Oh well. I found something fun, lighter fluid." He stepped closer to Duke. "I'm gonna fill your gut with it and try to drop a lit match down your throat." Arthur stood directly in front of his prisoner. He popped the top off the bottle. "Hey, where's the fucking knife?!"

That was Duke's cue. He whipped his head forward, the towel fell away from his face, the kitchen knife was clutched in Duke's fist and he lurched toward Arthur. The knife pierced the bottle of lighter fluid, forcing its contents to shoot into the air. As the flammable liquid sprayed the both of them Duke leaned farther forward pushing the knife into Arthur's chest. Duke fell to his face and the chair tied to his legs fell with him. Arthur stumbled backwards, with the knife stuck in his torso and the bottle of lighter fluid pinned to him.

Duke laid on his belly and reached for Arthur's legs. He tripped the convict and Arthur fell to his ass. The back of his head connected with the floor and made a nasty cracking sound. Duke pulled himself along Arthur's body and reached for the knife. His fingertips tapped the knife's handle and the agony it cause sent Arthur's arms thrashing through the air. The back of Arthur's hand slapped Duke's wounded face. The pain was excruciating. Duke let go of Arthur, rolled to his side and held the slash on his face. They laid side by side and screamed in unison.

Arthur sat up, wrapped his arthritic paw around the knife's handle and pulled with all of his might. It was stuck in the bone of his chest plate and he didn't have the grip strength to extract it. He grabbed the edge of the dining table and lifted himself off the floor.

Duke heard Arthur move for the revolver. He rolled back to his belly and crawled across the floor toward the fireplace.

"You dumb cyclopes motherfucker!" Arthur struggled to yank back the revolver's hammer. It gave Duke a few more seconds to drag himself into the living room. Arthur aimed with a shaking arm and fired. The bullet ripped into the couch next to Duke's head. He kept moving farther into the living room and slithered behind the knocked over coffee table. Another bullet punched a hole through the corner of the coffee table. It was blistering hot in the living room as Duke searched for something he could use as a weapon. There was a busted ashtray, stack of magazines, a throw rug, but no weapons. Next to the fireplace was a rack holding a fire poker, brush and a little shovel.

Arthur shuffled forward into the living room. "You bastard! You ruined my night. Now you're gonna eat a bullet!" He fired again. The round ricocheted off the stone fireplace. Duke had been counting and that was shot number five. Only one shot left. Duke reached for the rack of fireplace tools. Arthur leaned on the couch as he moved fully into the living room. There was nowhere left for Duke to hide as he scooted closer to the fireplace. The bottle of lighter fluid glugged as it drained down the front of Arthur's orange jumpsuit.

"Hold still you little prick!" Arthur looked woozy. The gun swung all over the place. He let go of the couch and used both hands to steady his aim. "What's that? A little shovel? Are you gonna slap away the bullet? You dumb son-of-a-bitch?"

Duke drove the head of the shovel into the fireplace, scooped up a mountain of red hot coals and flung them across the living room at Arthur. The man lit up like a desert morning sun. Whoosh! The revolver clattered to the floor and landed at Duke's side.

Arthur spun and twirled about the room with his arms flailing. He howled as every nerve ending on his body was seared to a crisp. He caught fire to the furniture and the curtains. The burning man stumbled back into the dining room and caught fire to the spilled lighter fluid on the floor. In five seconds most of the great room was set ablaze.

Every passing second Duke was less afraid of being poisoned and more afraid of burning to death. He lay on his back with the chair still under his butt. Duke stretched his legs and tugged at the thick knots. As the burning man crashed around the room it seemed impossible that he was still alive. The howling turned to shrieks. Even after going through the bleach torture at the hands of that mad man Duke felt pretty bad for the guy. Burning to death was a horrible way to go, but the convict didn't leave Duke many options.

A gunshot rang out through Duke's kitchen and Arthur's burning body fell to the floor in a hump. His sizzling skin fell off in patches as his body continued to burn.

Duke sat up as much as he could. In less than a minute the great room was already twenty degrees hotter. Duke peeked over the edge of the couch and spotted a red faced Deputy Spence holding a shotgun.

"Dominic?!" Duke was on the verge of crying.

Dominic lowered his gun and danced around the fire, "Jesus Christ Duke I thought I just shot you."

"That asshole was trying to kill me. You just put him out of his misery. Get these ropes off me!"

Dominic raced to Duke's side and caught a glimpse of his wound. "Your face!"

"Your face is jacked up too, buddy. You got a knife?"

Dominic set his gun on the floor and fished out a pocketknife from his slacks. "Here!"

The fire was spreading quickly and had begun to climb the walls of the cabin. Duke flicked open the blade. His hands moved with incredible speed as he sawed back and forth on the rope.

"You got any idea what the hell is going on?" Dominic picked back up his shotgun.

"Not really. It looked like four convicts judging by the way they were dressed. The three others left twenty minutes ago. Got it!" Duke hacked through the first restraint.

"They killed two people up at the Mountain Shop. Dropped a few trees over the highway that runs out of town and it looks like they killed the power to Sweet Home. Get a move on, Duke. This heat is murder on my face." Dominic stayed low to the floor. A growing cloud of black smoke filled the top half of the cabin.

"Got it." Duke slid the knife through the last of the rope. "Get me the hell out of here." Dominic helped him to his feet. Duke grabbed the Magnum on the way out of the living room. "Head for the kitchen."

They stayed hunched over and moved as fast as their legs could carry them. Fire seemed to be everywhere and the heat was

138

intense. The sweat on Duke's forehead evaporated as soon as it formed. They hit the garage door. It was a hundred degrees cooler standing by Duke's truck. Out of habit Duke tapped the button to open the garage door. No power meant it wouldn't budge.

"We have got to get clear of the building before the propane tank blows." Duke straightened his back and dug the keys out of his pocket.

"I should drive." Dominic reached for the keys.

"Over my dead body." Duke jogged for the driver's side door.

"You're missing an eye." Dominic protested.

"I've been driving with a patch on for a year. Get in." Duke opened the door and hopped into the truck. He fired up the engine as Dominic climbed into the passenger's side. Duke shifted into reverse and stomped on the gas. The tires burned rubber and the truck blasted through the garage door.

"Get us to the station." Dominic clicked his safety belt.

"No shit." Duke cranked the wheel, shifted into drive and barreled down his private driveway. Flames licked at every window and doorway of the cabin. Black smoke belched from the roof and looked like a dark spirit escaping from the fiery pit of hell and heading to the heavens above.

Duke spotted himself in the mirror. The split in his skin was deep and ran down his forehead into his eye socket. He hit the brakes, flung open his door and puked the rest of the bleach.

"It tastes worse the second time around." Duke spit as he closed the door. He reached for the mirror and cranked it up so he wouldn't be tempted to look at the devastation on his face. Duke's whole body filled with a festering anger. He wanted to find that fucker with the scarred face and get some numbers on the goddamn scoreboard. Duke stepped on the gas and pulled onto the main road.

Chapter 18

The steel door almost rattled off its hinges as a sledgehammer crashed into its knob. The knob bent at a thirty-degree angle, but it held. Zarren raised the hammer and held it like a baseball bat.

"You got this one, man." Regan cackled.

Zarren swung for the fences and nailed the door right above the knob. The force blew it straight out of the jamb and it flung the door wide open. Zarren stepped forward into the darkness and out of the freezing cold.

"It looks like no one's home." Regan snickered as he let Jacob pass him into the building. He closed the door behind them, even though a strong wind could easily push it back open.

The crew headed down a narrow corridor. On their right a door was labeled EVIDENCE. A little farther down the hall they passed another door. It had a handwritten sign taped to it that read CLEANING SUPPLIES. They rounded the last corner and the room opened up. A small holding cell was on their right and two desks filled the rest of Sweet Home's Sheriff's station.

Regan stepped quietly for the Sheriff's office. He rapped his knuckles against the glass and raised the pitch of his voice. With a falsetto southern accent Regan asked, "Sheriff? Are you there? I'm scared to death. There are four crazy convicts going around murdering people for sport." Regan's eyes bugged and his smile was ear to ear. The two others were not as amused.

There was no response on the other side of the door. They were not surprised. No cruisers in the parking lot meant there was a good chance they had all stepped out. Regan turned the knob on the door and found the office empty. He entered and walked around the desk. Regan pulled out the chair and sat at the desk.

"How many deputies we got?" Regan leaned back and kicked his feet up onto the table the same exact way Sheriff

MaCready had earlier that day.

Jacob raised his index finger.

"One deputy and one Sheriff. What a sleepy town. The guy on the highway must have been the deputy." Regan found the hand written note on the Sheriff's desk. "Someone called in about our work at the gas station."

On the Sheriff's desk next to the phone sat a longwave radio.

It chirped and squawked, "Sheriff? Sheriff MaCready, do you read me it's Marvin? The phones are down and I can't get a call out. Over..."

The sudden loud noise startled Regan. He laughed at the top of his lungs that he jumped with fright. "This things still got power. What the hell?" A little red LED was lit up under the words battery backup. "Okay, here we go." He picked up the radio's receiver and held it in front of his mouth. He cleared his throat and said, "Sweet Home's sheriff department. How may I serve you? Over."

Jacob moved closer to the open doorway. He carried a perplexed look on his scarred face.

Marvin's voice was panicked, "Duke Allen's cabin is on fire. It's burning to the ground Sheriff and there are trees blocking Route 13. Over."

Regan winked at Jacob as he grunted into the radio, "That's weird.... Oh yeah, over." He released his thumb from the receiver as he talked to Jacob. "Wasn't that the cabin we crashed, off route 13?" Jacob nodded his head. "Arthur must have started a fire. Check that one off the list I guess."

Marvin continued, "I can't get through to the fire department. I don't know what to do. Over"

Regan shrugged his shoulders as he talked to Jacob and Zarren. "No way to get a call out to the fire department and there's not much of a police force here. I guess we can move to the next stage of the plan."

Marvin asked from the radio, "Are you still there? Over."

"Yes, I'm here. Okay, here's what I want you to do, take a gun, stick it in your mouth and pull the goddamn trigger." He laughed into the radio. "Over!"

"Who is this? Where's the Sheriff?" Marvin yelled through the radio.

"Sheriff MaCready...? She's gone. I'm the new Sheriff in town." Regan slammed the receiver on to the radio's cradle, then he picked up the whole device, ripped out the power cord and tossed it against the wall. The radio left a divot in the sheetrock and cracked open on impact.

"I've always wanted to say that." Regan picked up the crystal award off the desk. He held it in his lap as he read the inscription to himself. "There ain't much action going on here. You boys can take off if you want. Go do your thing while I hang here for a little longer. If anyone shows up I'll take care of them." He tossed the award over his shoulder and the crystal shattered when it collided with the filing cabinet behind him. He spotted a large map of Sweet Home on the wall in the main office. Regan got to his feet and headed out of the Sheriff's office. He picked up a black marker from a desk and stepped in front of the map.

"Let's dice this bitch into thirds. That way we won't overlap." He located the station on the map it sat just about dead center of the town. "Okay, we are here. Zarren, why don't you take Main Street and head out to the school. That couple I took care of on the highway said there was some kind of thing happening at the school tonight. That's why they were all dolled up." He marked a line onto the map. Zarren moved in behind him and studied the landmarks. Regan jotted a capital Z on that section of the map. "Jacob, why don't you start with this place called, The Oasis, then head east?" He slashed out a line on the map. Jacob looked it over. Regan slapped a capital J on that part of the map. "And I'll take this cluster of homes in the south." He scribbled a line down to the bottom of the map and finished with a capital R. "This is just a suggestion. Feel free to cross lines. You know, go where the night takes you. It's just a good place to start."

The three of them nodded at each other out of respect. They knew there was a strong possibility that this was the last time they would ever see each other alive.

Zarren and Jacob headed for the front door.

"Jacob? Was it over one-fifty?" Regan crossed his arms and cocked his head to the side.

Jacob raised his hand and pointed his thumbs into the air.

Regan shook his head with disbelieve. "Higher than one-fifty? You have got to be fucking kidding?"

Jacob shook his head.

"Is it over two hundred?" Regan scoffed.

Jacob nodded his head.

"Crazy motherfucker. Whatever insane number you're gunning for, I hope you hit it you sick son-of-a-bitch."

Zarren tried to open the front door by just twisting the knob, but it didn't budge. He kicked at it and the sticky door cracked open. The two killers stepped into the snowy street and the door swung shut behind them. On their left was Main Street. Bill and Tad's Excellent Video Rental was a few buildings down. On their right only a block and a half away sat The Oasis.

Zarren took long strides as he lumbered away into the night. His trajectory was going to take him to the back alley behind Main Street. The flakes were coming down even harder and it didn't take long before Jacob could no longer make out the shape of the big man's body.

Jacob sucked in a long breath of fresh mountain air then he started to jog down the street. The night was filled with endless possibilities and he was so close to hitting his goal. He raced across the street and disappeared into the blizzard.

A moment later a set of headlights cut through the snow and sped toward the station. It was Sheriff MaCready's Bronco.

The spike of adrenaline coursing through MaCready's veins was a sensation she hadn't felt for a long time. She skidded to a stop in the station's parking lot, grabbed her flashlight and jumped out of the Bronco. She bolted for the front door. By the time she had reached the entrance, MaCready was already out of breath.

I have to get back into the gym and start running again.

I don't want what happened to mother to happen to me.

Her mother had been wheelchair bound from age sixty-five to the day she died. Not because of an accident or any medical reasons, it was only because the woman was so damn lazy that her body had simply atrophied away to the point that she couldn't leave the chair even if she wanted to.

MaCready put her shoulder into the door and marched in out of the snow. She stopped dead in her tracks. Two things jumped out at her right away. One, the door to her office was open.

That's not how I left it.

Second, was the crude drawing on the map of Sweet Home.

Z, J, R? What the hell is that?

She drew her pistol. "This is Sheriff MaCready! Come out with your hands up!" She whipped the yellow cone of light around the station. The room was silent and there was no movement.

Whoever had been here might have left already?

Why the hell would you kill two people and then head straight to the Sheriff's department?

Every ounce of her body wanted her to run in the other direction. It was insane to enter a building without back up.

Where the hell is Dominic?

Her mind raced and tried to think up a better way to get hold of the state police. Absolutely nothing came to mind. She didn't have a choice. The satellite phone was the only way to get the word out and call for help. MaCready moved slowly into the station. She checked her corners and behind the desks. The palm of her hand felt sweaty as she aimed the revolver around the room. MaCready was a pretty damn good shot, but that was standing on a safe, well-lit firing range. She wasn't sure she could hit the side of a mountain in this almost pitch black office with her body jacked full of adrenalin. Not once had she fired her piece while on the job and she had only pulled it twice since she pinned the star to her chest.

She inched closer and closer to her office door. The flashlight sent shadows creeping along the walls of the station and monsters appeared to be surrounding her from every direction. She was almost to her office when she realized she hadn't taken a breath since she stepped into the station. MaCready was getting dizzy so she forced herself to take in a lung full of air. She was ten steps from the phone and about to enter her office, when the door suddenly swung closed and crushed her wrist in the doorjamb.

The sound of her bones breaking caused her stomach to turn inside out. Then the pain hit. The person inside the room rammed a shoulder into the door again. Her wrist crunched a second time. She couldn't scream. She couldn't breathe. The only thing in her world right now was pain.

She dropped the gun and her flashlight as she gripped her wounded arm. The door swung open. The flashlight on the floor was the only source of light in the whole room and its beam was aimed directly into the office. It illuminated a beast of a man. He had a grotesque smile and a scar running down the side of his head. His orange correctional jumpsuit was filthy and stained with blood. He put his hand on his hips as he stepped from the office. It emphasized his barrel chest and thick arms.

"Hello Sheriff MaCready. I've been waiting for you." He giggled with a high-pitched, nails on a chalkboard, kind of laugh.

MaCready was crippled with fear. None of her training was kicking in to save her. All she could do was step back toward Dominic's desk and prop herself up on its corner.

The convict bent at the waist and picked up the flashlight from the floor. He aimed it toward her injured wrist. A sliver of white bone protruded from the skin and the hand hung at a sick ninety degrees.

"Ouch. That looks bad. What happened?" He mocked her. "I need to tell you something and it's a big secret." He stepped closer and towered above her. "I hate co-"

Halfway through the word her self-preservation went into overdrive. She reached behind her, grabbed a pair of scissors from a coffee mug on Dominic's desk and sliced the weapon at him. He raised his arm to block and the sharp edge cut him just above the elbow.

He recoiled and cursed, "You bitch!"

MaCready rushed for the front door. Every step she took caused her wrist to shake. The intense agony rippling up her arm had her on the verge of blacking out.

A heavy set of boots stomped across the office behind her. She got to the entrance, turned the knob but the swollen wood didn't budge.

He bull charged her and tackled MaCready through the door. They fell to the snow-covered sidewalk. The Sheriff tried to scream, but he caught her across the face with the back of his hand and hissed, "Shut your mouth." The con quickly checked the street. It was empty. "We gotta get back inside." He climbed off her, grabbed her ankle and dragged the woman back toward the office.

During the fall her shirt came untucked and was now scooping up snow as he hauled her across the sidewalk. The ice on her love handles helped wake MaCready up. She plotted how she could get away from this monster.

I can't fight him! He's too strong. She cradled her busted arm against her chest. Tears blurring her vision as the drops streamed down her face. Sheriff MaCready felt like giving up.

Just let the man kill you. Then the pain will be gone. Her logic was sound and it would have been easy for her to stop fighting, but the Sheriff was no quitter.

MaCready let go of her broken wrist, reached for the Taser on her belt, she lifted her free leg and brought the heel of her boot down on the hand holding her ankle. The kick broke his hold on her.

He turned back to catch her. "Where do you think you're goi-!"

Sheriff hit him in the thigh with 50,000 volts of electricity. The Taser ticked and his body seized. The con stumbled and fell to Dominic's desk, knocking the perfectly organized paperclips to the floor. He dropped to his back and she finally let up on the Taser.

Every muscle in his body contracted, but she did not have long. He was a big guy and the Taser would only keep him down for a few seconds.

MaCready unbuttoned the leather pouch that held her cuffs. She rolled to her side and wormed her way toward him. Working the cuff with only one hand was difficult, but she got one wrapped around his meaty wrist.

His neck craned up off the floor and he looked at her with pure hate.

"Shit!" She cursed at herself for not moving fast enough.

In the blink of an eye he grabbed her by the shoulders, twisted her away from him and wrapped his arms around her neck. The pressure on her throat was crushing. She reached for her Taser and tagged him in the back of his arm. It only made him squeeze harder. The world spun around her and she dropped the Taser. MaCready fired off an elbow into his balls.

He coughed out a rough, "Fuck!" His grip loosened and it was enough for her to turn her chin into the choke, blocking it from cutting off her air supply. She hit him with another elbow. He let go of her and cupped his throbbing testicles. Sheriff slid the mace out of her belt. She knew it was a horrible idea to discharge it inside, but even if they were both blinded she would have a little better chance to get away from the monster.

She was about to hit the button and blast his eyes with pepper when he let go of his testicles and grabbed her by the injured wrist and yanked on it. An ocean of pain swelled in her. Then he brought his forehead down on the bridge of her nose. It crunched on impact. Her vision filled with a flash of stars.

That did it. She had no more fight left in her. Once more his thick arms were around her neck and wrenching on her throat. Sheriff MaCready had two final thoughts.

She wished she could hear her favorite song one more time and the last thing that snapped through her synapsis was her regret for not letting Dominic go. She knew how badly he wanted out of this one horse town. His only goal was to get to a bigger city, help people and make a difference in the community.

She had called in a favor from an old friend at the Portland, Oregon Sheriff's department and asked them to botch his transfer request. She just wanted a few more years with him until it was her turn to retire. She knew it was selfish and sometimes it kept her up at night, but MaCready never had children of her own and she loved Dominic like a son. All of the years they worked together she never told him how she felt. MaCready was scared the feelings were not mutual. Dominic was a tough man to read sometimes. Maybe it made her a bad person, she didn't think she was evil and wasn't trying to be malicious. She just enjoyed his company. MaCready grunted one last gasp and the pain was finally gone.

Regan gave the tough old broad one final squeeze before he let go. Her body had gone limp in the normal amount of time, but she was tougher than most and might have been faking it.

He let her go and dropped her to the floor. "Goddamn my dick." He held his crotch as if they were precious jewels. "I hope all the bitches in this town aren't this tough." He sat up and rubbed the part of his forehead that had broken her nose and wiped the blood off his skin.

He spotted the Taser on the floor. "That little thing hurt like a bitch." He picked up the Taser and slipped it into his pocket. He found the keys for the cuffs and unlocked his wrist then tossed them next to the corpse. Her badge caught his attention.

"I am the new sheriff in town." Regan plucked the star from her chest and pinned it to his jacket. Regan's whole body ached as he climbed from the floor. Before leaving, he studied the map one last time.

Regan wiped the blood off his hand and onto his section of the map. "It's time to squeeze the life out of this little town." He pulled the keys for the blue van out of his pocket and headed down the hallway from which they had entered.

Chapter 19

Zarren liked the snow. He preferred it cold. The weather heightened his senses and he felt more aware of his surroundings. He was glad to be rid of the others, especially the bald man that was constantly talking with his filthy mouth. He disgusted Zarren to the core. Regan and his crusty old friend Arthur were the kind of humans Zarren hated most. Uneducated fools. The only one he could stand was the man without a face. Jacob was intriguing to Zarren. The man never said a word and was as deadly as they come.

How did such a creature come to be? Zarren thought to himself as he approached the backdoor of the video store. Then a thought occurred to him.

Jacob probably wondered the same thing about me.

The alley he traveled along was lined with garbage cans and dumpsters. Leaning against one of the walls was a large bathroom mirror that had a crack in it. Zarren's flashlight reflected off the surface and bounced the light back at himself. He didn't recognize his reflection at first. The thick black beard covered most of his features and he looked quite ridiculous with a wool blanket as a jacket.

What become of the young man I once was? Zarren posed the question to himself for the millionth time. He knew the answer. He knew exactly what drove him to this state of being. He wasn't born this way and it wasn't a slow transformation into madness. He became this monster overnight.

Zarren stood directly in front of the video store's backdoor. He raised his sledgehammer, readied a swing and was about to hammer a homerun when he noticed two overflowing ashtrays sitting next to the backdoor. Cigarette butts were everywhere.

What a bunch of slobs.

Someone that worked at this store had a nasty habit and they were too lazy to clean up this mess which meant they might be just lazy enough to keep the door unlocked. He lowered the weapon and tried the knob. It opened with a slight twist of his wrist.

Figures. He thought to himself as he stepped quietly into the storage room of the video store. He could hear the sound of voices arguing.

"Come on Steve. Pick a goddamn movie." Bill of Bill and Tad's begged as he stood behind the store's counter. The room was lit by a Maglite and a camping lantern. "You better have cash on you. We can't run any cards without the computer."

"How are you going to watch a movie without power?" Tad of Bill and Tad's asked as he kept himself busy. He was perfectly spacing apart the movies in the new release section.

A voice hollered from behind a black curtain at the back part of the store, "I got a generator."

"What do you think knocked the power and the phones out?" Bill rubbed at his potbelly.

Tad answered, "The snow?"

"It snows all the time and the phones never go out." Bill picked up his cell from the counter. It had zero bars. He barked to the back corner of the store. "Hurry up and pick a porn you dirty old pervert." Bill dropped his phone back onto the counter.

Tad moved to the next row. "Maybe it's an alien invasion and they're using the satellites to communicate with the mothership."

"That's a great movie idea."

Tad said it flatly, "Independence Day."

Bill remembered, "That's right? Good movie."

"Oh shit!" Steve dashed out of the adult section and tore down the curtain as he scrambled across the floor.

Tad spun around and asked, "What's going on buddy?" He aimed his light at the entryway. Standing at the threshold of the adult section was a man the size of a grizzly bear. He carried a sledgehammer and a tool belt was wrapped around his waist. "Hello, um. How did you get back there?"

Steve raced to the front of the store. "He's got blood on him!" He announced to the others.

At first the big man didn't move. He was counting how many people were in the store.

One.

Two.

Three.

He calculated his next move, then the move after that.

"Sir, are you injured? Would you like us to get you some help?" Bill stepped from behind the counter.

The man moved slowly at first. He reached for something in his tool belt.

Tad took a few footsteps closer. "Mister are you alrig-"

In an instant the big man whipped a long screwdriver through the air and down the aisle toward Tad. The tool entered his right thigh and slid all the way to the hilt. He crumpled to the floor, clutched his thigh and grunted.

The giant charged at Bill as he swung the big hammer. Bill ducked and rolled, just in the nick of time. The hammer collided with a rack of movies and the whole thing came tumbling to the floor. Bill scurried down an aisle and headed for his injured friend.

Steve saw his chance to make an escape and bolted for the front door. The man regained his footing, and sprinted after Steve.

"What do you want, man?" Steve screamed over his shoulder as he headed for the front entrance. The big man was quicker than Steve and he body-checked the fleeing victim though the front window. The large pane of glass exploded out onto the sidewalk. Steve had the wind knocked out of him as he crash landed spine first on the pavement. Chunks of glass protruded from Steve's neck and shoulders. However painful the wounds were, none of them were life threatening. Steve wheezed and coughed up blood as his eyes rolled back into their sockets.

Bill crawled next to Tad. "Fuck man, look at your leg!"

Tad's face had gone pale. "I see it. Get me the hell out of here!"

Bill pulled Tad's arm across his shoulder and heaved his

friend up off the floor. They limped across the store as they headed for their office.

"What are you doing?" Tad groaned.

"I'm getting the gun in my desk." Bill answered between heavy breaths. Bill came to an abrupt stop, let out a guttural yell then crumbled to the floor in pain.

Tad was dragged to the carpet by his injured friend. "What?! What happened?"

Bill thrashed on the floor. He reached for his hamstring and found a screwdriver sticking from the back of his leg.

"Come on! We have to keep moving!" Tad crawled for the office door.

The giant seemed to appear out of nowhere. The head of the sledgehammer came careening out of the darkness and caught Bill at the base of his skull. His head popped like a zit and covered Tad with blood, brains and bone fragments. The spray of gore got him square in the face.

Tad spit a chunk of Bill out of his mouth. There was no time to mourn the loss. The killer had reset and the hammer was above him now.

He raised his hands in the air to protect himself. "Please don't," was the last words Tad uttered.

The giant hit him on the crown of his skull and cracked his noggin wide open. Slop poured out onto the floor and Tad's torso went limp. The video store went silent aside from the wind gusting through the busted front window.

The devastation at Zarren's feet made him feel at peace, but it only lasted for a minute before the voice in his head told him to do it again.

Find someone and crush them.

These two freshly crushed bodies reminded him a lot of the first time he killed. It was 2001 and Zarren was a freshman at Stanford University. He was there to study environmental science and like a lot of students he was convinced he could help save the world one day. Zarren was always the biggest kid in his class and

152

coaches hounded him to play football and basketball, but he had no interest in contact sports or physical competition of any kind. He wasn't there on scholarship and everything at school was insanely expensive. Mom and Dad paid for as much as they could, but there was never enough money at the end of the month. Zarren, absolutely did not want to go into debt at school so when an opportunity to make a little extra cash popped up he jumped at the chance.

A major pharmaceutical company, Zarren was never told exactly which one, was testing a new anti-depressant. There was a long list of possible side effects and the one every doctor performing the test seemed most concerned with was the increased risk of suicide. Zarren was nineteen years old and of the mindset that he was special and death couldn't touch him. Besides the people putting on the test were paying out cash at the end of every day. He got a hundred bucks to take a pill, have them watch him and answer a slew of questions. It was easy money.

After a week of tests everything was going good. He was never one to suffer depression, but the drugs had given him an extra bounce in his step. He had an abundance of energy and had even worked up the courage to ask a girl in his class, Monica, out on a date. He showed up to take the tests like normal, but his paperwork had a new amount for him to ingest. The increased dosage was a misprint, but the administrator assumed it was because of Zarren's body size that he was given this new larger amount. By the end of that day's test he could feel a change. It was a creeping slow thought bubbling up inside him unlike anything he had felt before.

Afraid he might not get paid the money he needed for his date with Monica, Zarren lied at the end about the new thought that his mind was playing again and again. Suicidal thoughts were not his problem he was suddenly fantasizing about homicide.

The legal waiver he signed at the beginning discussed a one in one-hundred-thousand chance the antidepressant might affect him negatively, but it was a one in one-million chance of it flipping a switch permanently and that's exactly what happened.

Zarren went back to his dorm. He needed to get ready for his date with Monica. As he shaved and changed into a fresh set of clothes his two roommates were busy arguing about who would win in a fight, Superman or Batman. They droned on about it for what seemed like an eternity, until Zarren could no longer take it. He marched out of the bathroom, picked up the Xbox sitting next to the TV and bashed in their skulls. His whole body trembled. He dropped the game system and stepped back into the bathroom. His, hands, face and button up shirt were caked in blood. The old Zarren was dead and a new one had just been born.

He spent years moving from town to town crushing and killing with all different kinds of weapons. He finally settled on the sledgehammer as the best tool for the job. He spent a decade preying on small towns like Sweet Home and what Zarren didn't realize was his actions had gained him the attention of the FBI and a special agent had been sent to apprehend him. Zarren waltzed right into a trap set by a Special Agent Becker. He was quickly given three life sentences and shipped off to prison.

Thirteen months ago Zarren suffered a mild heart attack during a violent altercation with another inmate. Zarren beat a man to death with a reference book in the library. Just after crushing the man's skull he got dizzy and passed out. He was sent to the infirmary where the fresh out of college prison doctor told him his heart was undersized for a man of his stature and without major reconstructive surgery he would most likely pass in the next year. Zarren spent the next thirteen months between solitary confinement and the prison hospital until he was deemed a lost cause. What that really meant was the surgery was too expensive and it was best to let him die. He was shipped out with the others to rot at the maximum-security hospital until his heart gave out for good.

Zarren could feel pain growing in his chest. Today had been exciting but all of the running around was strenuous work. If he wasn't careful he could suffer a massive heart attack. Zarren calmed his breathing and the pain subsided.

Outside Bill and Tad's Excellent Video rental, Steve was stirring on the sidewalk. That was the signal for Zarren to get moving. He quickly pulled both of his screwdrivers from the dead men's legs and replaced them in his tool belt. He stomped down the aisles of DVD's and headed for the front door.

Steve was on his feet. Zarren was almost on top of him. Steve bolted when he saw the man making a beeline in his direction. The entrance to the video store crashed open behind him.

Zarren was in a full sprint. He moved like a speeding bulldozer. He got within fifteen feet of the fleeing man and launched the sledgehammer at him. Zarren had spent a lot of time practicing this move and he was deadly accurate up to twenty-five feet away. The head of the hammer caught Steve between the shoulder blades and sent him tumbling to the ground. He slid another five-feet in the snow until his momentum came to a stop. Nearly every time Zarren had done this move it resulted in the victim's spine getting broken. The chances of Steve standing up and running away were close to zero. Zarren stopped running and resumed his normal lumbering walk down the street. When he arrived next to Steve's dying body he extracted the stuck tool from the man's spine. He finished off Steve with a boot to the back of his whimpering head.

A quarter mile away a ton of lights kicked on all at once. Zarren could hear the faint sounds of a motor running. He moved out into the middle of the street to get a better angle on the action. The sign on that next block read Sweet Home High School. He continued in the direction of the bright light.

Zarren's brain repeated. *Find someone and crush them.*

Chapter 20

The smell of sex inside Stanley's van was musky. There was a pungent tang that could be tasted on the back of their tongues. Morgan climbed off Stanley's lap and took a seat next to him on the van's back bench. The light of a cellphone bathed the lovers in a sexy blue glow. Stanley couldn't believe Morgan had talked him into doing it three times in the back of his van, out in public no less.

Sex in the back of a van. He thought to himself. *Who does that other than hormonal teenagers?*

He was never one for public displays of affection.

Boy, if Cindy could see me now.

Stanley was raised to believe that what happened between a man and woman should only take place behind closed doors. Kisses or whatever you were into should be done where people couldn't see. It was one of the many reasons his ex-wife bugged out three years ago. Stanley did a lot of soul searching in the lonely three years after Cindy left. He decided if he ever found another lady willing to get naked and wiggle their bodies together he would be open to whatever they suggest.

Whose adventurous now, Cindy?

I'm doing three-ways and sex in public.

My horizons have been expanded, Cindy!

Stanley held a relaxed almost smug smile on his face as he slipped the condom off and tossed it with the other used rubbers. It landed with a wet splat in a crinkled shopping bag on the passenger's floorboard.

Three times, back to back, that has to be my all-time record. Stanley was sixty-eight-years old but because of his new workout routine, daily vitamin supplements and healthy diet, he was in the best shape of his life.

"Your thang is still rock hard?" Morgan reached over and tapped at Stanley's business.

He flashed his eyebrows at her as he looked back and forth from his erect Johnson to her makeup smeared face. "At fifteen bucks a pop, the little blue pill should last." Stanley giggled then he zipped up his jeans.

"And last and last. What are you doing? Get that monster back out."

His monster was sore and he needed to rest, but he didn't want Morgan to think he was weak. "We should get going." He checked his watch. "It's close to nine."

"Okay, party pooper. Where are my panties? Why's it so dark out?" Morgan sat forward and shuffled through the pile of clothes on the floor of the van.

Stanley hadn't noticed it before. Earlier he was too busy concentrating on the task at hand to pay attention to their surroundings. He ran his hand over the steamed up glass. It was black outside. Not just dark out, but black. The town of Sweet Home was completely absent of light. Stanley pressed his nose to the window and cupped his hands around his eyes to get a better look.

He whispered to himself. "That's weird."

Morgan heard him and asked, "What's weird?"

"All the street lights are out, HOLY SHIT!"

A horrible face appeared out of nowhere on the other side of the glass. It sat an inch away from Stanley. A flashlight lit up its disfigured features. The person held the light under his chin as if he was telling a ghost story around a campfire.

Stanley jerked away from the window. He backed into Morgan and the two of them fell off the bench seat. The cell, their only light source, was knocked from the seat, tumbled to the floor and was lost under the pile of clothes. It was now pitch black inside the van.

"What's wrong with you?" Morgan hollered from under Stanley.

He whispered as he righted himself. "Someone's out there."

"Is it that pretty bartender?"

"No."

"Well tell the pervert to go away or start paying if they

wanna watch the show." Morgan giggled as she found the phone, got to her knees and lit herself up with its screen as she shook her wonderful breasts. The full sized jugs swung playfully back and forth. "You wanna show? You pervert."

"Shhh." He covered her mouth with his fingers.

She quickly shook off his grip and talked at full volume. "Don't shush me."

"I think he's still out there." Stanley's hands searched the van for his button up shirt, but he couldn't find it.

"Well get out there and kick his perverted ass if it bugs you he was watching."

"Please be quiet. Where are my keys?"

"Why? What's wrong with you?"

Stanley pulled her in close and whispered, "His face was um, messed up."

"What? Is he fugly?" She raised her voice making sure the person outside the van could hear her. "Is he a fuck ugly weirdo wanting to watch us fuck our brains out?"

Stanley found his jacket and located the keys. He climbed his way into the driver's seat, fumbled through the keyring to find the correct one. Outside the van was a loud noise. Something struck the front quarter panel, then came the sound of air seeping from a small hole. Ten seconds later the same sound occurred on the passenger's side.

Stanley sucked in a gasp, "He's popping the tires." He found the headlights switch and turned them on. The parking lot filled with light. Through the steamed up windshield Stanley saw a man, dressed all in black, running toward the front of the van, he held a garbage can high above his head and launched it into the glass.

Stanley yelled, "What the hell?" He ducked below the dash. The metal can shattered the windshield. The man in black pulled the can back out of the gaping hole and continued to smash it again and again.

Morgan sobered right up once she caught a look at the man's face. "Get us out of here!" She grabbed Stanley's shoulder, shook it and screamed bloody murder in his ear.

Stanley worked the key into the ignition and cranked on the motor. At the same time the man outside forced the garbage can all the way through the windshield and into the front seat. The edge of the can cracked Stanley in the forehead and pushed his skull back against the headrest. He could no longer see. The man busted the driver's window, popped the lock, opened the door and yanked Stanley out.

His naked torso was instantly covered with goosebumps and his nipples became rock hard.

The man in black was on Stanley in a flash. The first punch landed square on Stanley's jaw. It was more pain than Stanley had experienced before.

In the van Morgan screamed her head off. "Kill him! Kill him! Kill him!"

For an instant Stanley thought she meant she wanted him dead.

Stanley raised his hands to protect his face, but the strikes were coming from all angles and were too fast for him to block. The man slammed Stanley into the side of the van then clutched the back of his head with both hands. The mystery man launched knee after knee into Stanley's naked ribs and stomach.

What the hell does this guy want?

The man delivered a devastating knee to Stanley's sternum, knocking the wind completely out of his lungs, then spun him around and tossed his limp body into the side of the van. The back of Stanley's skull cracked against the steel panel and his body left a torso sized dent. He fell to the ground wheezing and holding his ribs.

"Get the fuck away from him!" Morgan commanded. She stood topless and shivering in front of the van's headlights. A Derringer pistol gripped in her hands. The scar faced man paused and he looked at her. "Stanley are you okay?"

Stanley spit out a mouthful of blood and answered, "No."

"Can you get to your feet?"

"Maybe?" He reached up the side of the van and used the lip of a window to pull himself off the freezing ground.

"Listen here, asshole. You're coming with us to the Sheriff's station. If you do anything stupid I'll drop you."

The man sneered. A second later he pulled out a knife and was sprinting straight for Morgan.

She fired her gun and the .22 caliber round punched the man in his stomach, but it didn't stop him. He didn't even flinch.

The cold steel of the knife entered Morgan's chest and pierced her racing heart. The pumping muscle contracted around the tip of the blade. She was face to face with the monster. Her eyelids blinked double time. It was the first time all night she didn't have something to say.

Stanley yelled from the pit of his stomach, "You bastard!" and jumped onto the man's back. He let go of his knife and left it in Morgan's chest as the three of them fell to the ground. In a fit of rage Stanley straddled the man and punched at the man's face. "You killed her you son-of-a-bitch!" His hands were numb from the bitter cold and couldn't tell how hard he was punching this asshole in the face. Stanley was nailing him with some hard shots, but the man's expression never changed.

It was straight out of a nightmare, those horrible dreams where no matter how hard you try, you cannot land a good punch. Stanley stopped punching and wrapped his fingers around the man's neck. He squeezed and wrenched on his throat.

"Why did you kill her? Why?" Stanley begged for an answer and leaned into the choke.

With expert skill the man broke the chokehold, bucked his hips and tossed Stanley to his back. The man rolled along the ground and ended on top. Again a flurry of punches rocketed Stanley's face. Within a few seconds Stanley's nose was broken, jaw dislocated, eardrum ruptured, teeth knocked in and his eye socket was crushed. Blood pooled at the back of Stanley's throat. He coughed and spewed gore onto the man's horrible face, but the beating didn't stop until Stanley was dead.

Numbers two-fifty-six and two-fifty-seven. Jacob gloated to himself. His hands were drenched with the blood of his victim. He quickly got to his feet, pulled up his shirt and inspected the gunshot wound. He felt the pressure of the hit, but there was no pain. One tiny little hole sat to the right of his belly button. Blood seeped from the wound and ran down to his jeans. He felt around to his back and there wasn't an exit wound.

Damn it! A gut shot! Why now? He cursed at himself for not being more careful. Even if he cauterized the wound, which he would have to do quickly, it was only going to delay the inevitable. Jacob was bleeding internally and with all of the running, stabbing, fighting and killing he had left to do it meant he was going to bleed to death in the next few hours.

Shit, shit, shit.

He pulled his knife out of the woman's chest and put it back into its sheath. He ran his sleeve over his face and got the blood out of his eyes. He turned one-eighty and noticed the bar.

The Oasis would have what I need to slow the bleeding. Jacob found his flashlight in the snow and jogged to the bar.

Christy woke up to the sound of gunfire. The office was pitch black. At first she was completely disoriented until she noticed her diddling hand was still jammed down the front of her pants.

"Damn it, I fell asleep." The comfy leather chair squeaked as she sat forward. She felt her phone slide down the front of her chest. She pulled her hand from her jeans and picked the phone from her lap. She swiped right and the first thing to pop up on its screen was hardcore gay porn. Two men grunted loudly as they banged the hell out of each other. She'd been watching it to come faster. Christy had no idea why she liked gay porn so much. It was kind of rough stuff sometimes. She figured it was best not to dive into the mystery of why two beefy guys slamming each other's butts turned her on so much and just enjoy the results they produced.

Christy hit the pause button and the fantastic grunting stopped, but outside the bar someone was yelling. She sat still and tried to decipher if the yells were from someone in trouble or just Morgan and Stanley rocking the van.

It sounded like Stanley yelling "Why, did you kill her, why?"

Christy flipped on the phones light and headed out of the office. She tiptoed across the bar and crawled up to a widow that faced the bar's parking lot. She peeked out a corner of the window. Christy's hand shot to her mouth to keep the scream from escaping.

A man she had never seen before was straddling Stanley and beating him. Stanley's arms lay flat in the snow. He wasn't fighting back. Another body was on the ground next to them. A knife stuck out of her chest.

It's Morgan. She's dead!

Christy turned off her phone's flashlight and dialed 911, but the call wouldn't go through. She tried again, but there was no signal. She looked back outside and the man was coming her way.

Oh, god his face. Was Christy's kneejerk reaction. Then a thought occurred to her.

Maybe he saw me.

I've gotta hide.

He jogged across the snow and stood at the front door. He hit the door's window with his flashlight and sent glass across the bar's floor. He snaked his arm through the opening and unlocked the bolts. The door swung open and the man moved with purpose. He leaped up onto the counter and hopped behind the bar.

Christy shivered with fear and held her breath. She cowered in the corner of the bar at the farthest back booth in the building. She hid under the table and lay face down on the sticky floor. From the shadows, she peeked with one eye. The man rummaged through the bottles of alcohol and dug through the drawers until he found what he was looking for. Then he climbed onto the bar, sprawled out and lifted up his shirt. He aimed the flashlight at his stomach and gently touched a spot that was bleeding.

He was shot. Christy connected the dots.

The man laid on his side across the top of the bar and screwed the cap off a bottle of Everclear. He poured a few shots worth of booze out onto the bullet wound. It didn't seem to bother him at all. She was sure he was going to cry like a baby. He poured some more then used a rag to mop up the excess from his belly. He fired up a cigarette lighter and held it to his wound. The alcohol in the little hole burst into flames. Christy watched in amazement as he held the lighter to the wound and burned the skin shut. He did it all without uttering a single peep. He didn't even register pain or discomfort on his face. She had never seen anything like it before in her life. The smell of burnt flesh hit Christy and she almost puked.

Stay quiet! She commanded herself.

Her stomach held firm and she remained perfectly still. He climbed off the bar, tucked his shirt into his jeans and headed for the front door. From her spot under the booth she couldn't see him leave, but she heard the front door open then close.

Maybe he's gone? Maybe he's waiting for me to move so he can kill me too?

Her boss kept a loaded sawed off shotgun behind the bar. She wanted to crawl out to get it, but the fear was too powerful so she stayed put.

Chapter 21

Duke fishtailed his truck onto Main Street. The bumpy ride didn't help the perpetual feeling of nausea he had sloshing around in his body. Duke remembered when he was younger and went with his family to a county fair. There was a ride there called Maximum Spin. All it did was rotate three-hundred-sixty degrees. Faster and faster it went, until Duke felt like he was in a human centrifuge. It ruined the rest of his day. Duke was so sick he couldn't go on another ride or eat. All he could do was sit on a park bench and wait until his parents took him home. The uneasy knot in his stomach from the bleach and the loss of his eye was ten times worse than the sickness he had felt that day.

A blood soaked chunk of gauze was taped to Duke's face. Dominic was playing nurse. The quick turn caused Dominic to lose his balance and fall backwards from a kneeling position he had taken on the truck's bench seat. A first-aid kit slid across the dashboard, crashed to the floorboard and spilled all of its contents.

"Watch it, Duke!" Dominic barked as he got back to his knees. He found an Ace bandage on the floor and leaned toward Duke. "Hold still so I can secure this."

Duke dropped his shoulders and extended his neck as he kept his one and only eye on the road. Dominic wrapped the bandage around Duke's noggin. "Is that too tight?"

Duke moaned, "No."

"This is ridiculous. You need to see a doctor." Dominic fastened the bandage at the back of Duke's head. "I hope this holds." Dominic groaned in pain and cradled his hand as he righted himself in the passenger's seat.

"It'll be fine. We're almost there." Duke put his foot to the gas. "So what happened to you?"

"Whoever is doing this, rigged an explosive at the Mountain Shop. Goddamn gas station blew up in my face."

"Shit." Duke burped up a mouthful of bleach. He came close to ralphing on Dominic, but toughed his way through it and spit on to the floor.

Dominic sniffed the air. "Was that bleach?"

"We've both had a rough night." Duke passed by the same real estate advertisement he had seen earlier of Sharon getting doused by a veiny dong. He told himself that he hated her guts. Hated how she treated him when they were dating. Hated the condescending bullshit she would pull after a single glass of wine. Even with a heart full of hate he didn't want a psycho to tie her to a chair and cut her up. He was not sure what to do, but he knew he had to do something to help her. Just ahead was the station. Duke breathed a sigh of relief when he spotted the Sheriff's Bronco.

"Thank Christ." Dominic was thankful that the Sheriff was at the station. He sat forward and readied himself to hop out the second they came to a stop. Duke pulled his truck next to the Bronco and they jumped out together.

"Watch my back." Dominic took point and rushed for the front door. Duke readied his pistol and followed on the Deputy's heels.

The station's front door was wide open and the upper hinge had been busted out of the frame. The snow on the ground looked like a struggle had recently taken place. Dominic moved with caution as he stepped closer to the entryway. His flashlight panned across the station's threshold. Dominic tucked the butt of the shotgun into his shoulder as he took his first step into the building. He swiped the light around the room and checked his corners. On his second pass he found her.

This can't be happening.

Somehow he found his voice. "Sheriff?"

No response.

"Duke, stay by the door. They could still be in here." The Deputy inched closer to MaCready. He knelt down, reached out for her shoulder and rolled over her limp body. A set of cold black eyes stared up at him.

"She's dead." Dominic was hit with several emotions at once, but the winner at the top of the heap was, fear. Most of all he feared for his life and the lives in this town, but another, more selfish fear was the unnerving fact that he was now acting Sheriff. That meant he was stuck here, in Sweet Home, until this whole damn mess was cleaned up.

Dominic never liked MaCready. In fact he could barely tolerate being at the station with her. She had an old fashioned, golly shucks, way of doing police work that drove Dominic absolutely nuts. His boss was not the main reason he wanted out, but it was close to the top.

"What happened?" Duke asked from the doorway.

Dominic put his detective hat on and mentally combed through the evidence. Her gun was next to the office door. Blood splatters were on the door itself and on the adjacent frame. The Sheriff's cuffs were next to her body and most of his desk's belongings were on the floor. He noticed her busted nose and the bruising on her neck. He had found similar marks on the body of that plumber at the gas station. The damage to her wrist caught him off guard. He whispered to himself, "Shit, is that bone?" The map of Sweet Home sent ice down his spine. Z, J, R and a smear of blood stained the R section.

Duke said there were four of them. One got it in Duke's cabin. The remaining three have split the town into thirds. Fan-fucking-tastic!

"Deputy?" Duke itched for an answer.

Dominic mumbled under his breath. "She was strangled."

Duke dropped his head as he grunted, "Now what?"

Dominic searched the recesses of his mind for an answer. Saving a town from a group of murderers was nothing he thought he would ever have to face alone.

"I need to call the state police and the Feds." Dominic reached for his desk's phone and held it to his ear. The receiver found a nice big blister on his ear and he hissed in pain.

No dial tone. That was worse than the Goddamn blister.

"Phones are down." Dominic let the receiver fall. It rattled across the floor as it dangled from its cord.

Duke raised his head. "What?"

Dominic squatted next to the Sheriff's body and searched her pockets for her cell. He located it, but there was no signal.

"Cells are out too."

"They knocked out power and communication? Who are these guys?" Duke's nervous tone didn't help. Dominic felt his hands shaking and he turned his back on Duke to hide the fear that made itself at home on his burnt face.

It's the cold and my burns that are making them shake. He tried his best to convince himself his hands were a physical problem and not a mental one.

"How can you get the word out?" Duke pressed the man in charge.

An idea hit.

"There's a sat-phone in her desk. I can call the State Police with it." Dominic searched MaCready's pockets again and found her keys. He entered her office and used the keys to open the desk. There it was at the top of some papers, the sat-phone.

Dominic picked it up and hit the power button. Nothing. "Shit!"

"What?"

"Batteries are dead." Dominic searched the desk and located the power cord.

Duke motioned at the pitch-black station. "Good luck charging it here."

Right on cue a massive light fired up at the end of Main Street. It shined like a beacon of hope.

The sudden light caught Duke's attention. "Something's happening down at the school." He jogged out to the middle of the street to get a better angle.

Dominic worked the big phone into his jacket pocket along with the charger as he stepped from the station. "The school has a backup generator. It's the biggest building in town."

"I got it. A major disaster strikes, that's the best place in town for us to ride it out." Duke headed for his truck. "You should take the Sheriff's Bronco."

"Where are you going?"

Duke climbed behind the wheel. "To get Sharon."

"We should stay together," he said as he followed Duke to his truck. Dominic sounded more like the kid no one wanted to play with on the playground instead of acting Sheriff.

Duke rolled down his window. "I know." He turned the key and the engine rumbled under the hood. "But I can't wait for you." He put the Ford into reverse. "I have to make sure she's safe. See you at the school, Deputy."

"What if she's there at the dance?" Dominic was practically begging for Duke to stay.

"She ain't." Duke mashed the gas pedal, pulled out of the lot and headed in the direction of The Oasis.

Dominic found the key for the Bronco on the Sheriff's keyring. He shined his light into the backseat of the Bronco just to be sure and hopped in. Seconds later he was traveling toward the school. He flipped on the red and blues and put the pedal to the metal. He mumbled a prayer to a God that seldom listened.

Zarren watched from the shadows as the Bronco pulled into the school's parking lot. It raced for the main entrance. The officer was armed with a shotgun as he sprinted for the door.

That could be a problem. Zarren plotted out his next move, then the move after that.

Duke didn't get a block away from the station when he spotted Stanley's van in the parking lot of the bar. Its headlights were on, tailpipe was chugging exhaust into the air and the windshield was busted. Duke pumped the brakes and pulled into the lot. Once he made the turn he saw Morgan's naked body. She had a halo of pink snow surrounding her.

Duke's lips twitched around his clenched teeth. His fear and anger peaked simultaneously. He opened the door and rushed to her already cold body.

He fell to his knees as he rounded the front of the van.

"Motherfuckers." He pathetically stammered the word. He hadn't shed a tear when Sharon ripped out his heart and left him last year. Duke didn't cry when both of his parents passed away. Even when Old Yeller got shot he wasn't misty, but the sight of his oldest and dearest friend had the man weeping like a baby.

Stanley's face was unrecognizable, but Duke knew it was him. He tried to move closer, but his legs were worthless and he tumbled to his back. His throat was rough from the bleach. He couldn't scream in anger. It felt as if he was running a marathon just to cross the parking lot.

"Come on… You're okay… Get up…" Duke tugged at Stanley's hand. His friend was cold to the touch. Duke searched for a heartbeat on Stanley's wrist. There wasn't one. "You'll be okay. I'll get you to the doctor. Just hang on buddy." Duke's actions were frantic as he attempted to lift Stanley's body.

A soft voice whispered from behind him, "Duke?"

He raised his pistol into the air and aimed it at the voice.

It was Christy.

She stood at the rear of the van, the red taillights making her look as if she was coated in blood. Her fingers held a sawed off double-barreled shotgun as if it was keeping her alive. Her pretty little chin trembled as she shivered in the cold. "He's dead, Duke."

"Help me get him into the truck." Duke stayed determined. He hooked his hands under Stanley's arms and lifted him.

"He's dead." She stepped a little closer.

Duke lost his footing in the snow, slipped and fell onto Stanley's body. He got to his knees and cradled Stanley's head in his lap. "Please… Just help me get him into the bed of my truck. I don't want to leave him out here all night."

Christy nodded in agreement and stepped close to Stanley's legs. She hooked her arms under his knees and together they lifted the body. They shuffled slowly to the back of Duke's truck. It took all of the strength Duke had to hold Stanley as he lowered the tailgate on his rig.

They slid his body onto the bed. Duke wished he had a tarp or a blanket to cover him, but there was nothing. They got

Morgan's body and put her next to Stanley.

Slamming shut the tailgate was close to closing the coffin door on Stanley and it made Duke's legs want to give. The thought of plopping his ass in the snow and letting himself freeze to death was damn appealing.

It would be so easy to just let go. The phrase bounced around his skull for a second.

His knees were about to buckle.

Christy coughed. "I saw the one that did this. He was covered in scars."

That was the motivation Duke needed.

Vengeance.

He stopped his knees from going weak, cleared his eye and straightened his back. "Which direction did he go?"

Christy's chin bounced uncontrollably as she spoke. "I was hiding. I didn't see."

Duke headed for the truck's cabin. The warmth of the heater was calling to him. They climbed in and cupped their hands around the piping hot vents.

"Are we going to get the Sheriff?" Christy's lips and nose had turned bright red.

"She's dead." Duke put the truck into reverse and backed out of the lot.

Regan giggled a high-pitched laugh as he chased a woman through her kitchen.

"Where're ya going, baby?" He hollered after her. "I wanna play house." Children's toys were strewn about and occupied every corner of the living room.

She sprinted for a hallway that led to the bedrooms. Regan gained on her.

"Leave me alone!" The woman screamed as she raced for her bedroom door.

Regan passed one of the bedrooms and noticed the soft glow of a nightlight. Little angels were tucked into bed, sleeping.

"Baby, calm down, you'll wake the kids." He mocked her.

The woman entered her bedroom and attempted to slam the door. Regan shot his thick arm through the entry and blocked it from closing with his shoulder.

The woman was no match. Regan put his weight into her blockade and forced it open. As he entered he caught her fleeing wrist, drew her in close enough to get his other hand on her throat and tossed her onto the queen sized mattress.

Regan's full body pinned her to the bed. His meaty paw squeezed at her neck as he leaned in, "Where's the husband?" He released her vocal cords enough for her to answer.

"Reggie's at work. Please don't hurt my children."

Regan could smell the fear radiating off her and it was delicious. "When's he coming home, sweetheart?"

"I don't know. He could be here any minute." Tears formed and trickled down her cheeks.

"What's he do for a living, baby girl?"

"Lumberjack."

Regan gave her a wicked smile. "I don't think he's coming home, ever."

"What'd you do to him?"

"Can't be sure. Call it intuition, but Reggie is likely a goner."

The news devastated the woman. Regan gripped her jaw and shook her head back and forth.

"No, no. Don't go there, yet. What's the name doll?"

She struggled to speak, but managed one word. "Debbie."

"Debbie, I love that name." Regan made sure his bad breath hit her right in the nose.

Debbie spit white hot anger at her attacker. "Take whatever you want and go. You don't have to hurt anyone."

"You got the only thing I want." Regan licked his lips and squeezed her neck a little tighter.

"Please... you don't have to do... that."

Regan was offended. "Don't flatter yourself, babe. I don't give two shits about the wet spot between your legs, but I will get to know you more *intimately* than, *Reggie*, ever did."

It was clear Debbie was bewildered by his statement.

Regan decided to elaborate. "You want a little story?" He cleared his throat, not waiting for her to respond. "Once upon a time I was involved with someone. We were into everything. You name it we did it to each other. Sicker and more depraved the better. Sessions would go on for hours and hours as we experimented. We climbed to the highest highs of sexual exploration." Regan's vicious exterior softened as he recalled the last of his story. "But one day it all changed. A knife blade slipped. A simple accident, but someone got cut." Pain crept back into his grotesque smile. "The very things that make me a man were taken. So I said, bye-d-bye to my erection." He shifted his weight to Debbie's side but kept his grip firm on her neck. "Without a goddamn hard-on I said bye-d-bye to my partner. The person that took my manhood left me. How do you think that made me feel, Debbie?"

Her eyes darted back and forth as she searched for the correct answer. Debbie guessed. "Sad?"

"Yes, sad." Regan lay his head on the pillow next to Debbie and snuggled in. His voice cracked as he began. "It was the saddest time of my life." He paused as he relived the moment in his mind.

Debbie took a chance at the break in his psyche. "I'm so sorry. I ca-"

Regan cut her off and yanked her neck closer to him. "You have no idea what it was like. You live here in this perfect house with your perfect life. You don't know pain. The sadness turned into anger. The anger turned into hate. The hate turned into rage. If I couldn't have my partner, then no one could. They weren't gonna get the chance to replace me. That's when I discovered true intimacy." Regan released her neck, but shifted his arms around her so he was giving her a hug. "I was never closer with them until I felt their heart beat stop in my arms."

Debbie tried to pull away, but he wrangled her closer. "Where're you goin'? I'm just getting to the good part. I said I was going to know you more intimately than Reggie. Here's how." Every muscle in Debbie's body flexed and Regan squeezed right back. "I'm gonna be the one to feel your final heartbeat." His powerful arms wrenched her around and he tightened his grip as he slipped her into his clutch. Debbie swung fists into Regan's thighs, but it was too late. Her oxygen was cut off. He whispered in her ear, "I'm so sorry. I'm sorry for what I'm doing. Please, relax. Let go. It's your time. I'm sending you to a better place and he'll be there, waiting for you."

Regan focused and concentrated on her beating heart.

There it is! Regan was overjoyed. He could make out the slight thump and began to count the beats and registered the slower and slower pace until there was nothing. For that brief moment in time, Regan was absolutely in love with Debbie.

He let go of her limp body and pushed it to the edge of the bed. He felt exhausted. The rush was better than any orgasm, but twice as fleeting. He was ready to go find another lover. Regan raised from the mattress and headed down the hall. He stopped at the room with the nightlight. Regan calmed himself and relaxed his breath. He could hear the soft breathing of the children. He reached for the doorknob and rested his hand on its polished brass handle.

He whispered. His voice was barely audible. "I'm sorry."

Regan released the knob and headed away from the bedrooms. He entered the kitchen and went straight to the fridge. Regan opened the door to check for a tasty snack. He found a cup of chocolate pudding, snatched it out of the pack, peeled back the lid, found a spoon in a drawer and went to town.

He was reminded of an article he once read about chocolate simulating the same feeling as love. It said eating it released an opium-like endorphin.

I'm riding the wave of endorphins all the way to the beach, baby. Regan giggled to himself.

Behind him was a cough. Regan turned slowly, expecting Debbie to be there holding a gun and ready to snuff him out, but he found a sleepy three-year-old little girl standing at the edge of the kitchen. She had a pink Teenage Mutant Ninja Turtles t-shirt on and messy bed hair.

"Where's Mama?" she asked the stranger.

Regan slurped a spoonful of pudding. "She's, um, sleeping."

"I'm thirsty."

"You want a glass of water?"

"Yes, please." She rubbed the corner of her eye and walked farther into the kitchen.

"Where's the glasses, sweetheart?" Regan finished off the pudding and dropped it into the full sink. She pointed to a cupboard. Regan found a plastic cup with SpongeBob on it, poured her a glass from the faucet and handed it to her. The little one downed the whole cup in just a few swallows.

"Thank you." She raised the empty cup for him to take.

"Alright, off to bed with you." He took the cup, set it on the counter and watched the little one shuffle out of the kitchen.

He rubbed at the scar on the side of his scalp and mumbled. "Coulda, woulda, shoulda." He exited the kitchen and left through the busted front door.

Across the street was a two story split-level home. A sloppily decorated Christmas tree filled the living room window. A fire was going and the shadows of four individuals danced along the far wall. On the porch, next to Regan's foot, was a smooth stone the size of an eggplant. It had a yellow flower painted on it. He picked it up and felt its weight in his hand.

Time to fall in love, again. Regan giggled to himself.

Chapter 22

The cauterized wound on Jacob's stomach seemed to have stanched the bleeding, but he had no idea what that little chunk of lead was doing to his insides. He jogged along a dark street. Most of the houses he had come across were blacked out with no one home celebrating the holiday.

Well, this street was a bust. He thought to himself as he cut across a yard and headed for the next block.

There's one, finally. A flicker of candlelight called to him like a beacon. The car in the driveway was coated with a thin layer of snow. The Toyota Camry ticked as it cooled.

Someone just got home. Jacob inched his way to the living room window. Half a dozen candles dimly lit the space. He couldn't see anyone yet, but there were voices inside. Two ladies was his guess. He headed for the side of the house, hoping to catch a glimpse of the occupants. Before he kicked down the door he had to make sure they were worthy of his Reckoning.

A wrought iron fence separated the front yard from the back and connected to the side of the house. It ran all the way to the edge of the property. Jacob got to the fence and looked straight up at a bedroom window that sat eight-feet from the ground. There was no outdoor furniture or garbage cans for him to stand on, and the voices were clearly coming from this room. The sharp metal tips at the top of the iron fence would make it quite a challenge to stand on and look into the bedroom. It didn't leave Jacob a lot of options.

He eyed the lip of the windowsill. He judged his distance and was confident he could make the jump. He bent his knees slightly and readied himself. As quiet as a cat he leaped into the air, caught the lip with his fingertips and pulled his nose above the edge of the window. Inside was a well decorated bedroom and attached bath. Shadows flickered and the light reflected off a large full-length mirror that hung on the wall next to the closet, a vanity at the foot of the bed and on the ceiling, above the bed, was another full size mirror. From the bathroom stepped a woman and right behind her was her partner. Both were in their birthday suits and fresh out of the shower. They worked handfuls of lotion on to each of their bodies.

These ladies like to watch themselves in action. Jacob commented to himself about all the mirrors. He always enjoyed the female form, but there was no time to be a Peeping-Tom.

He posed the question. *Do I kick in the front door or the back?*

Then an idea occurred to him.

This is a small town. I bet I could knock and they would open the front door.

He dropped from the window.

Gwen flinched, "Did you hear that?"

Heidi's lotion covered hands crisscrossed her trim stomach. "Hear what?"

"There was a noise outside the window." Gwen stepped with caution to the sill and gave a quick look, but it was too dark to make out any details.

"I didn't hear anything." Heidi moved in behind Gwen. She slid her nipples across Gwen's soft back. She turned her slowly from the window, and with both hands she held Gwen's slender neck. Heidi pulled her in for a passionate kiss. That got her mind off the sound she heard outside. They moved with perfect grace for the bed. Their bodies pressed tightly against each other.

"What is it about New Years that makes me so horny?" Heidi whispered to Gwen.

"I have no idea, but I love it." Gwen's hands found the tips of Heidi's breasts. The night was just about to kick into overdrive when a loud knock at the door made both of them jump.

"Who the hell is that?" Heidi turned away from Gwen and lifted a silk robe off the back of the chair to the vanity. "I'll see what they want and be right back." Heidi cinched the knot on her robe and slapped Gwen's ass as she left the room.

Heidi wound down the steps that led to the front door. She cursed to herself, "Someone better be fucking dead to knock this late at night." She stepped up to the door and checked the peephole, but she saw nothing. It was black on black.

Heidi raised her voice. "Who's there?"

The door was beat with a heavy fist. The noise caused Heidi to jump back from the peephole.

Heidi tossed extra piss in with the vinegar, "What do you want?"

A sound grew from the darkness, it was like a wounded animal calling for help.

"Are you injured?"

The noise moaned and sounded like it was agreeing.

Maybe they were in a car accident. Maybe it's a trick.

Heidi had heard enough horror stories to know it was a bad idea to open the door. She needed a weapon, just in case.

"One minute," she spoke to the front door. Heidi and Gwen had been shoveling snow off the front walkway all week and they had left the shovel by the door. She lifted it and kept the wood handle perched on her shoulder as she unbolted the locks.

Holding the shovel like this reminded Heidi of her glory days out on the baseball diamond. She lettered in softball all four years in high school, but it had been awhile since she had spent time at a batting cage. The experience she gained standing at the plate gave her the confidence she needed to open the door.

She mused. *I can swat the hell out of any attacker attempting to enter this house.*

Heidi twisted the knob slowly and the door creaked open. She fully expected the boogeyman to jump out and carry her off into the night to play cat's cradle with her innards. There was nothing but darkness.

Something moved at her feet. Heidi stepped back and readied the shovel. A man lay on his side covering the doormat, dressed all in black. His back was to her and his face was covered by an extended arm. An odor wafted off him.

Iron?

No blood.

"Sir...?" A knot twisted in her stomach.

Heidi's thoughts began to panic. *Something's not right here.*

"Can you hear me?" Heidi used the head of the shovel to poke the man's shoulder blade.

Gwen called from upstairs. "What's going on?"

Heidi barked toward the steps. "Someone's injured. Get the po-"

It happened so fast. The man rolled to his back, grabbed the handle of the shovel and pulled. Heidi was yanked forward. She wasn't ready to release her grip on the weapon. The man spun around and sat up. A knife appeared in his hand.

There was no time to scream.

Heidi's pupils expanded. Her forward momentum couldn't be stopped and she fell onto the tip of the blade. At first it felt like he'd only punched her hard in the ribs. It knocked all of the wind out of her lungs.

With his free hand he hooked the back of her leg and dragged her to the floor. During the fall he twisted his wrist. That's when the pain exploded through her body. The knife blade ground along two ribs and opened a gash in her side.

All she could feel was the agony. She sucked in a mouthful of air, trying to catch her breath, but it felt as if she was drowning. She coughed and her chin was coated in blood.

Heidi landed on her back with a thud. He climbed his way up her writhing body and clamped his palm over her blood soaked, trembling lips, locking in the scream.

My god his face.

He pulled the knife from her side and held it above her heart for a nanosecond. The man plunged the blade to the hilt. The knife pinned her to the floor.

Footsteps stomped from the bedroom and were heading toward the stairs.

Seconds later Gwen was screaming from the landing. Wearing a matching silk robe. The lovebirds shared one last glance before Gwen turned on her heels and headed back for the bedroom.

The man sprung off Heidi's body. He left the knife buried in her chest as he raced. He climbed two steps at a time after Gwen.

The fresh coat of lotion on her feet caused Gwen to slide on the hardwood floor every time she took a step. The man was gaining on her.

He tackled her from behind just as they crossed into the bedroom. They tumbled onto the bed. Gwen rolled with it and landed on top with her back to him. They faced up at the mirror on the ceiling. She locked eyes with him. He smiled.

Gwen smashed the back of her head into his face and caught him in his nose. The cartilage crunched on impact and blood shot from his nostrils. She expected the man to let go of her and run screaming out of the room as he tried to reset the break. Instead he acted like nothing happened and continued to wrestle her. Gwen launched an elbow, but he caught it with his forearm. He used the shift in weight to roll them to her stomach.

He nailed her with a solid fist to the cheek. A halo of stars blurred her vision. The man grabbed a fistful of her hair and dragged her off the bed. She pulled back, but was dealt a fresh set of knuckles to her bottom lip. The man held Gwen by the hair on the back of her scalp. She clawed and scratched at his wild eyes. He caught her with a knee to the stomach and it doubled her over. Once she was bent at the waist he held her by the scruff of the neck and the belt on her robe.

The man lifted and tossed her toward the bedroom window. The top of her skull crashed through the pane of glass. Shards rained down on to her torso and legs leaving slivers of glass in her soft skin. Gwen felt weightless as she flew through the air. Her body twisted midair and fell on the wrought iron fence that stood below the window. The steel rods caught her and rung out with a sick *CHUNG.*

Jacob stared out the broken window. The half-naked, impaled woman stared right at him. He waited a full minute until her eyes rolled back into her skull. Then he could add her to the list.

There was no discomfort from the broken nose, but it was harder to breath.

Five years out of the game and my skills have dwindled.

Gut shot and a broken nose. What's wrong with me?

I've got to sharpen up if I expect to finish what I've started.

Jacob moved from the window and stepped to the vanity mirror. His face was within a few inches of his own reflection. Jacob surveyed the damage and reset his nose. The sound it made was nauseating, but he could breathe normally. His attention flicked up to the mirror on the ceiling and he turned back to face the bed.

That was pretty erotic, except for the look of absolute terror on her face. Jacob thought to himself as some of his blood ventured down south.

He checked out his growing member. *That's pointless.* He smirked.

Jacob found women attractive, but one of the worst parts of his sickness was his inability to reach a complete orgasm. His dick couldn't register touch. Other than expelling urine it was pretty much worthless.

Outside the bedroom window a sudden burst of light erupted down the street. Seconds later Jacob could hear bass notes from a powerful sound system. A house party was going on a block away and he was a deadly moth, attracted to the party flame. Jacob headed out of the bedroom and back to the woman that was holding his knife in her chest.

Jacob crept along the street as he moved closer to the lit up house. The garage door was half open and exhaust from the generator chugged out into the night's sky. A young voice would yell something out and it was immediately followed by laughter. Jacob crept closer to the house and snuck around into the backyard. He watched from a thick shrub as a small group of twenty-somethings stepped onto the back deck to have a smoke. He listened to their ridiculous chatter.

"You bang that girl?"

"Which one?"

"The tattooed one with the cat."

"Yeah, and her roommate."

"Nice."

"You catch that show."

"Which one?"

"The guy that can't see, but fights crime."

"Yeah, it was dumb."

"I didn't get it."

"I thought it rocked."

And on the nonsense went until they had finished their cigarettes and rushed out of the cold. Jacob peered through a kitchen window. He counted twenty-six young men and ladies milling about in the kitchen and dancing in the living room. Open bottles of booze were clustered on a counter. They had recently been baking something because the kitchen was a wreck. Mixing utensils and bowls were covered in chocolate batter.

One of the young men checked the oven. "Second batch of weed-brownies are almost done you guys." The group hooted and hollered.

Well, they all look healthy, under the influence, but beggars can't be choosers.

The clock is ticking.

Jacob had never taken on more than three at a time, so this was going to be interesting.

No way can I kill them all with just my fists, it'd take too long.

Jacob's hand rested on the knife's handle as he thought up a plan.

I need to do a quick set up before I start.

He slipped out of the backyard and back for the open garage door. He checked and made sure the coast was clear before he crawled on his belly and entered. Inside the garage he found exactly what he needed for the job.

The next few minutes of Jacob's life were a total blur.

He smashed in the sliding glass door at the back of the

house.

Screams erupted.

Jacob threw an armful of tools to the floor. A machete, square nosed shovel, hedge clippers, handsaw and hammer all skidded to a stop at the feet of the young men and women of the party.

There! Now they have weapons. Whew!

He zeroed in on the biggest targets in the room. His knife found a home in each of their hearts.

Two-fifty-eight, two-fifty-nine and two-sixty.

Jacob slid a razor sharp hatchet from his belt. He had a weapon in both hands and attacked like a ferocious wild animal. He swung the hatchet into the face of a young lady wearing too much makeup. Behind him he heard a clang of metal. Jacob turned, spotted a broad shouldered man with a wool sweater, racing toward him with the machete held high. As Jacob continued to pivot he launched the hatchet at the man. The camping tool whipped end over end. The blade struck dead center in the man's sternum.

Two-sixty-one.

The momentum of the man carried him straight for Jacob, who side stepped the incoming threat, grabbed the wrist of the hand that held the twenty-inch blade and guided it into the neck of a screaming girl.

Two-sixty-two.

Three more were hiding in the kitchen behind the island. Jacob extracted the hatchet from the sweater man's chest. At the same time he stabbed one person in the heart, and the other took the hatchet to the top of some girl's head. The blade wedged deep in the skull.

Two-sixty-three and two-sixty-four.

Before he could extract his two weapons the third person was on the run. Jacob grabbed him by the collar and tossed him into the still blistering hot range. Next to the oven was a hand held mixer. Jacob snagged it and drove both beaters into the young man's eye sockets. He left the motor running and the beaters drove around in circles, scrambling up his brains.

Two-sixty-five.

Jacob removed his blades from the two other victims. The rest of the group raced out of the kitchen and toward the front door. They pulled at the handle, but it wouldn't open. Before Jacob began his attack he had tied a length of rope around the front door's handle and attached it to the drainpipe. These partygoers were not leaving in one piece. Realizing they were trapped, two guys and one girl, picked up the tools and faced off against the madman.

Jacob ducked the advance of the shovel and landed a back handed swing of his hatchet. The razor's edge danced along the man's stomach and opened him up. A pile of guts fell to the floor.

Two-sixty-six.

Seeing their friends getting disemboweled and hacked to pieces took the fight out of the others. Jacob moved like a whirlwind from body to body. It only took seconds to kill one, add them to the Reckoning and jump to the next in line. It wasn't long before he got through the rest of them. The living room carpet looked like it had an inch of blood absorbing into the fibers.

A noise came from down the hall.

Jacob moved with caution in the direction of the sound.

Number two-eighty-three hid from him in the bathroom, behind the shower curtain.

What a dummy. Jacob thought to himself. He stepped closer to the thin hanging fabric with colorful seashells printed on it and wanted to scold the woman. *The hard surface of the shower amplifies every whimper, sob and desperate breath you utter, making it easy to pinpoint exactly where you're hiding, idiot.*

Jacob considered going through the tired old motions of pulling back the curtain, holding his knife high in the air, letting her scream her guts out and dropping the cold steel into her heart, but it had been done so many times.

He decided on something different. He tapped the knife against the rod, making sure she could see the blood covered finish. She crouched and let out a monster yell.

Jacob knew precisely where she was located. He fired a powerful sidekick through the curtain. The sole of his boot connected with the bridge of her nose and the back of her skull cracked against the tile. He pulled his leg back, she fell forward, and tore the curtain from the rod as her body slumped over the edge of the tub.

Blood drained from the gash at the back of her head and soaked the woman's dirty blonde hair. Fluid pooled on the floor below her. Jacob settled up to the bathroom sink. He turned on the hot water to clean his knife.

That was exciting. I'm getting back in the swing of things. His confidence swelled.

Chapter 23

Dominic charged into the gym, through the gold streamers and onto the basketball court. He scanned the room and found the four hundred partygoers facing the stage.

Thank god! It meant a third of the town was here. It would be easier for him to keep them safe if they were together.

A high-pitched voice howled at him. "Wow, Dominic, what happened to you?" The sheriff station's secretary, Rebecca, walked quickly from the crowd straight toward him. She looked his face up and down and noticed the bandage on his hand.

"There was an explosion. I'm fine. Where's the Mayor?"

Rebecca's jaw stayed slack as she continued to study his blisters. She reached out a comforting hand and touched his shoulder. "An explosion, did you call MaCready yet?"

Dominic shrugged off her touch, stepped closer to her and growled. "MaCready's dead. Where's the Mayor?"

Rebecca's complexion went pale. "What? How?"

A microphone popped and screeched feedback from the stage as the P.A. system was coming back online. Dominic looked to the stage and found the Mayor.

Good, she can help me get organized.

Dominic's heart began to beat double time once he realized who else was on stage. Dominic cut through the crowd.

Mayor Tyler tapped at the mic. A loud thud came through the speakers. "Okay, looks like we've got everything back on. It must be snowing like the dickens. Ben, you may continue." She handed him back the mic.

Ben smiled awkwardly at the sea of people. "Okay, I was about to say." Something in the crowd snagged his attention. "Oh fuck!" Ben blurted out as he saw Dominic was about to take the stage. Laughter fluttered through the crowd at Ben's expense.

Dominic marched up the stairs and out onto the stage. He

made a beeline for Lisa. Shock was the consensus of everyone on stage and in the crowd. As Dominic stepped closer to Lisa her eye's widened and she shook her head. Once he was within arms reach, her focus shifted to the floor.

Dominic's emotions had taken control. Logic told him there were bigger problems at hand, but his heart had different plans. With the night Dominic had lived though, he didn't care anymore. He didn't give a shit that a third of the town was watching this drama unfold. He no longer cared what people would think of him and he really didn't give a fuck that the love of his life was married to his best friend. He had survived an explosion. His life had literally flashed before his eyes. Dominic didn't want to waste anymore of his time on Earth not being with the woman he loved. Now it was time to get his love life on track and to be with his soulmate. He threw his arm around Lisa and pulled her body in tight.

"Thank God you're safe." He whispered in her ear. "I love you so much." He kissed at her cheek and rested his head on her shoulder.

Lisa went catatonic as she processed the insanity Dominic had dropped on her like a cartoon piano.

Safe from what?

He loves me?

This is a nightmare!

Dominic promised her they would never talk about what happened and were supposed to act like nothing was between them. He even put in a transfer request, just so they wouldn't see each other anymore.

Here he is kissing me! In front of Ben!

In front of the whole town!

Has he lost his goddamn mind!

The crowd was two steps ahead of Ben and had gone completely still.

What am I doing? Why am I just standing here? I've got to say something. Lisa wiggled away from Dominic and attempted to smile at her puzzled husband.

Dominic wouldn't let her go and he planted a few more kisses on her brightly colored red cheeks.

Ben's eyebrows scrunched together. "What are you doing, man?" The mic amplified the question to the crowd.

"I'm not going to live this lie anymore." Dominic held Lisa's hand. She wanted to run screaming out of the room, but her body wasn't responding. She had never, in her life, felt this level of petrified embarrassment.

Ben looked to his wife. "What's he talking about?"

"I...um," was all she could utter.

Dominic puffed out his chest. "I'm sorry Ben, but we are in love."

Ben cracked a smile as if it was all a big joke.

Lisa's expression told him it wasn't. Dominic was madly in love with her. She had known this for some time, even before they slept together she could tell how he felt. Lisa was confused. She wasn't sure what her feelings were toward him. She cared for the man, but wasn't ready to say, "In love."

Ben's features sped through a short list of painful emotions.

The sting of betrayal.

The bitter taste of their dying love.

The disgust.

Finally he landed on pure hate.

Ben swung a punch with the hand holding the mic. It landed square on Dominic's jaw. An audio explosion ripped through the P.A.'s speakers as the head of the microphone bounced off Dominic's cheek.

The people watching gasped at the sudden violence.

The strike popped a big blister as it knocked Dominic to his ass. His shotgun fell from his grip and tumbled over the edge of the stage.

Lisa pulled at Ben's arm and yelled, "Don't!"

He ripped his hand out of hers and pounced on Dominic.

He screamed, "You were my friend! How could you do this?!" Ben landed a solid combo of punches. The back of Dominic's skull cracked against the hardwood floor. Lisa yanked on Ben's collar, then clung herself to his torso as she attempted to pull her husband off Dominic.

He's going to kill him and it's all my fault. Lisa cursed herself for being so weak and giving in to temptation. A chorus of screams erupted from the crowd. They were loud enough to break into Ben's tunnel vision. He raised his head to see what caused the screams. Ben heaved air as Lisa hung from his back. His knuckles were coated in Dominic's blood. The deputy was knocked unconscious.

The mass of people became hysterical and swarmed like bees. They scrambled across the gym floor and headed in every direction as they attempted to make an escape.

The man they were fleeing from was the biggest human Lisa had ever seen. He was armed with a sledgehammer. He swung his heavy tool with pinpoint accuracy. He raced after the panicked crowd, popping skulls like they were blood filled balloons.

Five dice rolled across a coffee table and came up five of a kind. "Yahtzee, mother-*chuckers*!" Hayden's shoulders popped and locked as he danced in a seated position on the couch.

"You have to be cheating!" Andrew complained.

"His dice are loaded. No one's that lucky. And Mother-*chuckers*?" Colby questioned as he rubbed the bridge of his nose.

MaKelle popped a Reese's in to her mouth and talked as she chewed. "It sounds less crass if you change it to chuckers and he's going to say-"

The twins spoke in unison. "-It's all in the wrist."

Colby looked to Andrew, then back to MaKelle. "You guys know how creepy it sounds when you speak at the same time?"

In unison. "Yes."

"That's game." Andrew stretched as he leaned back on the couch next to Hayden. "What do you guys want to do now?" Andrew patted Hayden on the leg. As he looked at Colby and MaKelle something terrible outside scared the hell out of him. "Who's that?"

Everyone spun in their seats to check.

The man was standing on their deck, just on the other side of the window, next to the Christmas tree. The fireplace gave him an orange tint.

The man tapped at the window and shouted through the glass. "Hello young people. I'm Regan. Can someone open the door and let me in? It's cold out here." His smile twisted as he scanned their terrified faces.

The teens hopped from the couch and huddled together.

Hayden cleared his throat, "I'm afraid we won't be able to do that."

Regan became a sad puppy dog. "Why?"

They didn't answer.

"Is it because I'm a stranger? If you let me in we can get to know each other. Then we won't be strangers anymore. What are your names, guys?" Regan ate up the fear coming through the window.

Still they said nothing.

"It's okay, I got a key." Regan raised the eggplant sized rock with the painted yellow flower on it and pressed it against the windowpane. The sound of the stone hitting the glass was enough to turn the teens to jelly.

MaKelle regained some composure, stepped forward and crossed her arms, "If you don't get off our property, right now, I'm going to call the Sheriff!"

His eyes bugged out as he laughed. He called her bluff. "You didn't hear little lady, I'm the new Sheriff." He pointed to the star on his chest. Speckles of blood were on the symbol of authority. "I took this off the old lady I killed about forty minutes ago." What they thought might have been a bad joke just became too real for the young folks.

He tapped the rock against the window. "Open the door."

They didn't move.

He erupted, "If I cut myself, I'll make you suffer." He stepped back, cocked the rock above his shoulder and fastball pitched it through the glass. Regan aimed the rock directly at them. The stone punched a hole the size of a catcher's mitt as the rest of the pane completely spider webbed.

MaKelle grabbed Hayden and Colby by the wrists and took off for the hall that led to the bedrooms. The rock collided with Andrew's thigh and sounded like someone snapped a baseball bat in half. The young man crumbled to the floor, howling in pain. His leg bent backwards just above the knee. Andrew wrapped his fingers around the crooked limb. Hayden reached for his fallen friend, he hooked his hands under Andrew's armpits and tugged. Andrew screamed even louder.

Regan kicked at the glass and the last of the window fell. He used the Christmas tree for balance as he stepped over the sill and into the living room. Once both feet were set under him he knocked the tree onto its side. As he stepped into the room his boot crushed the photo of Hayden and MaKelle on Santa's lap.

Hayden had Andrew halfway down the hall, but Regan was on the move and closing fast.

MaKelle and Colby yelled from her bedroom, "Move faster!"

"Come on!"

"He's coming!"

Hayden was at the door and about to pull his friend to safety when Andrew's body came to an abrupt halt. Regan had a grip on Andrew's ankle. He easily yanked the boy from Hayden's arms. Regan bull charged at the door. They slammed it shut in his face, locked it and MaKelle tucked her desk chair under the doorknob.

Regan banged at the wood door with his fist. "Guys, you're hurting my feelings." He stomped his foot at the thin barrier and it shook violently in the frame. "At least you left me a playmate."

The three teens babbled and yelled at each other in a panic. Their hands shook and their voices cracked.

"What do we do?!"

"We got to save him!"

"Call Mom and Dad!"

"The phones are down!"

Andrew howled from the hallway. Regan had the boy and was doing God knows what to him.

Hayden wailed, "Don't touch him you animal!"

The howls turned to gargles.

"Open the door and I'll stop hurting him. I don't like torture, but you guys aren't leaving me many options."

Andrew begged, "No, no...don't...don't touch that, AAAHHHH!"

Hayden turned to his sister and choked through his tears. "We have to do something!"

She looked over her room then she bolted for her closet.

Regan continued to chat with Andrew on the other side of the door. "Hey buddy, I got a cool toy from the Sheriff. You wanna see it?" The sound of the Taser crackling was followed by more screams. "I'm in no mood to bust down the door. You guys open it right now and I'll put your friend out of his misery. I promise." Regan zapped him again. "If you don't open the goddamn door I'm gonna twist his broken leg three-sixty!"

Regan was on his knees and hunkered close to Andrew as the bedroom door swung open behind him. He turned and grunted, "Oh, shit."

MaKelle and Hayden both had bows drawn with a set of practice arrows loaded. They released the strings and SHUNK!

One arrow caught Regan in the lower back the other hit him mid-thigh. He dropped to his butt and cursed in agony. "Fuckin'-Fuck!"

They took the opportunity and raced out of the bedroom. Andrew laid on the floor and was the color of the moon. His face was soaked with sweat and he was on the verge of passing out.

They each grabbed a limb on Andrew and attempted to carry him away. Colby's body suddenly went stiff as the Taser ticked behind him.

Regan held the device to the back of the boy's calf, he huffed. "You ain't goin' anywhere."

Colby dropped to the floor. Regan extracted the arrow in his thigh and plunged it into Andrew's gut. "You little shits are gonna pay!"

MaKelle and Hayden continued to pull at Andrew's arms, but Colby was now in jeopardy.

Regan slid his arm around Colby's throat as he yanked the arrow from his back. "Let's see if he likes getting stuck!" Regan drove the bloody metal tip into Colby's side and pierced his kidney. Colby's eyes bugged out of his skull. He would have begged for mercy, but the arm around his throat impeded his ability to speak. Regan sat up and grabbed at Andrew's broken thigh. The boy thrashed about and wiggled out of the sibling's grip.

"These two are mine." Regan giggled. Even though he had been shot with two practice arrows the man was still as deadly as a rattler and no matter what, they wouldn't be able to save their friends. Regan shifted his weight and was getting to his feet. He released Colby's throat as he straightened his back. The man outweighed both the brother and sister put together. They didn't stand a chance going toe to toe with him.

MaKelle and Hayden clutched each other as they backed away from the convict. Colby's hands were outstretched in front of him and his expression pleaded for them to save him, but he mouthed the word, "Run." to MaKelle. Colby reached for Regan and stuck his finger into the arrow hole in the convict's leg. Regan squealed and dropped to his knee.

MaKelle and Hayden had to run. Colby couldn't distract Regan for long and if that monster got ahold of them it would mean their end. They raced passed the kitchen, MaKelle spotted Colby's car keys on the counter. She snagged them and raced for the door.

Regan clocked the teen in the nose and ripped the unwanted finger out of his leg wound. He picked up the Taser and zapped Colby once more to make sure he wasn't going anywhere. Both boys were laid out cold. Regan grumbled. "God, I hate teenagers!" He limped out to the living room and headed for the busted window. Cold wind whipped through the living room as the logs crackled in the fireplace.

The siblings ran full tilt toward the parked SUV.

Hayden ran his sleeve under his nose. "Where are we going to go?"

MaKelle tapped the key fob and unlocked the doors. "The school, we need to find Mom and Dad!"

They climbed into the ride, started it and pulled away.

Regan's fingers gently touched the wound on his back. "I'll see you two at the school." Regan turned on his heels and headed back to the hallway to finish off the boys.

Chapter 24

Blood dripped from Duke's cheek and into his mustache. He tasted iron on his lip. They were two turns away from Sharon's.

My bandage is leaking.

I've got to get to Doc Evans.

Duke kept checking his rearview mirror. He hoped Stanley would sit up and tap at the back window.

Stanley was a tough guy. He could survive a beating.

Humans have lived through worse. Duke's mind did its best to conjure up a miracle.

"You're bleeding," Christy said as she nodded toward Duke's face.

He ran his wrist across his mustache and wiped the blood from his lip.

Christy looked into the bed of the truck. "I'm so sorry about Stanley. He'd told me many times how you were his best friend."

Duke struggled to keep his composure. "He was a good man." He recalled the first time he met Stanley. It was twenty years ago and Duke had recently been through a horrible divorce. He needed a drastic change of scenery so he sold his half of his company and his six thousand square foot home in Bend, Oregon. He used the money to pay off his ex-wife and the rest he put down on the property in Sweet Home. For the first year he lived in a camper as he started to build the cabin. Stanley owned and ran the only hardware store in Sweet Home. Duke would come to town, looking for supplies and Stanley helped him pick out what he needed. Duke was there three times a week picking up odds and ends as he built the cabin all by himself. Duke quickly became Stanley's best customer. Halfway through the project Duke needed help on some of the plumbing and he asked Stanley if he would be willing to come out and help him in exchange for a twelve pack of beer and a nice thick grilled steak. Stanley agreed and the two men spent the whole day cracking jokes and laughing their asses off. Even though the job was hard work they still had a blast. Duke regretted never telling Stanley what his friendship meant to him and how much it helped him mend his broken heart, but he was pretty sure the man knew.

"What's the plan?" Christy opened the shotgun and made sure it was fully loaded. Two shells were at the ready.

"Get Sharon, get stitched up. After that..."

Is that the only plan? Duke thought to himself. *Find Sharon and get patched up by Doc Evans'?*

Duke squeezed the grip of his pistol. *No.*

"...I help Dominic find the guy that killed Stanley and did this," he pointed at his bandage, "eye for an eye." Duke made the last turn and it was no surprise to find that Sharon's house was dark. He pulled up to an intricate wrought iron fence. A keypad built into stone pillar sat next to the driveway.

Christy's jaw dropped. "That's Sharon's house?"

Duke sighed, "You've seen Sharon's advertisement?"

"Yeah."

"It's correct, she's been the top real estate sales person in the county for the last five years. Just ask her. She loves to talk about it." Duke rolled down his window and reached for the keypad.

Christy smirked. "The powers out."

"It's on a battery backup so the owner can't get trapped inside." Duke typed in the code and the door swung open. Duke slowly drove down the long driveway as he surveyed the house for signs of a break in. As the gate closed behind them he swore a dark blur squeezed through the closing fence. Duke pressed the brakes and the taillights illuminated the driveway behind them. No one was there.

I'm seeing things. My visions jacked and I'm sick from the bleach. Duke's thoughts were logical, but it didn't stop the spike of fear he felt at his core.

He continued a little farther down the driveway and parked the truck. He looked across the large, well landscaped winter wonderland that was Sharon's front yard and searched for more dark blurs.

Still nothing.

"Maybe you should stay here?" he said as he turned to Christy.

She narrowed her eyes. "Does that sound smart?"

Duke thought for two seconds and said, "No." They popped open the doors and Christy scurried around to his side. "You ever fired that thing?" Duke motioned at her gun.

She hesitated. He could tell she wanted to lie, but she landed on. "No."

"Pull it tight to your shoulder. Don't shoot until the asshole is within ten-feet. That thing is meant for close quarters action. It's going to kick like Van Damme, so be ready." Duke checked his gun and found only one round left.

Shit.

"Anything else?" Christy tucked the gun to her shoulder as she desperately tried to memorize everything he just said. Her nose and fingers were already red from the cold.

"Don't shoot me. Or Sharon." Duke trudged through the snow on his way toward Sharon's front door. He raced up three steps to the landing and pounded on the double-doors.

"Sharon! Open up. It's Duke." He peered through the small window next to the door. The foyer was solid black. Duke hammered the door again. A flicker of light appeared from a hall. The flashlight emerged and bounced around the room. It was carried by a shadowy figure and moving for the door, but Duke wasn't sure if it was Sharon. It could be anyone behind that light.

Duke barked, "Sharon?"

The light grew closer and closer. Duke cocked back the hammer on his gun. The locks turned and the door inched open.

"Well, well, well, Duke, you made it just in time." The light panned over the two shivering people at the entryway. Sharon stepped onto the porch holding a glass of wine. Some chardonnay slipped over the rim as the focus of her light jumped from Christy's gun, to Duke's gun, to his face. "Don't tell me that deer came back alive and took your other eye?" She snickered to herself.

Duke was relieved to see she wasn't diced into a hundred pieces, but it stopped there. At least that was what he kept telling himself.

Duke lowered his pistol. "Is that the end of the bottle?"

Sharon huffed, "It's New Years. This is bottle number two." She lifted her glass at Christy and said, "Hi."

Christy's teeth chattered as she said, "Hey," back.

Duke pushed Sharon into her home. "It's freezing. Let us in."

Sharon didn't put up a fight and stepped aside. Duke let Christy in, closed the door and locked it.

"All right what happened to your face? Tell me the sob story." Sharon sipped a little more from her glass.

Duke faced her and she lit him up with the light. "Four convicts smashed their way into my house, they cut out my eye, tried to poison me with bleach and lighter fluid, Sheriff MaCready is dead, Stanley's dead, I'm sure they've killed others. Plus they cut the power and phones."

Sharon studied them for a minute. "Bullshit."

"It's true. I saw Stanley get murdered." Christy stepped closer to Duke.

Sharon sighed and shook her head. "I know we ended on rough terms and our exchange at Safeway wasn't pleasant, but I'd never expect you to concoct such an outlandish story." She waved the light at Christy. "And you drag her into your lie. Is that fake blood on your fa-"

Duke lifted his bandage and showed Sharon his missing eye. A belly full of chardonnay emptied out of Sharon's mouth as she vomited across the floor.

She coughed and spit. "Jesus, Duke why are you here? Why aren't you at a doctor?"

Duke gingerly lowered the bandage, he moved toward Sharon, took her by the arm and headed deeper into the house. Christy followed close behind them.

It took Duke a bit to assemble his reasoning that would make sense to Sharon, but not give away his feelings. "I needed to make sure… you were… okay." Duke pulled her into the kitchen. Sharon had a dozen candles going to illuminate the great room that connected to the kitchen. Duke headed for a set of cabinets, opened them and found the Tylenol he was looking for. He set his gun down on the counter so he could use both hands to pop open the cap. Duke dry swallowed three tablets. "Get the gun I got you for our anniversary and a box of shells." Christy was still shivering uncontrollably. "Also grab a set of jackets for you and her."

"Why?" Sharon set her half full glass of wine on the counter.

"You're coming with me to Doc Evans." Duke picked up the glass and finished it off.

Sharon crossed her arms. "This is the same bullshit you pulled when we were together. I don't need a *man* to tell me what to do or protect me."

A storm raged within the *man*. Duke and Sharon were both alphas. It was an explosive combo in the bedroom, but you can't have two captains in charge at all times. Duke was seconds from entering into the same old fight they'd had time and time again, but this go round they had an audience with Christy.

Duke spoke clearly and softly. "I'm not trying to tell you what to do. I'm trying to keep you alive. It's freezing out. You'll need a jacket and it would be nice if you got one for Christy here." Duke lifted his pistol. "I have only one bullet in this gun and would greatly appreciate you getting yours and the extra ammo so I can keep you alive when the killers come to cut out your eyes and slit your goddamn throat."

"The yoga helped you lose the spare tire and it's calmed your soul." Sharon turned to Christy, who was standing at the edge of the kitchen. Behind her was a pitch-black hallway. "The old Duke would have yelled for half an hour then we would have fucked like wild beasts for the rest of the night." Back to Duke. "I'm not sure which one of you I like better. Why would I leave my house and come with you? I'm safe here." Sharon uncrossed her arms.

"These guys smashed my window and waltzed right in. You have thirty or so ground floor openings. Someone could bust in on the other side of the house and you'd have no idea until they were cutting into your guts." Duke found the open wine and swigged straight from the bottle.

As silent as a whisper a man appeared behind Christy. He pressed a knife to her neck, snatched the shotgun away and tossed it into the living room.

Sharon and Christy yelped.

Duke dropped his bottle mid sip. It clattered across the alabaster marble and chugged premium fermented grapes to the floor. Duke picked up his magnum and aimed it at the man's ugly, scarred face.

"Let her go!" Duke grunted.

The man shook his head as he hid behind Christy. A look of recognition played on his gnarled face.

"Please, don't kill me!" Christy pleaded.

The man said, "Shhhhh!" He held his hand like a child pretending it was a gun, then he held up his index finger and pointed it at the pistol. He knew Duke had only one shot remaining.

Duke's hand shook. His vision was blurred. The chances of him hitting his target and missing Christy were slim. Duke's thoughts worked quickly as he inched closer, attempting to get a better angle.

"If I drop my gun will you let her go?"

The man shrugged. He moved the knife half an inch, Christy winced. A trickle of blood rolled down her neck. Sharon stayed perfectly still as if she could disappear and be camouflaged by her surroundings.

Duke thumbed back the hammer. "You leave them alone and you can have me."

The man shook his head.

"It's all or nothing?" Duke asked.

The man nodded.

Duke stepped a little closer. His hand shook violently. Duke was right handed and with his missing right eye it was near impossible to aim so he switched the gun to his non-dominant hand as he crossed in front of Sharon. The expression on Christy's face was haunting. She was a smart girl and had crunched the numbers.

She knew her time was up. Tears flowed on her pale cheeks.

The man pivoted to keep his hostage between him and the gun. Duke stepped closer to the hallway that led out of the kitchen, keeping Sharon right behind him.

Duke went through every possible move he could conceive.

This guy won't kill Christy, not yet. He needs the human body armor.

If I pull the trigger there are three possible outcomes.

One, I miss and we all die.

Two, I hit Christy and we all die.

Three, I nail him on the forehead and we're all safe.

Only a tiny sliver of the man's face poked out from behind Christy's head.

Number three was impossible.

The only way to guarantee Sharon's safety was to run. Right now.

But that meant sacrificing Christy. He counted and recounted every avenue of escape. There was no option that would allow everyone to survive. The man with the knife seemed to know the score, he had gambled that the man with the shaky gun was going to pull the trigger and attempt some kind of a halfcocked revenge.

Duke backed out of the kitchen and pushed Sharon into the hall.

Christy shook her head and begged, "Don't leave."

Duke handed Sharon the keys to the truck. "Run," was all he told her. She did not argue this time. Sharon raced for the front door.

Duke spit as he spoke, "The next time I see your ugly fucking face, I will kill you!" He couldn't believe what he was about to do. It went against everything Duke stood for, but there was no other choice.

The man with the knife seemed to sense what was about to happen. He violently yanked a fistful of Christy's hair, exposing more of her soft neck. Blood seeped faster and soaked the collar of her skintight shirt. He was doing everything he could to goad Duke into firing the gun.

Sharon started up the truck.

She's safe.

Well, safer than before. Duke began a yoga breathing technic Lisa had taught him. It soothed his mind and allowed him to focus. The man peeked farther around Christy's head to see if his actions were working. Duke let out a lung full of air. He had made his final decision.

Fuck it!

Duke squeezed the trigger.

Chapter 25

At the high school gym, the man leaped across the blood slick floor and swung his sledgehammer. Chunks of scalp clung to the hammer's head. The tool made contact with its target. The skull of the screaming man didn't stand a chance. The plates of bone surrounding the brain caved, shooting gray matter out his ear, and crunching teeth from his mouth. The body dropped with a nasty thud.

Thirty bodies lay scattered across the maple floor as the maniac worked his way through the crowd. The terrified people bunched together like a bulk pack of sausages at *Costco*. The doors that led into the school were locked and the monster stood between the cowering town's people and the main exit. A slow, but steady stream of people escaped through the fire door. The alarm blared, adding to the chaos. The few people that tried to get past the man were cut down immediately.

Up on the stage the band members abandoned their instruments and jumped down to join the fleeing people.

Mayor Tyler yelled instructions to the audience, but no one could hear her.

Lisa climbed off Ben's back, grabbed his bloody fist and tugged at his arm. "We have to get out of here!" Ben's eyes were filled with heavy tears. He glanced to the passed out Dominic, then to his wife.

"Help me get him up." Ben got off Dominic and the two of them lifted him up onto Ben's shoulder.

Lisa surveyed the gym. The people were crowded into one corner of the building. The monster chopped them down, sometimes two humans per swing. The fire escape was clogged with panicked partygoers. The bar sat empty on the other side of the room.

"Ben, this way!" Lisa headed for the stairs that led to the

gym floor. Ben chugged slowly after her. He shifted Dominic's weight and moved his limp body into a fireman's carry. Mayor Tyler followed them. She fought her high heels and awkwardly stomped down the steps.

Lisa stayed close to the wall. The shadows were darker at the edge of the gym. With one eye on the killer, she darted for the bar.

One of the giant's swings tapped Rebecca, the sheriff's secretary, right in the kneecap. She collapsed to the floor. The people around her moved like a herd of hunted cattle. She was trampled by a stampede of dress shoes. The pointy heels stomped into her legs, stomach and arms. They busted her glasses and punctured her cheek.

The monster put her out of her misery when he dropped the hammer from high above his head and crushed her noggin. It looked as if he was at a county fair, trying to win a strongman game, but instead of shooting a puck up to the bell to win a prize, he shot her brain out of the top of her head and left a divot in the high gloss hardwood floor.

Lisa got to the temporary structure that made up the bar. She ducked between it and the wall. Ben waddled in behind her. Sweat dripped from his brow. Mayor Tyler's mouth was agape like a dead fish on the beach. She clutched at her heart to keep it from blasting out of her chest.

Lisa crept to the far corner of the bar and checked for the monster's location. Five men from the crowd summoned their courage and stormed at the giant. Two of them went for the handle of the sledgehammer. It kept him from knocking the fighters off. The three others kicked and punched at his ribs and stomach.

Lisa psyched herself up.

Here's our chance. While he's distracted we have to make a break for it.

It was a fifty-yard dash across a slick obstacle course of dead bodies. Lisa looked back at Ben. "Run now!"

Ben nodded, "Don't wait for me. Just get to safety." Mayor Tyler had her hand wrapped around Ben's belt. The fear of being left behind and smashed by the brute was apparently too much for her.

Lisa couldn't believe it. Ben had been completely blindsided by the Dominic bombshell, but his main concern was still for her safety.

How could I have done it? How did I let myself break his heart? She snapped out of her downward spiral. She could beat herself up later if she made it out of this horror show. Right now she had to concentrate on getting to that door. This was a race she had to win, for her children and the baby growing within her.

She charged out from behind the bar and traversed the row of corpses. Everywhere she looked was someone she knew.

John, the mailman and his wife were just a pile of goo.

So many teachers from the town's schools were mangled pretzels.

Council members and pillars of the community were drenched in their own fluids.

Tina, who ran the diner on Main Street, had her jaw crushed up over her nose. It looked like she was trying to eat her own face. Most of the bodies were completely unrecognizable. The gore that lay before Lisa was unlike anything she ever witnessed. Her stomach twisted into knots as she played hopscotch toward the exit.

The giant let go of his sledgehammer, grabbed a handsaw from his tool belt and spun three-sixty. The blade's sharp little teeth hacked hunks of meat from his attackers. They crumbled to the ground, pressing their hands against the ragged wounds. The creature noticed four people racing toward the door behind him. He liberated a screwdriver from his belt and zipped it after them.

Mayor Tyler stumbled. Her hold on Ben's belt yanked him along as well. Ben dropped to one knee and turned to see what happened. He found a lengthy tool sticking from the center of her throat. She gargled up mouthfuls of blood. Her eyelids blinked like hummingbird's wings. Ben grabbed her wrist and pulled it from his belt. Ben groaned as he rose to both feet. He took two steps when something hit him in the back. He let out a vicious scream.

The sound of her husband stopped Lisa in her tracks. She pivoted back to Ben. The look of agony on his face was worse than when he discovered the truth of her infidelity. She didn't know what was causing the pain until she spotted the yellow handle of the screwdriver sticking out of him.

Ben hissed, "Keep going!"

Lisa wanted to help him, but there was no way she could carry Dominic's body or Ben. She didn't have to rescue him, because Ben's feet were moving in her direction. Her husband was one of the strongest men Lisa had ever known. His physical and mental endurance was always something that astonished her. Whether it was in the gym cranking out an insanely hard workout or on the twenty-fifth mile of a marathon, he just seemed to be able to keep going. From the corner of her eye she watched him do just that. He had a tool protruding from his skin and was carrying the limp body of the man that had sex with his wife, but he kept going.

The giant watched for a second as the three people headed for the front door. They were out of his throwing range and he had enough people in front of him to take care of. He picked up his sledgehammer and got to it.

Lisa held the main door open as Ben jogged past her. The ice cold wind cut through her dress and the open toed shoes scooped up snow with every step.

Her voice cracked. "The keys?!"

Ben wasn't able to talk through his excruciating pain, but they both knew the keys to the car were inside his jacket, back at the coat check. Most of the people that escaped through the fire door were having the same problem. They scattered into the lot heading for their cars, but were not able to drive away. So they just kept running out into the dark night.

Lisa focused and tried to think of a plan, but the cold.

Oh god, the fricking cold.

The freezing temperature was so oppressive it was all she could think about. Every snowflake that hit her skin felt as if it was burning her.

Her jaw shivered when she spoke. "We have to keep

moving."

"Get...it...out." Ben turned his back to her. His shirt around the screwdriver handle was soaked with blood.

Lisa reached for the wound to comfort her husband. "If I pull it you might bleed out!"

Ben gasped. "It's...touching...bone...I can't take it anymore!"

Lisa knew it was a bad idea, but she wanted to ease his suffering. She wrapped her fingers around the handle. Just the slightest touch made Ben's knees go weak, but before he fell she yanked the screwdriver out of his back. He mashed his teeth together and heaved in lungful's of winter air.

"Can you move?" It was more of a command than a question.

He nodded at her. Lisa dropped the screwdriver and led the way as they headed into the lot. A few people had gotten their cars started and were hitting the road. They abandoned their fallen neighbors and left them to freeze.

She had to get them to Doc Evans' house. It was two miles away and on a good day she could run there in about fifteen minutes. This was not a good day. With Ben moving as fast as he could they would make it in about an hour.

He could die tonight. The fear of losing her husband pushed her to move faster. Divorce was one thing, but they would still see each other because of the kids.

The kids!

What if that animal hurt our children? Just the thought of something horrible happening to her babies was enough to make her want to jump off a bridge. Lisa wanted to sprint all the way home to check on Hayden and MaKelle, but Ben and Dominic needed a doctor. Her toes were numb by the time she got to the end of the parking lot and both of her thighs were threatening to cramp up. She glanced back at Ben and it was clear he needed to stop and rest.

How the hell are we going to get to Doc Evans'?
How will I make it home to see my children?

It seemed hopeless, but just as soon as she began to curse

her luck an SUV pulled in front of her on Main Street.

The window rolled down, MaKelle popped her head out and yelled. "Mom!" Hayden was in the passenger's seat. He was clearly upset about something, but at least they were alive.

The who, what, where and why could wait. Lisa opened the back door and helped Ben get Dominic into the backseat.

Inside the gym Zarren was having the time of his life, but a pain was growing in his chest. He ignored the troubling signs and focused on his joy.

Find them. Crush them!

Smash! His sledgehammer clobbered another victim. The blood shot out of their skulls and bathed Zarren in their warm sticky fluids. The gym had become his killing floor. He had lost count of exactly how many people he had obliterated in this gym.

Find them. Crush them!

Zarren sent an old woman across the room. She hit the wall with a splat. It left a basketball sized bloodstain on the sheetrock then her body slid to the floor. Fifteen or so people remained. It was hard for Zarren to tell with all the blood in his eyes. He crushed another, then another. Until there was nothing left. Zarren chased his last victim out of the fire escape and sent the body flying into a familiar van. The body left a dent and a smear of blood under the words Carl's Plumbing.

Regan rolled down the van's window. "Zarren, I need your help. Get in."

Zarren didn't like Regan, but he was exhausted from the all the exertion and needed his heart to settle down. Having a seat and taking a ride sounded nice right about now. Zarren went around to the side door and climbed in.

The teens hammered Lisa with questions.

"What happened?"

"Is Dad okay?"

"What's going on?"

"What's wrong with Mr. Spence?"

Lisa barked. "Head to Doctor Evans!" She slammed the door shut. The SUV's heater made her limbs tingle. The teens were turned around in their seats. An ocean of confusion washed over them. Lisa reached out and touched her children's shoulders to calm them. "Just drive baby, I'll tell you what happened later."

MaKelle turned around in her seat. She stomped on the gas, spun the wheel, did a one-eighty in the middle of the street and headed toward the Doctor's mansion.

Lisa turned her husband's back to her and she found the hole in his shirt. She used her fingers to tear the hole bigger. Blood oozed out of a wound the size of a dime.

Ben asked, "How bad is it?"

"You had a screwdriver in you, it's bad. Hayden, see if there are some paper towels or napkins in the glovebox."

"A screwdriver?" Hayden questioned as he popped it open, found a stack of napkins and handed them to his mother. She took them and applied pressure to the wound. They'd be at Evans' in two minutes. Ben would be okay, she was sure of it. Lisa looked over the strange vehicle then to her teary eyed son.

"Whose car is this? What happened to you?" Lisa couldn't help but sound like a Mom about to hand out some punishment to her naughty children.

Hayden tried to start, but busted into sobs.

MaKelle explained for him. "We had some friends over. A man showed up and broke into the house."

Lisa felt her heart stop.

MaKelle continued. "He attacked us. Andrew and his friend Colby... They didn't make it." Hayden cried uncontrollably into his hands. "This is Colby's car. He distracted the man and allowed us to get out of the house." MaKelle began to tear up too. "He saved us."

Lisa was disappointed that they had people over without asking, but in light of everything it was a minor and forgivable offence. They were alive and just saved her and Ben from the freezing cold. Now was the time for Lisa to be thankful and comfort her loved ones.

"Everything is going to be okay. Just get us to Doctor Evans' so we can patch your Dad up." Lisa patted Ben on the shoulder. He shrugged it off, turned his head to face her and gave her a look of disgust.

Not everything is okay, but we're all alive. Lisa was bound to stay positive.

Behind them a set of headlights kicked on its high beams and flooded the inside of the SUV with light. The car crashed into the back bumper of the SUV.

"Who the hell was that?" MaKelle spun the steering wheel to course correct after the impact. The vehicle pulled alongside them. She peeped a look out her side window. Her breath was stolen away. It was a beat up van and that maniac, Regan, was in the driver's seat, but the sight that broke her heart was in the van's passenger's seat. It was a crying teenage boy with a strip of duct tape covering his mouth. MaKelle whispered, "Colby."

Chapter 26

The bullet left Duke's magnum. The sound of it hit his unprotected ears with a thundering crack. His nostrils were instantly filled with the smell of gunpowder. The flash of muzzle fire was almost blinding in the dark room.

In that nano heartbeat Duke wished he hadn't pulled the trigger. It felt like a horrible mistake shooting at someone with his non-dominant hand, plus he was minus an eye, but there was no going back now.

The bullet zipped over Christy's shoulder, tore off the top of her ear, taking a loop earring with it and tagged the edge of the man's forehead. The man with the scarred face flung off Christy, landed on his back and his knife skidded across the floor into the darkness.

Christy grabbed at her two wounds as she stumbled forward. She collapsed into Duke's outstretched arms and sobbed like a baby.

"I got you girl. He's gone." Duke comforted her, but kept his eye on the body. It laid still.

Sharon rushed into her house and doused the two with her flashlight. "I heard a shot!" She noticed the body on the floor. "Jesus, Duke. You did it!"

Duke passed Christy to Sharon. "Hang onto her." He inched toward the body. Blood had begun to pool under the man's skull. A flap of skin was peeled back and bloody pink bone was exposed. Duke kicked at the man's leg. Then he stomped on the man's shin. Nothing.

Sharon whispered. "Is he dead?"

"I think so. A lot of skull is poking out." He turned to the ladies. "I'll grab the shotgun. Sharon, get the coats and your gun."

Sharon nodded and raced out of the room. Duke jogged into the living room, picked up the shotgun and hustled back to Christy.

"We are heading for the doc's place and he'll get you ship shape." Duke put his arm around Christy and rubbed at her shoulders.

Snot poured out of her nose as she looked up at Duke and said, "You saved me."

Duke pulled Christy's hand away from her ear to survey the damage he did. "Sorry about your ear."

"I'm still breathing."

Sharon appeared with coats draped on her forearm, flashlights in one hand, a plastic case and a box of ammo in the other.

She handed Duke the box of ammo and he crammed it into his front pocket. Duke also grabbed the flashlight and tucked it under his armpit as he took the gun case. "Let's get the hell out of here."

Sharon handed the jacket to Christy and the two ladies slid them on. Sharon zeroed in on the body. "If I ever sell this place I'll have to knock a hundred grand off because of that asshole."

Duke set the box down on a table and popped it open. A pearl handled, nickel plated .38 snub nose special with gold trigger and hammer lay in the foam lined case. Duke picked up the gun and loaded it. "I should have got you a bigger gun."

"We should have done a lot of things different." Sharon zipped up her jacket.

Duke let out a huff, agreeing with her. He slid the last round into the chamber and with a flick of his wrist he popped the cylinder into place. As he followed the ladies out of the house the urge to vomit hit him like a sucker punch to the abdomen. It wasn't from the bleach, although it wasn't helping, it was from the realization he just killed a man. He had been somewhat responsible for the death of that old guy, Arthur. He did set him on fire, but Dominic pulled the trigger and put the man to rest. This time the blood was all on Duke's hands.

Was it justified? He thought to himself.

Maybe.

That person, or that thing, killed Stanley and Morgan, took my eye and was about to murder Christy. He definitely had it coming.

Duke was a hunter. He had taken the lives of so many animals over the years, but that wasn't for sport. It put food on the table and helped keep the animal population in check. This was homicide. He had killed a man. It was not in cold blood, but the man was dead.

Can I live with my actions?

Duke reached the front entrance. His hand rested on the edge of the solid oak door. He took one more look at the body.

Hell yeah, I can live with it.

Duke slammed the door shut behind himself.

Regan crashed the van into the side of the SUV. MaKelle panicked and stomped on the brakes.

Lisa yelled from the backseat, "No, keep going!"

The teen stepped on the gas and the V8 lurched forward. She glanced another look and locked eyes with Colby.

Hayden pointed at the fiend driving the blue rig. "Mom, that's the guy that attacked us!"

The van smashed into the SUV again, causing MaKelle to miss the turn for Doctor Evans' house.

Regan screamed out the passenger's window. "This is my friend, Zarren!" The side door on the van opened and the hairy man emerged. He wielded a blood soaked sledgehammer with one hand as he clung to the van's roof. Zarren swung the hammer into the driver's side window. Clear square chunks of glass peppered MaKelle's face. She yanked on the wheel and turned into the Safeway parking lot. The van turned with her and continued to chase them down. The lot sat completely empty and was coated with untouched white powder.

"What should I do?" MaKelle yelled for guidance as she headed to the next exit.

Lisa watched as the van gained on them. "We've got to lose them!"

"They have Colby!" MaKelle's eyes began to well up.

"Baby, I don't know. Just keep driving."

The van collided with the back of the SUV and sent it into a tailspin. MaKelle spotted Colby three times as the SUV spun 1080.

"Turn into the slide and hit the gas." Ben barked at his daughter.

She did just that and skidded out of the lot and back onto Main Street. She regained control and within seconds the van was alongside them. Zarren hammered at the windows and sent glass all over the inside of the SUV, covering the three adults in the backseat. Lisa yanked the unconscious Dominic out of the way as the hammer hit the headrest, landing an inch away from the Deputy's nose.

Regan called to Zarren, "Use the kid!"

The monster disappeared into the van and when he reemerged he had Colby in his mitts.

Regan giggled as he drew up next to the SUV. "You pull that sweet ride over or we toss the boy!"

"Mom? Dad?" MaKelle whimpered.

Snowflakes blasted Colby as he hung out the side of the van, the teen shook his head at the girl.

"MaKelle, keep driving, if you stop they will kill us!" Lisa pawed at her daughters shoulder.

"Okay, if that's how you wanna play!" Regan sped passed them. "Do it!"

Zarren tossed Colby out the side of the van. His thin frame flailed through the air for only a second before he landed on the hood of his SUV and slammed face first into the windshield.

MaKelle flinched and hollered "NO!" at the top of her lungs. In her hysteria she yanked the wheel to the left. The safety glass spider webbed, Colby's forehead split open and blood exploded out onto the glass. MaKelle could no longer see where she was driving. The front of the SUV tagged the back of the van. The force of the hit spun the van out of control.

Regan cursed, "Shit!" as he headed straight for a telephone pole. The convicts came to an abrupt and loud stop as the driver's side of the van wrapped around the solid beam of wood.

Colby's limp body slid off the hood and was sucked under the back tires. The rear wheels jumped into the air as if they did a speed bump at fifty miles an hour.

MaKelle went into a frenzy. The SUV slid to a stop, she popped open the door and ran after the young boy's mangled body. Lisa climbed out the back door and cried. "MaKelle!"

The two women raced down the center of Main Street. Lisa caught up to her daughter, but it was too late, the teen had already seen Colby's twisted corpse. His torso was caved in where the tire had crushed him and bones stuck out from every limb. MaKelle cried on her mother's shoulder.

"I'm sorry baby. I'm sorry, but we have to leave him. We need to get your Dad to the doctor." Lisa dragged MaKelle to the car and helped her into the backseat.

Ben wrapped his arm around MaKelle's shaking body. "It's okay. We're going to be okay."

Lisa shut the driver's door and put the SUV back into gear. Hayden took her hand. The boy's shirt was soaked with tears. "Mom, I don't think we are going to be okay."

"I know," said Lisa as she stepped on the gas and left the wrecked van in the dust.

Jacob's eyes opened. He found himself staring up at the ceiling of a mansion he had just broke into. His ears were ringing like someone had pulled a fire alarm in his brain.

What happened?

He sat up and something dripped into his eye. He rubbed at his face and his hand came back slick with his own blood. He reached farther up onto his forehead and felt the flap of skin lift away from his skull.

That son-of-a-bitch shot me.

How the hell did he do that?

He had a missing eye and was shaking like he had Parkinson's.

Jacob tucked his knee under himself and struggled to get to his feet. There was no pain. Only the ringing in his ears, but the shot had thrown off his equilibrium. He looked around the room.

They must have fled to the doctor that they were talking about.

Jacob spotted a shiny reflection off something in the dark corner of the room.

There's my knife. He stepped toward it and his knees buckled. Jacob crashed to the floor.

This isn't good. Damn it. Nothing had gone according to plan since he entered this house.

Shot twice in one night. I really have lost my touch.

Jacob crawled along the floor until he got to his knife. He slid the blade into its sheath and tried again to get to his feet. He got himself upright and noticed the pool of blood where his head had been.

That's why I'm so woozy. I have got to get bandaged up so I can hunt down the asshole that shot me.

Jacob limped into the kitchen and headed for what looked like the master bedroom and bath. A handful of candles lit up the bathroom. Jacob stepped close to the mirror and inspected the flap of skin on his head. The skull had a groove where the bullet had struck him and a hairline fracture that led up under the attached skin.

Well that was lucky. I guess. It could have been a lot worse.

It wasn't a good idea to cauterize this wound, he might burn out an eye, but he would need to close it up somehow.

Jacob carried a candle into Sharon's home office and found what he was looking for.

He walked back to the bathroom and looked into the mirror. He held up a black stapler, pressed it to the flap of skin and punched at it with his fist.

CHUNK!

Jacob drove staple after staple into his skull until the wound was sealed.

That should hold. Jacob thought to himself.

Now I really look like Frankenstein's monster.

Jacob headed back to the kitchen and poured a drink of

water. He hoped replenishing his fluids would help with his dizzy brain. He guzzled at the water and hatched a plan.

I owe that bastard a stab to the heart for shooting me.

I've got to find the doctor he was talking about. What was the name? Edwards? No, Evans.

Jacob emptied his glass and looked around the kitchen. A cordless phone hung from a wall. Below it was a desk. He moved closer to it, slid open a drawer and found a phonebook for Sweet Home. Jacob flipped it open, there he was, Doctor Evans and his home address. The front pages of the phone book had a map of the town. He zeroed in on the address. It was a few miles away from where he was standing.

Damn. I'm bleeding too much to walk.

I need a ride.

Jacob's blurry vision found a brightly colored purse sitting on the kitchen table. He limped toward it and unzipped the bag. Right on top was exactly what he was looking for. He lifted up the set of keys and on one of the rings was a little black stick with a *Cadillac* symbol on it.

Jacob sat behind the wheel of a top of the line luxury *Escalade* parked in Sharon's garage. The engine purred under the hood. His foot found the gas pedal. The Escalade launched forward and obliterated the garage door. Jacob spun the wheel around and headed for the wrought iron gate.

Jacob was six bodies away from reaching his goal and nothing was going to stop him.

He grinned to himself as his daydream began.

I'm going to cut out that bastards other eye after I force feed him those two lady's hearts.

Then I'll add him to the Reckoning.

Chapter 27

Regan groaned as he popped open the van's door. A layer of blood coated his bald head and ugly face. "That sucked!" He coughed out a mouthful of gore onto the snow. "Zarren? Zarren, are you dead?"

A grumble came from the back of the van. "No."

Regan shuffled his way around the front of the vehicle and headed for Zarren. "Are you hurt or injured?" he asked as he ran his sleeve across his features to clean the blood from his eyes.

"Injured." Zarren tumbled out of the side door of the van and landed on his back. He groped at his right shoulder.

Regan's knees gave out and he fell next to the big man. "Me too." Regan dug his hand into the snow, raised a ball of ice to his forehead and placed it on the gaping wound. "I'm sure I have a concussion."

Zarren spoke so softly, Regan felt as if he was a child getting bad news from a parent. The giant cleared his throat and said, "My shoulder is out of socket and I believe I am about to suffer a heart attack."

Regan removed the ball of ice on his scalp and checked to see how pink it was, the ball of snow was bright red. "One upper." Regan jested with Zarren. "I can set your shoulder, but what do we do about your thumper?"

"I need nitroglycerin pills."

Regan sat up and tossed the bloody ball of snow. "There's gotta be a doc somewhere in this one horse town. We can beat a prescription out of him." Regan painfully got to his knees and took Zarren's injured arm by the wrist. "Okay, big guy, this is gonna sting a bit."

"Shut up and do it." Zarren gritted his teeth in anticipation of the agony.

"One, two and-" Regan tugged with all of his might. "Three!"

Zarren's shoulder made a sick noise as the bone returned to its joint. Zarren's eyelids fluttered and he was seconds from passing out.

Regan tapped at the giant's face. "Stay with me. Come on. It wasn't that bad." Regan giggled. "Let's get moving before we freeze to death." Regan helped the big fella up off the ground. "You want me to carry your sledgehammer?"

Zarren kept his gaze focused on the ground as he willed his heart to slow down. "Yes, please."

Regan lifted the heavy tool from the back of the van and carried it on his shoulder.

Lisa tapped the brakes and made a quick turn. She felt Dominic violently jerk awake behind her. His arms flailed about the cabin as if he was blocking ghost punches. His hand knocked into her headrest.

He blurted out, "Get off me!" before he was able to register where he was. Sitting next to him was a terrified teenager. "MaKelle?" He looked around the vehicle. "Ben, Lisa? What the hell happened?" Dominic shook off the rust in his brain and gently touched his sore jaw. His fingers felt where the blister had popped and a spike of pain raced along his nerve endings.

Lisa cranked the wheel and said, "We're there," As she pulled into a driveway. The vehicle fishtailed up onto the front yard. Every window in the big brick house was black. The clock on the dash read 11:32pm.

Evans probably conked out three hours ago.

This is going to be a rude awakening. Thought Lisa. She checked the house for signs of a break in. Everything looked clear.

"Kids, help me get your dad." Lisa popped open the door and was assaulted by the cold wind.

"I can manage." Ben growled as he exited the back of the SUV.

Lisa lifted her dress past her knees. It allowed her to take longer strides toward the front door. She rapped her knuckles on the solid oak door the same way she had earlier that day.

"Doctor! Doctor, it's an emergency!" Lisa barked at the door as she continued to knock. Her children huddled close to her for warmth. Ben and Dominic ignored each other. "Evans, please open the door!" She kicked at the solid oak once her hand became sore.

"Maybe he's out of town." Suggested MaKelle.

"He's not." Lisa pounded at the door with her other fist. "Evans, open up! It's an emergency!"

The door cracked open and she stopped striking it. Doctor Evans sounded half asleep with a frog in his throat. "Lisa? What are you doing here, again? What's the second emergency of the day?" He stepped into the entryway of his home. He had on a robe with his initials embroidered on his chest. His hair was wild and jutted in all directions. Doc panned a flashlight over his five late night guests and was startled by the Deputy's face. "Oh my."

Evans worked by the light of a lantern that MaKelle held high above the Doctor's shoulder. Hayden hovered close to his sister and rested his teary eyed head on her shoulder. Evans' wrinkled hands moved with grace as he stitched the hole in Ben's back. "That is one wild tale you are all spinning."

The rest of the room was dimly lit with candles and another lantern. The soft glow of light, an office full of medical tools, killer convicts on the loose, it was safe to say the place couldn't feel any creepier. Ben sat on the edge of the examination table and stared blankly out the front window. Dominic propped himself up in a chair, facing the opposite direction. He gently held a cold pack to his face. Above him on the wall was a clock. It claimed it was 11:48pm.

In Dominic's other hand was the dead sat-phone. He set in on a counter as he whispered to himself. "Without power this thing is useless."

"People killed at the high school? It's just crazy enough to be true." Evans made another loop through Ben's skin.

"It is true." Lisa entered the doctor's office. She donned a fresh pair of gym socks, an oversized sweatshirt and matching sweat pants she had found in the Evans' bedroom. She cinched the drawstring tight around her hips and pulled the shirt down over her waistline.

Evans tied a knot and snipped the string. He taped a bandage and covered the closed slit. "That should stop the bleeding, but without an x-ray of your torso, we won't know the extent of the damage the screwdriver really caused." Evans turned to Lisa and said, "We need to get him to Salem as soon as possible."

"Doctor, what did you mean by, second emergency, of the day?" Ben turned and faced Evans.

The Doctor looked to Lisa and stammered, "Uhhm, well." He turned back to Ben. The man's eyes burned with a piercing intensity.

Lisa felt like a trapped animal, as if she was cornered and her paw was stuck in the vise grip of a steel jaw. She had hoped to have a few weeks where she could dance around this secret and plot out a clear plan to tell the man she loved about her surprise, but nope. Here it is. The moment of truth and all Lisa wanted to do was lie.

"I'm pregnant."

All eyes were now on her.

Dominic sat forward and lowered his cold pack.

Ben's words were ice cold. "How far along are you?"

Tears formed as she choked. "Five weeks."

Dominic did some fast math. "Oh shit!"

She nodded at them.

Ben fumed.

Haden and MaKelle looked at each other and had the same thought, but she was first to say it. "We're confused. Should we say... congratulations... or...?"

Hayden found his voice and asked, "What's going on with the three of you?"

A high-pitched giggle echoed from out on the lawn. It put everyone in the office on edge. The group's attention flipped from Lisa to the window.

Regan stood alone next to the SUV. "Would you look at this?" He aimed his flashlight at the window and illuminated the six faces. "How goddamn lucky am I?"

Dominic noticed the Sheriff's star on Regan's jacket. He

reached for his sidearm, but it was missing. The gun must have fallen out when he was unconscious. He patted at the rest of his belt. There were his cuffs and only one other weapon.

"I'm here to see the Doctor." Regan stepped closer to the front of the house. "A little bitch forced me off the road and now my head is all cut up. Plus two teens shot arrows into me and it hurts like hell."

Lisa glanced at the kids. MaKelle nodded back at her, agreeing to the man's accusations.

Regan's light focused on the siblings. "There they are. Hey, Mom and Dad, I'm gonna make you watch as I squeeze the life right out of your precious little babies." He clicked off his flashlight and ducked into the shadows. The man disappeared right before their eyes.

There was a full minute of complete silence in the office. Terror had its evil grip on them.

"All right, I'm going out there to arrest him. Doctor Evans, do you have a gun?" Dominic tossed his cold pack onto the counter and zipped up his jacket.

It sounded like the frog in his throat just died. "No, I'm sorry I don't."

"Of course." Dominic stepped across the office.

"Are you insane?" Lisa moved in front of the Deputy.

"This is my job. To protect." Dominic reached for a lantern.

"I'm coming with you." Ben straightened his back, gritting through extreme discomfort.

"No, you're not. You're injured and have no police training." Dominic headed for the door.

"You're injured too." Ben argued.

Dominic opened the office door. "Ben, I am so sorry for everything I have done, but you have to stay here and watch over... *your* family." His voice waivered as he spoke. "And Lisa..."

She couldn't help but let a tear fall. "Yes?"

"I have and always will, love you." Dominic exited quickly.

"What is going on?" Hayden grabbed his mother by the wrist.

Dominic stepped out into the cold and closed the door behind him. He waited for the sound of the bolt turning from inside before he continued. "This is the police! Come out with your hands up!" He held the lantern out in front of himself and stepped down to the snow-covered walkway. He clutched something tightly in his bandaged hand. The pain equaled the fear he felt. Spikes of adrenaline poured through his veins. He was venturing into unknown territory. In his tenure as deputy he had only arrested individuals for drunk driving or disorderly conduct.

Come to think of it most of my arrests were because of alcohol.

The arrested citizen would always come peacefully. He never had to physically restrain or fight any of them. This time he was coming outside to square off against a madman. This must have been the guy that killed MaCready and judging by the shape he left her in, this was going to be a junkyard dog style street fight to the death.

No way in hell I'm letting that monster get into this house. Dominic psyched himself up. He was ready to kill if he had too.

Lisa is in there and... my baby. Dominic always wanted to be a father and now he was going to get the chance. It was too early to figure out how they would all function as a family, but it didn't matter. He was going to do the right thing and take care of his child. This new reason to live hardened his resolve.

He barked. "This is the police! Come out peacefully! You are under arrest!"

"What's the charges?" Regan appeared five-feet behind Dominic.

The Deputy spun to face him. "Murder!"

"Oh yeah, that." A crooked smile wormed across his lips. "What the hell happened to your face, officer?"

"Gas station outside of town was rigged to blow." Dominic tossed his cuffs at Regan. They hit him in the stomach and fell to his feet. "Put them on!"

"Oohh, that explosion was me too. Man, I'm just guilty in

spades and no thank you. I don't do jewelry. You'll have to put them on me yourself. " Regan's eyes bulged from his skull. "And I aint gonna make it easy on ya."

Dominic flicked the wrist of his injured hand. A retractable baton extended at his side.

"Well, that might help ya." Regan charged at Dominic just as he swung the baton. The lantern fell to the ground. A circle of yellow glowed around it in the snow.

Regan blocked the weapon's strike at the same time he delivered a heavy fist to Dominic's stomach. He doubled over as all the wind escaped his lungs. He felt the man's hands grab him by the back of his head and Dominic could tell what was coming next. His forearm blocked against the advancing knee heading straight for the Deputy's nose and swung the baton again, aiming lower on the convict's body. The metal rod made contact with Regan's thick thigh. The impact stung Dominic's burnt hand almost as much as it hurt Regan's leg.

Regan jumped back in pain. "SHIT!" He rubbed at his leg. It gave Dominic just enough time to catch his breath.

They began again. Expert punches were thrown and blocked. Kicks flew, but missed their mark. It was clear Regan was as well trained as Dominic in the art of fighting. Back and forth they went. Neither could get an advantage over the other and their wounds were taking a toll on both of them.

Dominic felt exhausted and sick to his stomach. The burns on his face exploded with pain after every punch the psycho landed. He extended himself too far and Regan slipped the Deputy into his clutch. Regan's thick arms wrapped around Dominic's throat with such speed he couldn't believe it. The pressure was crushing. He already felt the effects of asphyxiation. Dominic tried to slip his good hand between his neck and the man's deadly arm.

I needed a small pocket.

A little space to breath.

Regan whispered into Dominic's ear. "I've killed better men than you with this move. Just relax. It'll be over soon."

Lisa pushed her children away from the office window. She couldn't let her kids watch Dominic get murdered. "We need to move!"

"I've got to go out there!" Ben leaped for the door. Ready for a fight.

Lisa caught him by the elbow. "I know! I know! I love him too!"

Ben ripped his arm away from her. His lips curled around his teeth. He was about to breath fire.

She waved it off. "You know what I mean! Ben, you can't go out there! He'll kill you! We need you to stay with us!" She was flanked by her children. The conflict on Ben's face was clear.

"Daddy, please." MaKelle brushed a set of tears from her checks.

"We need you." Hayden reached for his father.

Ben dropped his head.

Lisa pushed her family out the office door. "Evans, is there a safer room?"

The flustered Doctor was right behind her.

Dominic fought for that pocket of air and he got it. Now he had a second to think. In his panic he had forgotten about the baton. He swatted it at Regan's ankle, then quickly brought it up to the bald man's head. The connection was brutal. Regan's death grip loosened. Dominic spun out of it and landed a powerful elbow to Regan's chin. Dominic gasped for air as Regan fell backwards and landed in the snow with a thud.

The Deputy clung to the side of the SUV in the front yard. He coughed and spit as his lungs struggled to fill with air.

"He got out." Regan chirped to himself in amazement from the ground. Dominic pulled his shoulders back trying to help his body draw in more oxygen. He glanced at the convict on the ground. It was obvious the bald man's world was spinning. Dominic searched the ground for the cuffs. He didn't have long before the monster would be back on his feet.

Regan didn't move his body, but his mouth kept running.

"You thought this was a singles match. Nope! This is a tag team event. Zarren, you're in buddy!"

Dominic found his cuffs but it was too late. A mountain of a man emerged from the side of the Evans' mansion. His eyes were black and held no emotion. It reminded Dominic of footage he had seen on *Shark Week*. He carried a blood soaked sledgehammer. He had a tool belt wrapped around his waist. The giant moved slowly at first, but the closer he got the faster his legs turned. By the time he got to Dominic the hammer was held high in the air, ready for a killer blow.

The Deputy timed it perfect. He tucked and rolled out of the hammer's way. It missed him by an inch. The momentum of the running swing caused Zarren to keep going a few steps.

Dominic popped to his feet and darted across the lawn for the giant's back. He thrashed the baton into Zarren's torso, landed hit after hit to the big man's kidney, ribs and spine.

Zarren shrieked to the heavens and retaliated with a backhand across Dominic's cheek. The oversized fist hit the Deputy like a cinderblock and tossed him up onto the hood of the SUV. A galaxy of stars exploded into Dominic's vision. His bell was rung harder than he thought possible. His body was splayed out across the front of the car. His baton fell from his bandaged hand.

Zarren's heart felt like a jazz drummer was tapping out a solo. The baton to his kidney was no joke and he was sure he would pee blood for a month. His recently dislocated shoulder throbbed in agony. Lifting the sledgehammer was now a painful chore.

I should switch to a saw. Zarren thought to himself, but then the phrase played like a song.

Find them. Crush them. He picked up the hammer and moved to the front of the SUV. The cop looked like a dead pig ready to be butchered.

Regan felt like a beaten old dog. Every part of his body ached as he steadied himself and rose to his feet. "That's my boy!" He hollered at Zarren. A flash of light caught Regan's attention. It was on the second floor of the Doctor's mansion. A set of faces looked down on the action.

I have an audience. Regan grinned.

He began to chant like a cheerleader. "KILL HIM! KILL HIM!" He yelled it again and again. Louder and louder his voice grew with excitement.

Zarren didn't need all of the hoopla. He needed the nitroglycerin pills. It was time to smash this cop and get into the doctor's office, before his heart came to a stop.

Regan kept screaming in his ear. "KILL HIM! KILL HIM!" It was so annoying, but it did make him want to get the job done faster. Even though it was pure agony for his shoulder he raised the sledgehammer high in the air. He focused his aim at the man's burnt nose. The muscles in his arms were about to contract when he was hit with a wall of light. Zarren peeked out the corner of his eye and saw a set of headlights racing straight toward him. He hadn't heard the truck's engine with Regan screaming. The front driver's side headlight and fender clipped Regan. The hit spun him like a top and tossed him to the ground.

The headlights were on high and it wasn't until Regan's body shattered one that Zarren was finally able to see the truck's hood ornament. A rack of antlers charged right for him. It looked like a motorized deer pouncing across the yard on a collision course. Zarren turned and faced the oncoming creature. All twelve points punctured Zarren's broad torso at the same time. He was ensnared. The truck kept racing across the yard. The tires stopped spinning, but the snow gave no traction. It crashed into the brick mansion with a hellacious CRUNCH. The mortar cracked in the shape of an arch around the big man. Zarren was pinned to the wall. Blood spurted out of his body. Every major organ was impaled and the truck's bumper had cut both legs off just above the knees.

It was the first time in a decade that he didn't have those words on repeat. There was no more.

Find them. Crush them.

Zarren was filled with a sense of peace. He was sure it was

from his body going into shock, but he didn't care. He was finished with this life. Zarren was cold, but that was how he liked it.

Duke stepped from his vehicle, his gun at the ready. Smoke poured from the engine block of his beloved truck. The giant was skewered like a shish kebab against the wall. The killer's black eyes never broke contact with Duke. Not until he took his final breath. The massive head of hair dropped and tilted forward onto the truck's hood.

It was poor timing but Duke couldn't stop himself from thinking.

Dominic was right, it was a public safety hazard.

Sharon climbed out the driver's side and joined Duke on the front yard. "Where's the other one?"

Christy slid out of the door behind Sharon and motioned to the yard. "He was right there a second ago."

Duke turned to look where Christy was pointing. Blood was splashed across the snow, but no body. "Maybe he crawled off somewhere to die. Let's grab Dominic and get inside."

Chapter 28

Jacob buzzed down Main Street. A fleeing car or a group of people running through Sweet Home would occasionally snag his focus. The thought of stopping and padding his numbers was so tempting, but he wanted the man with one eye.

That bastard left me for dead.

At every intersection he read the street signs and searched for the correct turn that would take him to the doctor's house.

Six more to go.

Six more bodies and my Reckoning will be complete.

When he woke up in his cell this morning it seemed like an impossible mission. One he would never accomplish, but life is full of surprises.

He spotted the street sign he was looking for and made the turn. A little farther down the street, in the middle of the road, there was a pink and red thing. As he closed in, he identified the thing.

It's a body.

There wasn't time to swerve and miss it. The front of the *Escalade* bounced into the air. A severed arm flung up onto the windshield and rolled up over the roof.

Half a block later his headlights lit up a van wrapped around a telephone pole. It was the blue one they had lifted off the plumber. It was totaled, but no bodies were inside.

Regan had a little accident.

Some blood leaked over his eyebrow and into his eye. He wiped it from his lashes.

The staples aren't working. I need something better.

I can't have my blood blinding me mid kill.

He made one more turn and was a few blocks from the doctor's house.

I'll walk from here so they won't see me coming.

He pulled the vehicle to the side of the road and killed the engine. Jacob opened the glovebox to see if there was anything to help with the bleeding.

Nothing there. He checked the center console.

Jackpot.

He lifted a roll of packing tape from the compartment. He angled the rearview mirror at his forehead. Jacob pulled a length of clear tape from the roll and made three circles around his noggin.

That should seal in the juices. Jacob felt giddy. He rarely had humorous thoughts.

Maybe the shot to the dome knocked a box of screws loose. The image of a big box of screws spilling across his psyche brought a smile to his face.

Jacob dropped the roll of tape and climbed out of the *Caddy.*

Duke and Sharon lifted Dominic off the hood of the SUV and shuffled for the front door. The Deputy's face had already begun to swell up as if he was stung by a swarm of bees.

Christy kicked at the door and yelled, "Open up!" A moment later Ben stood in the entryway, his eyes were bloodshot and he held a large kitchen knife in his fist.

"Ben?" Christy gasped.

The color drained from Ben's face when he realized who was at the door. "Christy? What are you doing here?" He noticed the blood on her neck and ear then he nervously looked back into the house.

Duke grunted. "What do you think?"

Ben took over for Sharon and helped Duke get Dominic back into the building. Christy locked the door behind them.

Ben shouted up the stairwell. "Evans, we got more injured people here!"

The group hustled into the Doctor's office. They laid Dominic on the observation table.

Doctor Evans hurried down the steps and entered his office. Right behind him was Lisa and the kids. The room suddenly felt very crowded.

Evans went to Dominic's side. He felt his neck for a pulse. Then he gave a listen to the officer's breathing. "He's unconscious, but stable." If Evans knew this was the third time today Dominic had been knocked out, he would have been more concerned for his patient. The old physician's hand shook with fear as he adjusted his glasses. "Okay, uhm, who is next?"

Sharon and Christy spoke at the same time. "Duke."

Duke motioned at the man's shaking hands. "Doc, I'm going to need you to calm down before you patch me up, please get something to stop the bleeding on Christy." Duke slid the bandage off his head and showed everyone why the ladies thought he should go first.

Evans groaned. "Sweet Mother Mary."

Hayden touched his stomach and looked queasy.

MaKelle gasped.

Lisa noticed Ben wasn't looking at Duke's horribly destroyed face. Something else in the room was making him act weird. Well, even weirder since his world got dropkicked out from under him. He kept glancing back and forth from Christy to his wife. It made Lisa start to stare at the bloody bartender too.

The Doctor took a step closer to the cyclops and studied the dark red ravine. "I need someone to stay and hold the light. Lisa, can you help Christy? Everyone else please evacuate the room."

Sharon grabbed the lantern. "I've got it."

MaKelle raised her hand into the air as if she was in school and asked, "What about the two crazies outside?"

Duke smirked as he took a seat in the Doctor's medical recliner. "Don't worry about them little lady. Ol' Duke took care of it."

Lisa snagged a lit candle and a first aid kit from the cabinet and led the way into the mansion's living room. She was followed by Christy and her family.

The Doctor's living room was well decorated. It was clear he had paid a professional to make the room the outstanding centerpiece of the mansion. The building was constructed in the sixties and had a classic mansion style with exposed beams in the ceiling, an ornate fireplace and French doors separated this main room from a solarium. The dining room sat on the other side of an archway. An inviting, fourteen-place dining table and crystal chandelier filled the large room. The kitchen and living room were separate and divided by a swinging door. In the corner of the living room, next to the fireplace, was an elegant Christmas tree. Two new leather couches faced each other and a coffee table the size of a Mini Cooper separated them. It was the first time Lisa had ever been in this part of the mansion. She thought to herself as she placed the candle on the coffee table.

I should have gone into the medical field.

"Ben, why don't you and the kids start a fire? We'll need the light?" Lisa said as she set the first aid kit next to the candle. She took a seat on the couch.

"Here." Lisa patted the cushion next to her.

"What?" Christy wasn't paying attention and she looked at the couch like she had never seen one before.

Lisa didn't know Christy very well. She had only been to the Oasis a few times and Christy wasn't a member at their gym so she didn't know how the bartender acted on a day to day basis, but Lisa was sure it wasn't like this. Christy looked rigid and uncomfortable in her own skin. She moved like a lizard, glancing back and forth from Ben to her. She seemed confused by everything in the room. Lisa chalked it up to blood loss and the stress of this horrible night.

Christy finally took a seat next to Lisa.

"Let me take a peek." Lisa nodded at the woman's ear.

"What?" Christy was distracted.

"Your ear."

"Oh, right." Christy let go of her wound and leaned closer to Lisa's face.

Lisa focused on the missing chunk of skin. Ben squatted in front of the fireplace. He had a kid on either side of him. Again he stole a glance over his shoulder at the two women on the couch. Ben stacked logs onto each other. MaKelle and Hayden scrunched newspaper pages into balls.

MaKelle nudged her father and whispered so only the three

of them could hear. "What is going on? We are very confused." She pushed her ball of paper into the fireplace.

Ben didn't say a word as he reached for the box of matches.

Hayden stuffed his ball of paper between the logs. "Did Mom and Uncle Dominic...uhm... and now she is having...uhm...a baby."

Ben struck a match. Their faces were bright yellow. Before dropping the match onto the paper he said, "Yes."

The teenager's minds melted.

Lisa placed a large rectangular piece of gauze on the top of Christy's ear and taped it into place. "So what happened to you?"

Christy's voice cracked at the top of the sentence. "A man. He attacked us at Sharon's house. It was terrifying. His face was covered in scars. He held a knife to my neck. I thought for sure that I was going to die, but Duke shot him and that's what happened to my ear."

"That is horrifying. What the hell's going on in this town? Where did these maniacs come from?" Lisa placed another bandage on Christy's neck. "That should hold until Doctor Evans can stitch you up."

The fire roared and the room filled with light. Lisa got up from the couch and faced her family. The tension in the room was thick.

Lisa's throat felt dry. "I'm going to raid the Doctor's fridge. You guy's thirsty?" She noticed another awkward glace from her husband to the bartender. "Come on kids. Grab the candle."

MaKelle plucked the candle from the table and the teens followed their mother through a swinging door that led to the kitchen, leaving Ben and Christy alone.

Ben watched the door until he was sure Lisa or the kids wouldn't be stepping back into the room.

Christy turned to him and whispered, "Does she know?"

He moved through the living room and sat on the coffee table across from her. He matched her whisper. "I didn't say anything. Did you say something?"

232

"She keeps staring at me." Christy sat forward.

"Well you are acting like a goddamn weirdo."

"So are you."

Ben's mouth turned into a tiny slit. His jaw was tight. "She doesn't know anything about us and I need to keep it that way."

An open can of soda dropped to the floor. It fizzed cola out onto planks of dark rosewood. Lisa stood at the doorway to the kitchen. Her jaw sat on the floor next to the emptying red can.

Ben stood and faced his wife. "Lisa?"

She turned around and headed back into the kitchen.

"Lisa?" Ben called after her.

Christy sunk deep into the couch as her cheeks went flush.

"Shit." Ben cursed himself.

MaKelle and Hayden were busy lighting a group of candles they had found on the kitchen island. The mansion's kitchen was quite different than the living room. It looked more like a restaurant than luxury kitchen. It was built to be used by a chef and their staff, not to entertain in. The swinging door fluttered behind Lisa as she stepped to the kitchen's sink. She rested her hands on the counter. Her chin dropped to her chest.

"Mom, are you okay?" Hayden grimaced. "I mean, I know it's not okay... it's like...uhm... MaKelle?" He turned to his sister. She had zero to say.

Ben burst through the kitchen door. "It meant nothing. She meant nothing. It was six months ago and I've regretted it every day since."

Lisa kept her head down and her back to him.

Christy heard every word and it was doing nothing for her self-esteem. "This is a new low." She said as she rubbed her hands together.

Ben moved close to his wife. "We haven't been good for a long time. Obviously." Ben's fists became claws and a vein jumped out on his forehead. "I don't know why I'm justifying myself! We are in the same goddamn boat, but at least I wasn't stupid enough to get her pregnant!"

Lisa looked at her husband. "You're right. We are in the same boat and I was stupid. Does that make you feel better?" She was cold enough to freeze fire.

The vein on his forehead smoothed out. Ben's hands went slack at his sides.

Doctor Evans extracted the needle from Duke's cheek. "It's just a local anesthetic. I can stitch the skin, but the eye, that will need a specialist." Evans nodded to Sharon. "Were you there when this happened?"

"No, I was at home." Some of the wine in Sharon's belly threatened to come up.

"When did you sustain this injury, Duke?" Evans prepared his workstation for the procedure.

"I was at home. Four bastards broke in and did this to me."

"Then you drove across town to Sharon's before coming here?" Evans threaded a needle.

"I never claimed to be a genius Doc." Duke attempted to smile at his own joke, but his face was beginning to numb up.

Sharon understood what Evans was hinting at. She shifted her weight and adjusted the lantern. "Looks like you get to keep wearing that eyepatch." Sharon stared out the window.

Duke cleared his throat. "It goes with my-"

Sharon said it with him. "-motif." she continued, "Yeah, I've heard it before. The matching scars through your eyebrows will look pretty badass." Sharon reached for Duke's hand.

Evans placed a medical pad, with an opening in the middle, on Duke's face, leaving only the wound exposed.

"Why'd I let you escape?" Duke squeezed her hand.

"Cause I'm a bitch and you're an asshole."

"You're right." Duke peeked out from under the pad. "But can you imagine if I were a little less of an asshole."

"And if I was less of a bitch?" She glanced down at him.

"Yeah."

"It's something to imagine."

Evans had the needle ready and moved into position. "As a medical professional I should mention that after I finish with Duke he needs to rest."

Sharon smiled at the Doctor and pulled Duke's hand close to her heart. A thick arm snaked around Sharon's neck, a bloody hand crossed her lips trapping in a scream, and her body was yanked to the other side of the office. Doc Evans spun on his stool as Duke sat up and pulled the pad from his face. A broken looking bald man with a scar running down his scalp had her.

The madman whispered. "Hey folks, I'm Regan. Don't make a fucking sound or I'll snap this bitch's neck."

Chapter 29

Christy had little else to do other than wait for her turn for the Doctor and feel horrible about her life choices. This was the one and only time she was the *other woman*. It was absolutely mortifying. She recalled that night.

Ben had been sitting at the bar, starring at his beer for an hour. He looked like a sad and lost puppy. She remembered thinking.

He is so handsome.

His body was amazing.

As if he is carved out of marble.

She started with some small talk and it didn't take long to get him gabbing like a teenage girl. He was so funny and witty. She only gave him a little of her attention and that was exactly what he needed to feel good about himself. Christy knew he was married, but she kept thinking.

Why isn't this guy happily married?

Christy was aware that his wife was less than five miles away from the bar, but it did not stop her from pulling him into the office at the Oasis and taking his body for a ride.

He was so good.

It was as if he hadn't had sex in a decade and he was really enjoying himself. Christy had often thought of that night in the last six months, whenever she was in the mood and the hardcore gay porn wasn't doing it for her. She sank farther into the couch and deeper into depression. She was twenty-feet away from a family that had completely fallen apart at the seams.

...and I'm the asshole that tugged the string and started its unraveling.

Christy looked around the living room. "Wonder if Doc is a drinker." She caressed the bandage on her neck and a horrifying notion became clear.

The last man to really touch my body since Ben tried to kill me.

A pocket of sap popped loudly in the fireplace. Christy jumped with fear and giggled at herself for being ridiculous. Then she heard the sound of a floorboard creaking behind her. She craned her neck to see and started to scream.

Back in the examining room, blood pooled at Regan's feet. The pant legs of his bright orange Corrections jumpsuit were mostly crimson now. He favored his right leg. Blood poured from the top of his scalp, he blinked wildly. It was all he could do to keep the fluids out of his eyes. Sharon's chest heaved as she hyperventilated. Duke looked for his .38 special, but he had set it across the office, on the table next to the unconscious Dominic.

Evans kept his voice low and said, "Calm down and tell us what you want, Regan?"

He was rattled and it made Regan babble. "We just wanted to have a little fun, right. Terrorize a town. Ya know. Put some bodies in the ground and we did it, but the last hour has been rough. It might be pointless, but I need ya to fix this busted up body of mine." Regan recognized Duke. "Ain't you the one we tied up in the cabin?"

Duke eased forward in the medical recliner.

Regan hissed, "You don't move another goddamn inch or I pop her like a zit." He readjusted his arms around Sharon's neck and tightening the grip on his clutch. "What happened to the old guy, Arthur?"

"He's dead."

"How?"

"I burned him." Duke motioned toward Dominic. "And the deputy here blasted him with buckshot. Let the woman go and take me instead." Duke sat up a little farther. Hoping the news of his fallen brother would enrage the madman enough to let Sharon go and attack him.

Regan twitched. His eyes bugged out of his skull. He wasn't taking the news very well at all. His anger grew into a raging storm.

Then a high-pitched scream from the other room grabbed his attention.

Duke flew like a bolt of lightning. Regan saw Duke coming, but the blood loss slowed his reaction time. Duke's fist crashed into Regan's nose, breaking it. The man's thick arms let go of Sharon and reached for the busted cartilage. He held his broken nostrils for a second, then began his assault on Duke.

Regan raised his knee and it crashed between Duke's thighs. Duke squeaked like a stepped on rat. Regan quickly threw two punches before his knee left Duke's family jewels. One to Duke's ear, the other in his ribs. The retired electrician hadn't been in a fight since high school. Duke's equilibrium was flipped upside down. He stumbled backwards and crashed into a glass cabinet, shattering it on impact. Duke slid down the cabinet until his butt was resting on the floor.

Sharon raced straight for the .38 special the second she was free of Regan's arms. She picked it up, spun on her heels and started to aim. Regan caught her wrists and kept the gun pointing in the air. Her finger slipped and she fired off one round into the ceiling.

Ben and Lisa stood in the kitchen, blankly starring at each other. The teens silently looked from Mom to Dad as if their parents were playing an invisible tennis match. It was still unclear who they should root for or who was in the wrong. It appeared to be a tie. It was 30-all and anyone's game. A cabinet rattling scream came from the living room.

Ben opened the swinging door. Lisa and the kids were right behind him. A man, dressed in all black, had Christy on the coffee table. The light of the fire glinted off the polished blade in his hand. He plunged it into her chest and pinned her to the table. Her scream trickled off until it was nothing more than a raspy cough.

The man looked up from his work and spotted the family at the door. All four of them screamed. He leaped from the table and raced after them. Ben scooted his family back into the kitchen and braced himself against the door. He prepared for the impending crash.

The woman made it two hundred ninety-five.

Jacob was giddy with excitement. He charged at the kitchen door, but came to a sudden stop once he hit it.

The man on the other side is strong as hell.

This guy is going to be a challenge.

What a way to finish the night.

Jacob drove his shoulder into the wooden barricade but it wouldn't budge. He kicked at it and nothing. He reared back with his knife and tried stabbing into the door.

A blade punctured the wood and grazed Ben's cheek. Blood trickled from the fresh cut. He pulled his head back from the door and continued to hold it with only his hands and one foot acting as a doorstopper. The blade disappeared back out of the door, then it reappeared between his middle finger and ring finger. The blade chimed against Ben's wedding ring.

Ben's eyes doubled in size.

A gunshot thundered through the house.

Jacob heard Regan struggling down the hall where the gun had been fired.

I'm not getting through this door. I should check on Regan.

He looked pretty bad when I found him outside.

Jacob kicked the door once more, but it still didn't move. A wooden chair was within arms reach. He grabbed it and forced the back of the chair up under the door's handle. He gave it a quick hard pull and the chair held. He sprinted down the hall for the office.

A ligament snapped in Regan's busted knee. Sharon heard a pop and saw the pain in his crazed eyes. She used it to her advantage and drove Regan across the room. The joint in his leg buckled and he fell backwards onto Dominic. The deputy began to stir. Sharon pushed down on the gun and aimed it toward Regan's skull. The barrel inched closer and closer. Sweat mixed with the blood on his face. All of Regan's strength and confidence fell away. He was too injured and out of juice.

Regan panted and thought to himself. *This lady with the big fake jugs is gonna kill me.*

A knife blade jabbed its way through her cleavage. Thick dark crimson drained from her chest and poured onto Regan. She coughed and choked. Blood and spit dribbled out of her mouth and down her chin. A look of disbelief twinkled in her dying eyes until they turned off for good.

Jacob's scarred hand grabbed a fistful of blonde hair and yanked her off of Regan. He tossed her limp body to the floor. The gun clattered out of her hand and skidded across the tile.

Two hundred ninety-six.

Jacob surveyed the room. The Doctor cowered in the corner of the office. The other two men appeared to be dead or dying.

Regan heaved in a lung full of air. He had difficulty focusing. "Let me squeeze on these two." Regan licked his lips. "I'm gonna need the doctor too. So please don't kill him." He winked at Evans.

I should slit Regan's throat right now. Jacob toyed with the idea for a second. He so wanted to feed that woman's heart to the man with one eye.

I want my revenge. Jacob tightened his fist around the handle of his knife.

Regan moved closer to Duke. He grabbed him by the collar and dragged him across the floor toward Dominic. Regan rested his elbow on the Deputy's chest. "I call dibs." He spit a mouthful of blood on the Deputy's jacket and another mouthful on Duke. It was Regan's version of putting his tongue on the last two slices of pizza.

If Regan wants these two so badly, he can have them.

There was no time to argue. The family of four in the kitchen would get him to his goal. He needed to check on them before they tried to run. Jacob nodded at the broken convict. He turned to leave.

Regan called after him. "I wanted them teenagers too, but I

ain't got it in me. Have fun. You sick son of a bitch." He giggled his high-pitched laugh, but it ended in a couching fit.

Jacob paused in the hallway and listened. He could hear the family arguing in the kitchen. From this angle and judging by the echo of their voices Jacob made a discovery.

There's another way into the kitchen. He had one quick stop to make before he searched for the kitchen's other entry point.

Ben stayed solid against the swinging door. "I think he's gone!" Ben noticed a sliding lock above the doors handle. He pushed it into place.

"Where did he go?" Lisa spun around. On the opposite wall was another swinging door.

"I don't know, but there's no one pushing against this one."

"We should run!" Hayden tugged at his mother's arm.

"Where?" MaKelle stayed close to her father.

"Anywhere but here!"

"You still got the keys to the SUV?" Ben questioned Lisa.

"Yes!" She pulled them from the pocket of her sweatpants. "Let's go this way!" She pointed to the other door. "It's the way out!" Lisa led the kids through the kitchen. Ben pivoted and raced after his family. Lisa was three feet from the other swinging door when it began to move. She put on the jets for the last two steps. Lisa crashed into the door, but she wasn't fast enough.

An arm shot through the gap. A long hunting knife grasped in its bloody fist. The arm swung at her and glided down her forearm. The blade sliced through her sweatshirt, her skin and bounced off the bone.

Lisa leaped back and crashed into the others. She held her wound tightly. Blood seeped through her fingers and dripped on the floor. They huddled together as the door swung open. The man in black's body filled the escape route. Ben quickly put himself between the man and his family.

"We don't want any trouble!" That's when the whole family spotted what the man had in his other hand. It was a burning log from the fire. The timber glowed red hot in his bare hand. No glove.

Nothing. His skin blistered and popped, as patches dripped from his fingers and plopped to the floor.

Jacob enjoyed the fear oozing off the family. The burning log was a nice touch and the look of panic on the parent's faces made the whole endeavor worthwhile. Jacob let the door swing closed behind him. He noticed a sliding lock and pushed it into position. He set the log on the floor. Jacob stood there, menacingly, as he waited for the burning wood to do its trick. It didn't take long for it to catch. Flames licked at the white entrance turning it black. The paint blistered and peeled.

He wished he still had a tongue so he could thank them for their sacrifice. He was about to do something most people would never even come close to accomplishing. A lifetime of work was finally coming to an end.

Shit. They don't have any weapons.

He was sure they would have picked up a kitchen knife or at least a pan.

Nothing ever goes easy.

Lisa watched in disbelief as the monster with the knife slid the blade back into its sheath, then he lurched at the terrified family.

Chapter 30

Dominic knew it was a dream, but he did not care. He stood on a beautiful stretch of exotic beach. The blue ocean lapped softly as the salt water rushed over his ankles. His feet sank farther into the sand with every new wave. The sun poured hot rays onto his face, it was so hot he felt as if he already had a sunburn. Suddenly, next to him was Lisa. She wore a white linen dress. The fabric flapped in the breeze. Her skin glowed with a healthy tan. She looked radiant. Lisa reached for his hand and they interlaced their fingers.

This is love. Maybe he said it out loud. He couldn't be sure.

In her other arm she held a six-month-old baby. He knew right away it was his child. The little one was breathtaking.

Perfect from head to toe. The baby reached for its father. Dominic gently took the child from Lisa and held it to his chest. Its tiny arms wrapped around his neck and gave him a little baby squeeze.

The hug tightened like a noose. Dominic could no longer breathe. Lisa and the baby disappeared. He was left all alone on the beach. The sun went black and a cold breeze floated in off the ocean. The hug morphed into a choke. The water at his feet turned to blood and the sand became tar. He sunk deeper and deeper into the bloody tar as his lungs struggled to suck in air. The pain around his neck was excruciating. He fell to his knees. A tidal wave of blood crashed into him. The bloody water did not recede. He was drowning in gore and at the same time something continued to strangle him. The dream went black.

Regan's blood dripped off him and landed on Dominic's face. He grunted and thrashed as the grip tightened. Dominic's body jerked with a spasm, then it fell flat. Regan released his clutch on the deputy. He spoke softly to the crying Doctor. "Whew, that boy did not wanna let go. What's the problem Doc? You ain't ever lost a patient before?"

Evans' hand reached for a napkin. "No." He took the Kleenex from the box and sucked in a sharp breath of air. The pistol was sitting next to him, hidden from Regan by a cabinet. He tried not to react. Evans covered his face with the thin sheet of paper, wiped away his snot, and plotted a way to reach the gun.

Duke sat on the floor, propped up against the table that held Dominic's body. He lifted his head slightly. Regan pointed. "This one's coming around. I better act fast." He swung his arms to give them a quick stretch. "I'm gonna be sore tomorrow." He giggled at the Doc.

Ben took a fighting stance against the man in black. He had trained with Dominic for the last year, but had never been in a real fight. He threw a fast hard jab at the oncoming man. The punch seemed to have caught him off guard and it tagged the man in his gnarled lips. The man in black's head snapped back as a shockwave of pain rippled up Ben's arm.

That hurt so goddamn bad! Thought Ben. He dreaded the idea of throwing another punch.

Lisa pushed her children toward the opposite door. She slid back the lock and pressed against the white painted wood, but it was extremely hot to the touch. She yelped in pain. Tiny blisters rose on the tips of her fingers. Not only was the door hot, but it also didn't budge.

"What's wrong?" MaKelle reached for the door herself. Lisa caught her before she touched it.

"It's hot."

"Look!" Hayden pointed to the floor. Smoke curled from under the door. The paint had turned black and was blistering into large bubbles.

He set a burning log on this door too. Lisa really began to panic. There were only the two doors in and out of the kitchen. Above the sink sat a medium sized window. It was their only way out.

Lisa corralled the children toward the sink.

Ben exchanged blows with the maniac. He nailed the freak with a nice three-punch combo, but the man kept coming. Between shots, Ben took in all the horrible details of his ugly mug. There was the band of clear tape that circled his forehead. Staples were under that. They made a jagged U shape. Chunks of his lips were missing.

He couldn't press them all the way together even if he wanted!

Ben got rocked by an unblocked punch. The madman's fists were taking their toll on Ben. Dominic pulled his punches whenever they sparred. This guy wasn't. Ben already had a split lip and he knew for sure he was going to have a black eye in the morning.

If I live to see the morning.

The part that terrified him the most was when he landed a solid strike, it didn't phase the psycho at all. Ben was backed into a corner. Punches came from everywhere. He kept his arms up to block, but he kept getting tagged in the ear. Uppercuts would slip through and threaten to shatter his jaw.

Lisa and Hayden helped MaKelle up on to the counter. It was the only way to reach the window's locking mechanism. She worked her thin fingers at the old stubborn lock. It turned ever so slightly. Lisa heard Ben grunting in pain. Her husband was cornered and taking a savage beating. She yanked on a cabinet drawer and found a large kitchen knife. The handle slipped at first. Lisa's fingers were slick with her own blood.

She raced around the kitchen's large center island and charged right for the crazed killer. Lisa had only a pair of socks on her feet and she slipped a little as she rounded the corner. She held the blade out in front of her as she came to her husband's rescue. The tip of the knife pierced the man's back, but her grip on the handle was too slick. Her fingers slid down the handle and along the knife's razor sharp edge. Her sock covered feet didn't come to a stop and Lisa's torso collided into the back of the killer. Her stomach pushed her knife farther into his body. The blade found its way through his organs and poked out of his stomach. Her impact into him sent the man forward into Ben and the first inch and a half of the knife drove into Ben's guts. They looked like a sandwich with Ben and Lisa as the slices of bread. Ben and Lisa howled. These fresh cuts were just the beginning.

Duke's eyelid fluttered as he floated back into consciousness. He was slumped against a table and his butt was going numb from sitting on the tile floor. Just above him was the giggling nut job.

Duke wondered. *When would the nightmare end?*

"It's your turn buddy boy. This one's for Arthur." Regan tugged at Duke's collar and yanked him off his butt. Duke caught a glimpse of something on the floor that snapped him awake.

Sharon!

His ex-girlfriend lay in a pool of blood on the floor. A gaping wound carved in her chest. Her unblinking eyes stared coldly at the ceiling. Duke got to his feet and before he could react, a powerful set of arms draped around his neck.

Regan whispered in his ear. "I've got ya and I'm sending you to see your lady. Just relax. Let go."

Duke was dumbfounded, his heart ached for his losses, and it was worse than the pain at his throat.

First Stanley and now Sharon. He pawed at Regan's forearm. Trying desperately to breathe, but he couldn't get the monster to loosen his grip.

Maybe he's right. I should let go. What else do I have to live for?

They took my friend and my woman.

They burned my home and I wrecked my truck.

I've got nothing left.

Duke's light flickered. His world got soft around the edges. Black shadows crept from the dark corners of the room. They surrounded him, drawing out his soul.

"Duke!" A voice yanked him from the cold clutches of

shadows. It was the Doc. Sharon's .38 special shook in his fist. Duke grabbed the observation table that held Dominic's body and twisted himself. Regan came along for the ride and his back was to the Doctor.

Evans fired five shots. They ripped into Regan's thick jacket, and little pink puffs of blood erupted from Regan's back. He hollered and spit. His body went rigid for a second. Then he fell forward on Duke, who landed on the observation table next to Dominic. The broad torso of the convict covered Duke's thin frame completely and he disappeared under the dead man.

MaKelle stood on the countertop. Hayden swatted at her leg and she turned from the window.

"Look!" He pointed at their folks. The three adults were pinned together in the corner of the room.

The man in black threw a rear elbow and caught Lisa in the temple. He headbutted Ben on the bridge of his nose, it crunched and blood poured out his nostrils. MaKelle jumped from the counter to the island. The top of her head glided along the ceiling. From the island's countertop she launched a kick at the man's face. It sent his noggin into a cabinet door and cracked the white wood. Both parents dropped away from the psycho and slithered to the floor. MaKelle jumped from the island and landed on the man's back. She wrapped her arms around his neck. The weight of the teen threw off his balance and he stumbled backwards.

"Hayden!" She called for her brother. He was on the move, armed with a cast-iron skillet.

Jacob spun and reached for the island. The wiggling girl on his back kept cranking his neck and pulling him backwards. He fought to regain balance. The second he had it the other damn teenager caught him in the nose with the pan. A flash of white light washed over Jacob. It didn't hurt but damn it was difficult to concentrate. Jacob took a large step backwards. Another hit from the pan dislocated his jaw. The sick popping noise echoed around in his skull. The teen boy threw a sidekick. It landed dead center on

Jacob's chest. He tipped backwards. The girl on his back planted her feet to the floor, twisted her stance and popped her hip into his lower spine. She yanked on his neck. It flipped Jacob. His legs flew into the air and he crash landed on the top of his skull. He landed on his face, splayed out like a starfish.

Damn I hate teenagers. Jacob grumbled to himself.

The kids raced away from him shouting, "Mom, Dad!"

They used weapons.

Jacob reached for his knife as he got to his feet. Both doorways were covered in flames and black smoke floated along the ceiling.

Almost done. Jacob gloated to himself.

Duke grunted as he pushed himself off the table.

"Thank heavens you're still alive." Evans lowered the pistol.

Regan's dead body slid to the floor. "If he wasn't such a big guy, I wouldn't be." Duke faced Evans and reached for the gun.

"Mom, Dad!" came from the kitchen. The Doctor handed it to him. Duke fished out the box of ammo from his pocket and quickly reloaded the pistol. As he slid the rounds into the cylinder he looked at Sharon. Duke wanted to drop to the floor, hold her and blubber like a baby, but there wasn't time. The Williams family sounded like they needed help. He would mourn her passing later. Duke twisted his wrist and the cylinder snapped into place.

Chapter 31

The side of Lisa's skull throbbed. She had never been hit in the face before. She was sure the crazy man's elbow knocked her down a few I.Q. points. Her hand and forearm burned intensely. She was in so much agony and didn't want to move, but her son was tugging and screaming "Mom!" at her.

Ben's fingertips tapped at the cut in his stomach. He could not stop himself from checking out the damage. Pain shot through him like a charge of electricity. He wanted to barf. Ben lay on his back. His busted nose drained blood into his throat. He couldn't breath and coughed out a mouthful. He felt his daughter yanking his arm and yelling at him to get up, but his body wouldn't respond.

I must be going into shock.

Jacob straightened his back. He did a quick survey of the kitchen. Both doors were on fire and the cloud of smoke was growing above their heads.

This is it.

My final match.

Between the gut shot, the blast to his skull and the knife in his torso Jacob knew he was a goner. It was just a matter of time.

I'm going to make sure I go out with a bang.

The kitchen had a large old gas range and without power the igniters wouldn't spark. Jacob tried to smile, but his dislocated jaw didn't move. He stepped toward the range, turned a knob on the cooktop and gas hissed from the orifice.

I've got to work fast before I'm blown to hell. Jacob charged at the family.

Duke raced into the living room. The Doctor was on his heels. The room was ablaze and the door to the kitchen was completely blocked by flames. A pool of blood dripped off the edge of the coffee table. Christy's complexion had already gone white.

"Doc?" Duke stepped closer to her.

Evans felt for a pulse on her neck. "She's gone. Quick, there's another way in!" The Doctor headed down the hall.

MaKelle's tears blurred her vision. Both parents weren't moving and the psycho was heading their way. She barked, "Hayden!" and took a fighting stance between the man in black and her folks. Her brother joined her armed with the frying pan. She had fought a few matches at the different tournaments her parents signed her up for, but that was totally different. She wore protective gear and there were rules. Plus a referee would break up the fight if it got too heated.

This was an adult, not a teenager. He had no rules and was armed with a knife. MaKelle felt a shot of adrenaline kick in.

Good, it will help me fight this asshole.

Her heart filled with fear, but she wasn't going to let it cripple her. There was no way she would stand by and watch him carve up her folks.

The man in black swung the knife at her. The blade sliced through the air. She used an outside block. Her wrist met his and stopped the attack. She whipped a front kick at his knee and sent the joint backwards. His leg hyperextended and he stumbled.

Hayden crashed the pan onto the top of the man's head. It sounded like he rang a gong.

Neither hit slowed him down. He retracted his blade and sliced at them again. Hayden ducked. MaKelle's instinct was to block the oncoming hit and the blade sliced her elbow. She screamed and clutched the wound. Hayden landed another hit to the man's face with the pan. It dislocated his jaw in the other direction. The man didn't care. He threw his blistered fist at Hayden and cracked him in the eye. It was a knockout blow and the kid fell to the ground.

That enraged MaKelle.

No one hits my brother!

She came at the madman with all her best moves. She nailed him in the face and the chest. She kicked his knees and tried to break them. She sidestepped and evaded the knife when he swung it at her. She blocked his punches and kept advancing.

I'm doing it. I'm going to beat him! Her confidence grew, but it was a premature thought. The man threw a front kick and tagged her in the chest. It knocked the air from her lungs and she crumbled to the floor.

He towered above her, grabbed a fistful of hair, pulled her head back and exposed her neck. The blade hovered for a moment. MaKelle saw it coming but couldn't do anything to stop it. Her arms wouldn't let go of the agonizing pain in her chest.

Evans and Duke rounded the corner and headed for the smoking white door at the end of the hall. Duke squared his shoulders and launched his boot at it. The damn thing cracked but didn't budge. He kicked at it again.

The pounding at the door grabbed Jacob's attention. He turned to see if he had any unexpected company. When he looked back the family's mother was chugging toward him like a steam engine. She looked pissed.

Lisa tackled the man to the ground like she was sacking a quarterback. She landed on top, but he bucked his hips, pinned her arm and reversed it. She slapped wildly at his face and tried to gouge out an eye. He reared back and the knife plummeted toward her chest. Lisa blocked his arm and kept the blade from piercing her skin. Years of yoga had given Lisa incredible upper body strength. It was just enough to keep the knife from ending her. The man leaned forward putting the weight of his body onto the knife's handle. The tip of the blade inched forward. Lisa ripped out a scream as the tip of the knife entered below her sternum.

My baby!

Duke pivoted from the door. A bathroom was across the

hall. He entered it, yanked a thick towel from the rack, turned on the shower and soaked it. He sprinted from the bathroom, wrapped the wet towel around his shoulders and charged at the door.

Lisa's scream woke up Ben. He sat up from the floor. His view was blocked by the island. Hayden was knocked out next to him and MaKelle was crawling away. She was heading around the corner of the island, from where the scream had originated.

The sheer terror MaKelle felt as she watched the man drive a blade into her mother helped her forget about the pain in her chest. She reached, grabbed the handle of the knife sticking through the man's torso and twisted it. He lashed out at MaKelle with the back of his hand and sent her skull into the wood base of the island.

CRASH! The burning door fell from its hinges and Duke appeared in the kitchen. He tossed the towel from his shoulders and raised his gun.

Jacob pulled the blade from the screaming woman and threw it at the man with the gun. He hit his mark and the blade slid to the hilt in his stomach. The man stumbled backwards out into the hall. Jacob wrapped his fingers around the woman's throat and squeezed.

Duke lay on his back. He could feel the knife tip grinded on the floor below him. Duke desperately pumped himself up.

Come on you old kook.

Don't let this psycho kill another friend.

He grunted and bit his bottom lip as he sat up. Pain surged throughout his body. He heard Lisa gasping.

I wasn't there to save Stanley.

I couldn't save Sharon or Christy.

You've got to save Lisa!

His stomach contracted around the knife's razor sharp edge and cut deeper into the muscle fibers. He outstretched his arm and yelled. "Hey, ugly!"

Jacob looked up at the insulting man. The muzzle flashed, then half of his vision was gone.

He shot me again! He touched his face and felt where the bullet hit.

Duke smirked at the killer. "Eye for an eye!"

Lisa managed to get one full breath before the killer choked her again. *How? How can he still be alive?*

Jacob gritted his crooked teeth. He leaned in close and squeezed. *Die, so I can kill your family and finish my Reckoning!*

Ben put his arm around the killer's throat and pulled him off his wife. He locked the madman in a vicious chokehold. It was a move Dominic had shown him and he had it wrapped up perfectly.

Jacob noticed the lack of oxygen right away. He let go of the woman and pawed at the man's strong arms. He sat upright and straddled the lady. He didn't have long before the gas would blow them all to hell. He just had to wait a little longer.

Goddamn it! This was a bust!

Jacob wanted this to count so badly toward the Reckoning, but it wouldn't. The rules he set were clear.

They must die by my hands.

He could have been setting fires to churches and hospitals the whole time and his numbers would have been in the thousands, but that wasn't how he wanted it. He wasn't an arsonist. He was a cold blooded murderer. It looked like he was going to miss his goal by four.

At least I can finally get the peace and quiet that only death brings.

This horrible life has been so tiresome.

Lisa took in a deep breath. She smelled the odor of rotten

eggs in the air along with the smoke. The burning sensation where the knife cut her tummy had driven her mad.

He killed my baby! Lisa reached around the psycho's body, found the knife stuck in his back and pulled it out. She gripped it tight with both hands and plunged it into his stomach. She sawed back and forth working the blade up through his belly. She screamed and forced the cutting tool to his sternum. A tangled pile of guts poured from him and on to her. Ben lifted the body and tossed it to the floor. It landed with a wet thud. He quickly turned off the gas burner. A towel hung from the oven's handle. He grabbed it and pressed it to her belly.

"It's going to be all right. I promise. Everything will be okay."

Tears streamed down her temples as she shook her head. Ben lifted Lisa and held her tight in his arms. They bawled on each other's shoulders.

His lips brushed her neck. "I love you so much. I'll never let you go again." He planted a passionate kiss on her trembling lips.

"I hate to break up the moment, but we've got to get out of here." Duke coughed from the floor. Evans moved to Duke's side and helped him to his feet. "This place is still burning down."

Ben and Lisa released each other and raced to the children. Ben helped MaKelle from the floor.

"Did we beat him?" she asked as she rubbed the knot on the side of her skull.

"Yeah, sweetheart. We did." He lifted and carried her like a baby as they inched toward the exit.

"My head hurts."

"Me too kiddo."

"You can put me down. I can walk."

"Nah, I got you."

MaKelle rested her head on her father's shoulder as if she were a toddler.

Lisa held the towel tight to the cut on her belly as she shook Hayden's shoulder. "Wake up baby. We have to go!"

He sat up and blurted out. "I had the worst nightmare." He looked at his Mother and noticed the blood on her. "Shit, it wasn't a dream."

Lisa lifted him to his feet. "No, it wasn't and don't curse."

They limped for the door. Lisa noticed a clock hanging on the wall. It was 12:03.

Happy New Year! She snorted back a tear. Then it hit her. "Ben, we got our kiss in at midnight."

Ben faced her with a smile. "Well that's a good start to the year."

Evans opened the front door and a gust of cold wind hit the six of them. It felt amazing. The fresh air was a blessing.

Inside the burning kitchen, Jacob's bloody hand reached up toward the gas range and turned on all six burners.

Lisa reached out and handed Evans the keys. "You'll have to drive." She let Hayden go first and was the last one to leave the mansion. The falling snow pelted her. It felt good to be out of that kitchen. Her body hurt everywhere and she wasn't sure she would make it across the yard by herself, let alone make it through the rest of her life after this horrible night. Then Lisa remembered what Evans said to her earlier when she found out she was pregnant.

'It might be years from now, but it all will work itself out and you'll be okay.'

Maybe, just maybe. She gingerly stepped from the mansion. A set of scarred hands shot from the dark doorway. A rope was thrown over her head and wrapped around her neck.

That wasn't a rope! It's an intestine!

Lisa choked out, "Ben!"

Her husband turned and saw her getting dragged back into the house. "Lisa!" He put MaKelle down and raced back toward the door. Lisa struggled to get free, but the man in black was choking her with a noose made from his guts. A ball of flame exploded from the front door. The last thing Ben saw before he was knocked to the ground was a black silhouette of his wife.

Chapter 32

Ben sat at a table across from a young couple. His nose was a little crooked, but he was still handsome. "Okay, I'll have you sign here and here." He pointed at two spots on the form. The man picked up the pen, signed the paper and handed the pen to the lady.

"This place looks brand new. How long have you been open?" asked the man.

"I opened ten years ago, but I recently updated the entire facility. I take it you guys are new to town."

The lady signed and handed him back his pen. "Yes, we moved in two weeks ago. The house prices here in Sweet Home were incredible."

Ben forced a smile. "A town full of empty homes can do that."

The lady continued, "It's such a beautiful place to live and raise a family."

"Do you have any children?" asked the man.

Ben looked over the forms. The couple's names were Chad and Darcy. "I've got a few running around here."

Chad's smile became uneasy. He leaned in as if he was asking Ben a terrible secret. "Were you here...in town...last year...when it happened?"

Before Ben answered Darcy chimed in. "It was all over the news. It sounded like an absolute nightmare."

Ben remained professional and switched subjects. "Here's your membership cards, welcome to the Sweat and Tears Gym and if you need anything or have any questions please feel free to ask me. I'm always here." He reached out, shook the couples hand and stood up from the table. The couple picked up their gym bags and headed for the locker.

The bell dinged above the door as it swung open. A patron

stepped into the building. The man wore an eyepatch and a cigarette hung from his lips.

"Put it out, Duke."

Duke's good eye drifted to the bright red tip of the cigarette. "Gadzooks, how long has this cancer stick been here?" He sucked it to the filter and tossed the butt out the front door.

"Same joke. Different year. Happy New Year by the way."

"To you too. I'll get my writers working on new material." Duke hung his jacket on the rack next to the front door. He noticed the young couple heading for the lockers. "Another new family?"

"Yep, soon us townies will be outnumbered by the transplants." Ben dropped their forms on the front desk counter.

"If Sharon was still with us she'd have been in hog heaven. A hundred houses for sale all at bargain basement prices. It's a goddamn buyer's market."

"I guess I can't complain. Most of the new families have joined the gym and business is booming." They looked around and almost every machine had a person on it trying to stick to their New Year's resolutions. "How's the cabin coming?"

"The exterior is all done and the team is working on the last few details of the interior. I can't wait to move in. Living in a camper is not all it's cracked up to be. You know, I've been thinking we should take the money we got from signing that movie deal and buy a bunch of homes before the prices rise."

Ben crossed his arms. "Maybe, but I feel like I've already profited enough from this town's misfortune."

Duke nodded his head in agreement. "That's true. That's true. I still can't believe how much Hollywood paid us for the rights to our story."

"Did you hear? They've started production on Sweet Home the movie so we'll see another check next month. It's just in time too, I got my bill from the hospital and even with insurance they want six figures for my family's stay last year. So I'll just about break even when it's all said and done, but hey, it could be worse."

"It could be worse." Duke sounded like an echo. Then his face lit up. "Speaking of spending our cut from Tinseltown, did you see my new toy?" Duke pointed outside. In front of the gym was a brand new Ford Super Duty. It was chromed top to bottom and mounted to the front grill was his deer.

Ben shook his head and asked, "What's the new sheriff say about your hood ornament?"

"Don't know. I haven't met him yet."

"Happy New Year Mr. Allen" A young female voice spoke from behind him.

Duke turned to find MaKelle and Hayden putting a new weight bench together. "Thank you. Your Dad has you guys hard at work over the Christmas break? What a bummer."

"He's a real taskmaster," said Hayden as he handed his sister a bolt. "I can't believe you're here on New Year's. Why aren't you home enjoying the holiday?"

"Home's a fifty square foot camper, besides Doc Evans says I wouldn't have survived last year if I wasn't in such good shape, so here I am."

Ben crossed his arms. "Are you going to the memorial at the school tonight?"

"Maybe, I had plans to honor Stanley and Sharon in my own way, but I might stop by and show my handsome face. What about you?"

"We can't convince the kids to babysit," said Lisa as she emerged from the back office. On the back of her arms and neck were scars from their ordeal, but she was just as lovely as ever. Clung to her chest was a four-month-old baby in a pink onesie.

"Dominique is getting so big." Duke took a step closer to the mother and child.

"She's a good eater. Say hello to Mr. Allen." Lisa held the child's arm and extended it toward Duke. He offered his index finger and the Dominique's chubby little hand latched on tight.

"So cute," said Duke as his smile grew. "The baby's nice too."

Ben laughed off Duke's joke. "Okay, that's enough. Someone's got a class to teach. Give me that little bugger so you can get to work." Ben reached for his daughter.

Lisa and Ben exchanged a quick, yet loving, peck on the lips as she handed the child to Ben. "She's got a belly full of booby milk and diaper full of old booby milk."

Ben pulled the baby close to his chest. "I've got it." He kissed the top of her head. "Hayden, MaKelle, we have a code brown."

"Ew, Dad."

"You ready for a hell of a workout?" Lisa led the way to the classroom.

"I am," said Duke as he caught up to her. "Isn't this your first class back in action? You must be excited."

"It is good to be out of the house, feedings, diapers and napping every day can be very repetitive."

"How is the third go round of motherhood?"

"Compared to this year of, surgeries, skin grafts, physical therapy and child birth, motherhood is a breeze. Ben's an amazing father and the kids are so much help."

"That's good." He nodded at the scars on her. "They do look better."

Lisa ran her fingers down the bumpy terrain of her skin as she examined the rough tissue on her arm. "I wish Jacob's body would have blocked a little more of the blast, but all in all it could have been worse. He's dead and I'm not. I'll see you in there."

"Sounds good." Duke entered the gym's locker room as Lisa continued on toward the yoga class. A group of ten people were already waiting for her inside.

Lisa smiled with pride. "It's a full house."

The man's vision was blurred and it sounded as if he was underwater. Slowly the room and his hearing began to focus. Bright lights illuminated the handful of people bustling around him. A bank of computer monitors filled one wall of the room. Different human body parts occupied most of the screens. The pictures flipped quickly and a time-lapse video showed the slow transition from a wounded and disfigured arm to a healed and healthy limb. Scars disappear completely and healthy new skin regenerates in its place.

A man wearing a lab coat and surgical mask moved into the

man's field of vision. "Can you hear me? Nod if you can."

He nodded.

"Good. Don't worry, you are not in prison. This is a private medical facility. A secret one. You have been in a coma for the last year. Do you remember who you are?"

He nodded.

"I've been looking forward to meeting you for a long time. You are quite unique and it's my privilege to make you into something…spectacular. My team and I have already begun to fix you. We are now ready to start the next stage of treatment. We are going to make you faster and stronger than you were before." The man in the mask moved in closer. "Would you like that Jacob? Would you like another chance to kill?"

Jacob smiled and nodded again.

The End.

Thank you for checking out Sweet Home. I hope you had as much fun reading it as I did writing it. It would mean the world to my family and I if you could take a couple of minutes and leave an honest review. Books on Amazon are measured by reviews and total downloads. The more reviews I can get the more people will have a chance to see my books. Then they too can join in on the fun I have created. When people see honest reviews it helps them decide if they want to take a chance on me. It also helps me figure out what I need to add or take away in the sequels to make future books even more fun. I check every review I'm given and they truly help me become a better writer. Thanks again for your time.

Made in the USA
Columbia, SC
04 November 2019